CALLED

"Drama, suspense, humor and wisdom: *Called* has it all. Packed with profound spiritual truths, it's a 'must read' for metaphysicians and ET buffs alike."

—Tony Stubbs, author of *An Ascension Handbook*

"CALLED incorporates many themes . . . ufology and ufo crash recoveries, ET contact, and expanding human awareness. . . . Most unique is the fact that the author has articulated her personal interpretations of TRUTH, SOUL, and EXISTENCE/EXPERIENCES, finding ways to express her knowledge of each by weaving specific insights and awakenings into her unusual, engrossing plotline."

—Paul Davids, Executive Producer/Co-writer, *Roswell* and Producer/Writer/Director, *Starry Night*

ACCLAIM FOR **CALLED**

"This is a very important piece of work, coming as it does during a period of great change in our world and our acceleration towards the heavens of other worlds. Many of us have not overlooked the significance of events occurring on Earth itself, which includes the thousands of UFO reports from all parts of the globe. We have had to wait until now for the first cracks to appear in the government's secrecy surrounding the subject. As we move into the 21st century, the French and British governments admit that there are objects in our skies suggesting something or someone has 'Called.'

"As I read through this book, it became apparent that there was such resonance to the story that it did more than cement the story into place but registered an eerie kind of message to us.

"Current scientific findings and technological advances bring us to a place where we should be thinking constructively about our wider future in the universe. Visions cast today will undoubtedly become reality sometime in our tomorrows—*Called* is a book to be enjoyed, but it shouldn't be taken too lightly either.

"A great read, this book will deeply touch people who have had unexplained experiences and who continue to suffer in silence, rather than chance rejection by friends and colleagues. All thinking people will feel the timing of the material. *Called* did not arrive on our bookshelves a day too soon."

—Colin Andrews, author of *Circular Evidence*,
and president of Circles Phenomenon Research International

"*Called* . . . appeals to both adults and young adults. . . . Many will enjoy it as a wonder-filled tale . . . for some—those often called 'wanderers' or 'starpeople'—it will affirm their sense of identity and purpose here and 'elsewhere.'"

—Jody Boyne, Librarian, University of Hawaii
and Transhuman Counseling Psychologist

OTHER WORLDS
The Series

VOLUME I

CALLED

Lauren Zimmerman

PELICAN POND PUBLISHING

Copyright © 2001 Lauren Zimmerman

Published by Pelican Pond Publishing,
Fine Literature for All Ages,
fiction imprint of Blue Dolphin Publishing, Inc.

For inquiries or orders, address
Blue Dolphin Publishing, Inc.
P.O. Box 8, Nevada City, CA 95959
1-800-643-0765
www.bluedolphinpublishing.com/pelicanpond/

ISBN: 1-57733-098-6

Library of Congress Cataloging-in-Publication Data

Zimmerman, Lauren, 1948–
    Called / Lauren Zimmerman.
        p. cm. — (Other worlds ; v. 1)
    ISBN: 1-57733-098-6
        1. Human-alien encounters—Fiction. 2. Life on other planets—
Fiction. I. TItle.

PS3576.15117 C3 2001
813'.54—dc21

                                                        00-065830

First printing, February 2001
Second printing, May 2001
Third printing, September 2001

Cover design: Lauren Zimmerman

Printed in the United States of America

10   9   8   7   6   5   4   3

Though this book was written in fiction form,
many of the events described
were based on actual events. . . .

FOREWORD

As with many of the titles we publish, *Called* speaks to the heart of the reader by sharing Universal Principles which, when understood and accepted into consciousness, will change reality and the way we each experience our own existence.

We live in a changing world, and Lauren Zimmerman is a change catalyst. She has had a vast array of "paranormal" experiences, including contact with friends from the stars. She draws upon these while speaking, writing, and teaching.

Though *Called* is presented as fiction, we believe that it may very well be more fact than fiction.

Paul M. Clemens
Publisher

ACKNOWLEDGMENTS

Creating and bringing to completion a project such as
OTHER WORLDS: The Series
is an enormous task ...
but extremely fulfilling on each and every level.

I wish to thank all of those who have
given of themselves without hesitation.
Without the help of those who love me,
my dream would never have seen the light of day.
*You know who you are and I thank you
and bless you for being a part of my life.*

CHAPTER ONE

THE DREAM WAS SURREAL. A massive craft that spread across the night sky. An empty control room, dimly lit by an unidentified light source. Large black chairs set solidly before a control panel, small phosphorescent lights blinking occasionally. Beyond the expanse of windows above the panel, the Universe waited silently. Shadows of other-world beings could be sensed moving around behind him, though Paul couldn't see them.

Suddenly a hand touched his shoulder. He turned his head to look. The hand had only three fingers. He slowly moved his eyes until he was looking into the solemn, almond-shaped eyes of a small being with ivory skin. He felt a rush of peace fill him as the memories that he'd shared with this being flooded him. A flash of light as bright as a sun ray burned itself into his brain. Instantly the memory of another place dominated the dream, sliding him, as dreams often do, into another world. He was in a nebulous world full of remembrances of another life in another time, a loving face, raven-black hair wrapped around his arms and drifting across his chest like clinging seaweed, a love so deep that his soul ached for it. He felt himself sliding away from her at the same moment he recognized her. He reached to hold her, but in vain. Waking, he shook his head. He was filled with conflicting emotions. He knew instinctively that he would never be the same. The dream world felt too real to be fiction, his emotions too raw from the memories to be ignored.

Paul laid still, giving himself time to adjust to the morning light that was just beginning to enter the room. At twenty-nine, he liked to think that he wasn't afraid of anything but this morning he could feel an unnamed fear stirring up his stomach. He decided to skip his morning coffee and instead mulled over the dreams. Dominating his thoughts was the memory of a triangular face with large black eyes, the touch of a cool hand, the hint of a mystery far beyond his present understanding. The dream echoed through his mind, trying to find a place to become real.

He identified a fear deep within himself as he searched the dream. Accepting the dream as fact, and knowing that he had been in another place while his body was sleeping, wasn't the source of his fear. He probed his discomfort like a sore tooth. His body ached as if he had the flu. A dull pain stood behind his eyes. All of this was familiar to him … even the dream.

These dreams had been romancing him for years. Other worlds, other realities, other universes. Each dream was a nebulous seduc-tress, enticing him to believe in something other than the reality that he was living. The thrill of possibility danced through his spine every time he allowed himself to believe that there was something more, something beyond what everyone accepted as reality.

No. He was not afraid of encountering other worlds and other-world beings. His fear was that now it was time to do something about it. The time had come for him to face the challenge of admitting to the world that he was from elsewhere. But the first thing had to be his own acceptance and understanding.

He pushed himself into a sitting position, rested his back against the backboard, and linked his arms around his knees. The dream had confirmed what he had always felt about himself. He was from elsewhere. All of his discomfort, uneasiness, and boredom with life were now explained. What remained was the decision of what to do about it.

A thought crossed his mind. Would his life have been different if he had always been aware of his origins? Would he have been able to stop his father's drinking, his mother's abuse and martyrdom, his brother's rush to fate and death as he escaped into drugs to avoid his pain? Realistically, he knew that he could not have changed the people but perhaps he could have changed his own reaction to his experience.

Would he have leapt from one woman to the next, seeking that certain someone that he could sense but could not put a face to? Would he have spent his life searching? Would he have taken so much time and made such an effort to fit in, to attempt to be something that he could never be?

He had always been athletic and lean. He worked out at the school gymnasium after hours at least three times a week. At 6'1", he weighed 192 and was good-looking enough to be called handsome by the ladies that he'd dated. At the present time he was, he thought, an efficient but lackadaisical coach at the high school that was only blocks away from his small apartment. He still lived in the city where he'd been born and raised. He drove a beat-up, old Bronco and, on occasion, he tossed a few clothes and some food in the back of it and headed into the nearby foothills on a weekend quest for peace and quiet.

Paul shook his head, realizing that his introspection was serving no purpose. He threw off the covers and headed for the shower. Later, shirtless and barefoot, he paced the length of his apartment as his memories became clearer. He was in the past and in the present at the same time. Watching himself from a distance, he studied the memories as if they belonged to someone else.

There were five small beings guiding him through the atmosphere of Earth. They ranged between three and four feet tall and had smooth, ivory-colored skin covering their small, thin frames. Their heads were large in proportion to their bodies. Their great, almond-shaped ebony eyes were made even darker by the compassion that poured through them.

Paul was in spirit form, drifting through the atmosphere without effort, flanked by his comrades. The light that was cast by his spirit touched the forms of his five friends, giving them a slightly haunted appearance. Beneath them, the roof of the house where he was going to live loomed black and, to Paul, ominous. Though he had volunteered for this mission, he was not happy about it.

He and his companions merged their cells with the cells of the roof and ceiling and moved easily through the apparent solidity of them. They were now looming above the sleeping form of a small, four-year-old child.

"Learn what you can," Zere said, extending his small, three-fingered hand toward Paul's spirit.

Paul nodded and turned toward the child. Immediately, as if summoned, a small light emerged from the child's body. After emerging, it grew in stature until the full light of a tall spirit stood before them.

Paul nodded in acknowledgment. "Thank you for holding the focus for me," he said.

The tall spirit nodded in return and extended its light to embrace Paul. "I wish you all the best," he whispered. "I know this won't be easy for you."

A deep sense of dread rushed through Paul. It had been a common emotion since the Council had accepted his decision to incarnate on Earth. Now that the moment of incarnation had arrived, a sense of hesitation and misgiving gripped him. As if all of them were sharing the same thought, they all exchanged solemn, questioning glances. All eyes turned toward Paul. After only a second of hesitation, he nodded slowly. The others resumed their work. Paul watched without speaking as Zere and the others busied themselves with disconnecting the departing spirit and attaching his to the small body that lay still on the bed beneath them. When the operation was complete, Paul watched as the freed spirit soared eagerly through the ceiling and away. He turned to his five companions with a sorrow unmatched. Their eyes reflected his pain.

"We'll be with you," Zere said quietly.

Unable to speak, Paul nodded once again. He scanned the eyes of each of those who were so dear to him. There was nothing more to be said. His decision had been discussed and debated for several months. All of the details had been hashed through, all possible issues that might arise had been addressed and solutions hammered out until, finally, everyone was satisfied that they had done the best they could to prepare for this mission.

But now that the moment of separation was upon him, Paul could think of thousands of things that could go wrong. And his family would be millions of miles away.

He choked back a sudden wave of longing and lifted his eyes to meet theirs. "I will be back with you soon," he said stoutly.

Each of them nodded eagerly. He didn't think any of them believed his words at all. He certainly did not. His life on Earth would take up nearly eighty Earth years. It would take that long to complete the work that he had assigned himself.

One by one he embraced them. He watched solemnly as they merged with the ceiling and disappeared from sight. He was alone in a darkened room with a small, foreign body that was going to be his home for the next eighty years. Beyond the door of the bedroom slept the strangers that would serve as his parents. Beyond them sat a foreign world, a world filled with people who would challenge him in ways that would take all of his strength to master and understand. The very thought of it took every ounce of resolution from his spirit. Exhausted, he sank down next to the body and wearily closed his mind to the future. The cord that now attached him to the body lay across him like an abandoned umbilical cord, dull and unwanted.

The phone beside him rang softly, startling him out of his memory. Unnerved by the sudden call to reality, he scrubbed his long fingers through his sandy-colored hair and picked up the receiver.

"Happy summer vacation," Sandi chirped, her pert voice grounding him firmly into the day.

"Thanks. Same to you." He realized that he sounded dull but he didn't have the energy to do anything about it.

"What do you have planned for the first day of your vacation?" she asked.

Paul frowned at the phone, feeling trapped by the sudden necessity to make plans. He knew that she was falling in love with him. It was time to tell her that he didn't feel the same. It wasn't fair for her to continue to believe otherwise. "I haven't really thought about it," he told her. "I wanted to give myself some time." He cleared his throat nervously, thinking about his next words.

Sandi's voice became hesitant. "Oh. Sure. I can understand that."

Paul could feel her back off, like she always did, ever anxious to please him. He felt compassion for her rise in his chest. He saw her as vulnerable and somehow defenseless in a world that was too large for her, too complicated. He wanted to protect her because she was his friend. But for the first time he realized that he needed to put his own needs before hers.

"Did I wake you?" she asked. "You sound distracted."

Paul shook his head. "No. But I need to tell you something." He hurried on before she could interrupt. "You're a wonderful person and I wish I could be the right man for you. But I'm not."

He heard her draw her breath in quickly but he didn't stop. It needed to be said. "You're going to find the right one, Sandi." A rush of intuition and vision flooded him. He suddenly knew who the man was. He saw, in his mind's eye, the two of them standing before a minister, exchanging vows. He chose to believe in his vision and hurried his words in order to give her the hope she needed. "You already know him, Sandi. You just haven't opened your eyes to him yet. Think about it. Open your heart to accept him and he'll be there."

Paul closed his eyes briefly, feeling his own sense of loss as he let her go. "You'll be very happy," he said quietly.

"Paul?" Sandi said hesitantly. "Are you all right?"

"I'm fine, Sandi. And you will be too."

"I don't understand you," she told him softly.

"I know," he whispered. He sighed deeply as she gently set the phone down.

CHAPTER TWO

LATER, STILL SHIRTLESS AND BAREFOOT, Paul again paced through his apartment as his thoughts raced through the frustrations and circumstances of his life. He was now certain that he was from somewhere else. The frustrations of his life had been genuine. Also real were the dreams that had been walking by his side as regularly as his shadow.

Without warning he heard a voice inside his head.

"Your memories were deliberately taken away," the voice told him. "Recall that it was our decision so that you could concentrate on where you were rather than where you wanted to be."

Undisturbed by the voice, because it sounded the same as it had when he had last heard it, Paul smiled sarcastically. "It did not work," he said softly. "I wanted to be there without even knowing where it was that I wanted to be."

He thought he heard a slight chuckle. "We know. We have been monitoring you all the way, as we said we would. But then," the voice chuckled, "you always have been fairly stubborn."

Paul laughed aloud at the accuracy of the statement. "Well," he said hesitantly, "have I blundered the entire plan?"

"No," the voice assured him. "As a matter of fact, now is when the real work begins."

"Meaning?" Paul asked.

The voice made no comment. Instead Paul was hit with a sudden, driving inspiration that plunged him into an almost frantic sense of urgency. He'd had flashes of intuition all of his life. Some he'd ignored. Some he hadn't. This one was too strong to ignore, even though he sensed that to follow it meant that he would be changing his life irrevocably. He dove into the bedroom, finished dressing, threw a suitcase onto the bed and began tossing things haphazardly into it. Within minutes he was packed and ready to go. He drove directly to the bank, withdrew his savings, gassed up the Bronco, and got on Interstate 5 heading south. Only mildly surprised at his impulsiveness, he allowed the feeling of rightness to flow through him.

Dry and desolate, the desert landscape through Nevada did little to inspire him. He perked up when he saw that the scenery was turning green ahead. Tall ponderosa pines edged the freeway, taking over the barren scenery. Finally, breathing a deep sigh of relief, he pulled off of the freeway and into the town of Flagstaff. The evening light was bathing the town as he drove onto the main street. He guided the Bronco through the sparse traffic, looking over the sights and the people. A friendly-looking restaurant was advertising "home-cooking." He pulled into the parking lot, ran a comb through his hair, and stretched as he stepped from the car.

Everything on the menu sounded great. He finally decided on fried chicken, mashed potatoes, and salad. Savoring the crispy, honey-coated chicken, he closed his eyes with pleasure. When he opened them, he discovered a man watching him intently. He appeared to be about thirty-five. His face was round and tanned to a rugged brown, framed by straight, shoulder-length, black hair. He wore dusty jeans, worn-out cowboy boots, and a red plaid shirt with torn elbows. Recognizing that he was of Indian descent, Paul searched his memory in an attempt to remember what tribes lived in the area. The man silently appraised him, his lips locked in a firm, solemn line.

Now uncomfortable, Paul gave him a faint smile and dropped his eyes to his dinner. He was not surprised when the chair opposite him was dragged away from the table by a strong, tanned hand. The Indian flipped the chair around, straddled it, and scrutinized Paul without speaking.

Paul cleared his throat nervously. "Um, what can I do for you?"

"Probably nothin'," the Indian responded dryly.

Caught off guard by the comment, Paul smiled as his nervousness was replaced with curiosity. He gestured at his plate with his fork. "Are you hungry? You want some chicken?" he asked, wondering if possibly this might be a homeless man who had identified him as someone who might be willing to help. He could have been right. Paul's soft-heartedness had given him a lot of wanted and unwanted experiences throughout the years.

"No."

"A man of few words." Paul paused and stared at the man, waiting. He began to feel a tickle of suspicion, as if the man was going to tell him something profound. He even fancied that he would hear the message and then the man would simply vanish into thin air. He'd read stories of such things. He had made up his mind during the drive that he would be open to anything and everything that might happen during this trip. He was looking for adventure. An adventure that would change his life forever. Could this man be the beginning? When the man still didn't speak, Paul spoke again. "Well, you must be sitting at my table for a reason. You want to let me in on it?"

The Indian nodded.

By now Paul was totally intrigued. He wiped his hands on his napkin and stretched his right hand across the table. "My name is Paul. Yours?"

"Marlen," the stranger said, taking Paul's hand in his and giving it a brief shake.

Amused by the gruffness of the single word, Paul grinned. "Okay, Marlen." He picked up a piece of chicken, took a bite, and gestured at his plate again. "Are you sure about not having any?"

"Yep."

Both men fell into silence, Paul deciding that when the man was ready to say what he had to say, he would say it.

Marlen finally broke the silence. "Yes, you are the man I saw aboard the mothership. You were told to come here and that you have a mission. I will show you where you need to begin."

Paul looked at him in amazement. Apparently he had been open but not really prepared for the appearance of a mystery. Without being aware of it, he set his chicken down and wiped his fingers carefully. He was no longer hungry. His voice came out in a choked whisper. "What do you know?" he asked.

"They told me you would come. They also told me that I should meet you here. And here I am. Here you are."

Paul thought about what he'd heard. "Okay," he said slowly.

"All things can be known if you decide to be open enough to know them."

Paul looked at him curiously. "If you say so," he said, dismissing the comment. "But why are you interested in me and what I'm doing?"

"I'm going to be your guide," Marlen said simply. He didn't watch for Paul's reaction, instead choosing to gaze around the restaurant at the other patrons.

Paul struggled with his inner conflict. It was illogical for him to believe in aliens and other worlds and, at the same time, choose not to believe in powers and happenings that he did not yet understand. He had been inspired to come to this place he'd never been. He hadn't questioned the inspiration. And this journey had led him to this moment. Studying the nonchalant man who sat across from him, he made the decision that he was going to change his life forever. "So," he said abruptly, "where do we start?"

Marlen pointed at Paul's plate with his large, square chin. "I suggest that you pay the people for the meal and then we leave." He stood and flipped the chair back under the table. By the time Paul had paid the bill, Marlen was leaning against the side of the Bronco, picking at his teeth with a toothpick. He waited impassively as Paul unlocked the doors. Lowering his bulk into the passenger's seat, he rolled down his window and rested his deeply-tanned arm on the window edge.

Glancing at him, Paul thought that he was probably enjoying the edge that he had over him. He leaned against the steering wheel and turned to stare at him. "So … what do you know about why I'm here?"

"Let's talk while you drive."

"You're going to have to tell me where I'm supposed to be going," Paul said with a slight edge to his voice. "And while we're at it, it might be a good thing if you tell me who you really are." He set the palms of his hands sternly against the wheel, determined not to move the Bronco until he had a better understanding of what was happening.

Marlen watched him with a slight smile of amusement. "If you think about it, you will realize that you already know who I am."

Dazed by the comment, Paul took in a deep breath. Fear of strangers, he decided, was something that he'd been taught. In this case what he'd been taught was not necessarily what he needed to believe. It was time to learn to fully trust his own instincts, develop his own intuition. With a certainty as potent as one hundred-proof alcohol, he knew that Marlen had been ushered into his life for a reason. Putting his trust in him might be a mistake. But not putting his trust in him could turn out to be a far greater mistake.

He felt Marlen's gaze on him. He turned to find him smiling with a faint hint of sarcasm.

"Now that we've decided to trust each other, maybe we should get moving," Marlen suggested.

Paul shrugged. "South?" he asked.

"Southeast."

Paul smiled, shook his head slightly, and set the Bronco into gear. Two hours later the back of the Bronco was filled to capacity with camping supplies and groceries. Satisfied, Marlen settled back against the seat and finally told Paul where they were headed. Night had taken the daylight away as Paul turned the Bronco onto Lake Mary Road and headed toward a town and a future that was uncertain.

The night was too dark, too deep, for him to see much of anything other than the headlight-kissed pavement of the road.

They passed a small community with one store and one filling station. After that, the forest was deep and tall, with pine trees hovering over the road, stealing the moonlight. With the window open slightly, Paul managed to fill his lungs with the fresh scent of night branches.

The streets of Payson were silent and empty as they pulled the Bronco into the only open gas station. Paul stepped out and stretched, breathing in the night air and the sense of peace that seemed to pervade the entire town. Marlen joined him and the two of them stepped into the bright lights of the interior of the station. Paul headed for the restrooms on the right. The narrow hallway was stacked with boxes. Just as he reached for the men's room door, the door beside it flew open. Jumping back in surprise, he stumbled against a case of motor oil and hit the wall. The blond-haired woman who had thrown open the door stopped, stared at him, and immediately burst into tears.

"Hey!" Paul cried, alarmed. "I'm sorry if I scared you." When she continued to weep, he reassured her, "I'm not hurt. And you're all right." He reached a tentative hand toward her but she shrank away as if terrified.

She stared at him with tears clouding the strong, violet-blue color of her eyes. "I'm terribly sorry," she said, her voice thick with tears. "I don't know what's the matter with me."

She dropped her head immediately, sending her long, blonde hair falling over her face like a veil of protection. She was short, petite, and had an aura of vulnerability that, if Paul had stopped to think about, spelled trouble.

The woman began to cry again. Now Paul knew for certain that something was terribly wrong. Their simple mishap had stirred up too much emotion. "Look, are you okay?" he asked, studying her intently. All of his protective instincts kicked into high gear. "Can I help you?" he asked softly.

As if the words were a catalyst, the woman threw her head back and stared at him, her eyes blazing like the challenging stare of a cornered stallion. Contrary to her glare, her continued sobs filled the station, disturbing Paul with the intensity of his own reaction. He sensed someone behind him and turned to find Marlen scrutinizing them both. Paul shrugged and lifted his arms in a futile motion.

"Is there anything we can do for you?" Marlen asked the woman in a voice so tender that Paul stared at him in surprise.

She brushed at her tears and raised her head to meet his eyes. Paul thought that what he saw in her eyes was fear.

"No. There's nothing you can do," she told Marlen quietly. "I'll be all right. Really," she added.

She reached to brush her hair from her eyes. Paul winced at the bruises that marked her arms. Now he noticed the red hand print that stood out on her cheek like a brand.

"My gosh!" he cried, reaching out for her without thinking. "What happened to you? Who did this?" He looked around angrily, hoping to see her attacker.

"No!" she cried, backing away from him.

Marlen stepped in front of Paul, glaring at him briefly. "We have no intention of interfering if you don't want us to," he said quietly.

She stood and trembled before him, like a frightened child. "I just want to go home," she said unsteadily.

"We can take you home," Marlen said gently. "But first we need to know if the guy who did this to you will be there."

She shook her head. Her long hair fell over her face once again, hiding the abuse. She turned away slightly, shying away from their intense stares. "He's not there. It will be all right. He's just stressed out lately," she added defensively.

Flashes of memory besieged Paul. His mother weeping. Bruises unsuccessfully covered with make-up. "So that means you deserve to be hit?" he asked tightly, his strong jaw locked around his tension.

Marlen threw him a quick glance and turned back to the woman, stopping the protest she was preparing to throw at Paul. "We can take you home," he repeated.

She gathered herself to answer but instead clenched her jaw. Her right hand grabbed for her ribs, her face drained of color. Marlen grabbed her just as she fainted. Gathering her into his arms, he nodded at Paul to precede him and headed for the door. Tossing a twenty at the startled clerk, Paul rushed after Marlen and the wounded woman.

He drove as fast as he dared. The hospital was only blocks away. The emergency nurse took one look at the woman and ordered them to follow her. She pushed through a set of double doors and pointed to a small, curtained room on the right. As Marlen was laying the unconscious woman on the table, the nurse was already barking orders into a telephone and setting up an IV.

"What happened?" she demanded, glancing from one to the other as she worked.

"We only know that she's been beaten," Paul said. "We ran into her at the gas station and she passed out while we were trying to help her. She grabbed her right side before she fainted."

The nurse's name tag read "Marci." She fit the name. Her halo of short, auburn hair shaded her sad, brown eyes. "You just met her?" she asked. "You don't know her name?"

Paul shook his head. "We were trying to find out when she fainted. We were going to take her home. We had no idea she was hurt this bad."

"Well," Marci said in a soft, reassuring voice, "we will find out how bad this is. Maybe she passed out from stress or shock or maybe she's got some broken ribs. If you want to wait outside, I'll let you know how she's doing." She nodded toward the curtain, inviting them to leave.

"I hope she's going to be all right," Paul said worriedly. He glanced at the unconscious woman and caught his lower lip between his teeth. He was surprising himself with the extent of his concern for her. Just the few minutes of encounter had convinced him that he wanted to help this woman in any way that he could. He breathed a sigh of relief as a doctor and two nurses rushed into the room. He moved to get out of their way. The curtain closed behind them as he and Marlen left the small, now-crowded room.

An hour later the police had finished interviewing them. Marlen seemed to be dozing, his long legs stretched out in front of him, ankles crossed. Paul couldn't rest. His mind darted here and there, uneasy with the thoughts that were plaguing him.

Why did he feel as if he had seen this woman somewhere before. Why had he, for just a minute, pictured her with hair as black as a raven's wing when clearly it was blonde? Why did she seem so familiar? And ... would he ever see her again?

"Existence is nothing more than a experience," Marlen murmured sleepily.

"What?" Paul asked, turning to him with surprise, the realization dawning that Marlen had been reading his thoughts.

Marlen opened one eye and peered at Paul before closing it again. "Existence is a place where we, as explorers of existence, learn all things in all ways. That takes lifetimes. And we meet a whole lot of people as we travel along these roads. It's simple. She's one of those people that you've traveled with before."

Paul studied him for a silent minute. "What you're saying is that we've had another lifetime together."

"Exactly," Marlen murmured, his eyes still closed.

"So is there a reason for meeting up with her again?"

"There's a reason for everything," Marlen said simply.

Paul sighed. He was tired. He was not up to playing mind games. "I mean, is there a particular reason for this meeting? Am I supposed to do something? Or does this mean we'll spend time together in this lifetime?"

"Consider the possibility that you're trying to repeat a memory, Paul. You had a lifetime with her. That doesn't necessarily mean you'll have another one together." Marlen lifted one eyelid and peered at Paul with interest. "Whatever you choose to do will be fine. People talk about pre-destiny ..." He shook his head. "I believe that the only thing predestined is that we'll experience existence and we'll accomplish certain things. How we accomplish them is up to us and the people in our lives. People make choices every day." He lifted one shoulder in a shrug. "Every single choice leads everyone else to make choices based on those choices." He shrugged again. "I can't choose to take this path with you if you choose not to take it with me. If you hadn't come along, I would have had other choices to make. The future unfolds depending upon the choices each of us make. And no one person is separate from all others."

He opened both eyes and looked intently at Paul. "Like this situation ... you're already enamored with this woman. You can choose right here and now to abandon the mission you and I have and stay with her. But," he lifted his index finger and wagged it slightly, "she has free will too." He grinned mischievously. "She could choose to hate the sight of you when she wakes up." He chuckled lightly and closed his eyes again, readjusting his back against the chair.

Paul was not certain if he should laugh or be offended. He chose the first and gave Marlen a dry, humorless chuckle. "Cute," he commented.

Marlen shrugged without opening his eyes. "You never know." He re-crossed his ankles and pushed himself further back into his chair.

"By the way," Paul said lightly, "stop reading my mind."

Marlen smiled like a satisfied cat. "Stop thinking so loudly," he shot back quickly. "And keep in mind, all thoughts are readable if you stop creating your own long enough to listen to someone else's. In other words," he said with a lop-sided grin, "learn to shut up inside your own head. You'll probably end up a lot wiser if you do."

Paul regarded the limp form of his new friend skeptically. "Is that really true?"

"All things are made up of energy," Marlen murmured. "Thoughts are energy. A wise man learns to read energy and becomes an even wiser man."

Before either of them could make further comment, Marci appeared in the doorway. Paul stood upon her approach. Marlen opened his eyes at the activity and leaned forward in his chair, his elbows on his knees, his eyes watching the nurse thoughtfully.

"Well, she's going to be all right. This time anyway. It appears that this isn't the first time. She's got some bruised ribs. Nothing's broken. She hasn't been eating right. It looks like she fainted from hunger and shock. We're going to run some more tests but it looks like she'll be all right." She looked from one to the other. "I don't suppose you saw the guy who did this, did you?"

Paul shook his head. "We were the only car at the gas station." He thought about it. "As a matter of fact, I wonder how she got to the station. There were no other cars around."

Marlen spoke up. "She was in his car. She locked herself in the bathroom when he stopped to get gas. He took off without her when he couldn't get her to come out. It's a good thing he did."

Marci looked at him curiously but didn't comment. Paul simply nodded, rapidly becoming accustomed to Marlen's knowledge about things he shouldn't have known. His shoulders sagged with sudden fatigue. He was aware of the unspoken warning behind Marlen's words. Perhaps the next time the woman would not be lucky enough to escape with only minor wounds.

His stomach clenched with anxiety. "I can't deal with this," he said suddenly, to no one in particular. "I grew up with this kind of thing." He stood and walked to the window that overlooked the serene, unaware night. Struggling against his emotions, he swallowed a sudden surge of rage and helplessness.

Behind him he heard Marlen ask if they could see the injured woman. He felt himself resist the idea. Instantly he regretted his selfishness. They were the only friends she had at this time of night; she needed them. But was he going to be walking into his past again? He remembered the stark and desolate nights of pain and weeping over his mother's bruises. He had put a lot of effort into walking away from the memories. Getting involved would bring them all back.

Without warning he heard a small voice inside his head. "Wounds are not healed if you put them away untended. They must have air and light in order to heal. Until they are healed they will always fester, waiting beneath the surface to rise again and again until you finally accept them and stop resisting them."

He turned and followed Marlen and Marci down the bright hallway and into the small, curtained room.

Lying small and helpless, the woman seemed paler, more vulnerable, more open to his sympathy than she had before. Her bruises made the pale of her skin seem as fragile as century-old china. Paul winced in sympathy and struggled to control his emotions.

Her eyes were open, watching them approach. She looked from him to Marlen and back again. The bright blue-violet innocence of her eyes tugged at him like a beacon of hope sent from Beyond.

"My name's Stephanie," she said, her voice low and tired. "And you two are my rescuers. I need to thank you for your help." She licked her dry lips and looked away briefly. "I'm sorry I was so much trouble."

"You weren't trouble," Marlen said quickly. "We're both glad that we were there to help."

Paul spoke. "My name's Paul. This is Marlen."

Her eyes caught and held his. Suddenly Paul was in another time and place. She was lying in his arms, her silky black hair spread warmly across his chest. The sun embraced them. Nearby, the gentle grace of a small waterfall fell into a pool of liquid at its base. The pool was crystal clear, the stones at the bottom purple and blue in color.

Paul blinked in shock. The moment was lost. He stared at Stephanie in an attempt to bring back the vision, the memory, the serenity and love that had momentarily taken him to a place of peace. But the moment was gone, as surely as the lifetime that he had just glimpsed.

Marlen looked at him sharply and turned back to Stephanie. "We should let you rest, but we wanted to be sure you were all right."

"Is he talking about leaving already?" Paul asked himself, surprised. Marlen was touching her hand in farewell. Not knowing what else to do, Paul followed suit. Seconds later he was reluctantly following Marlen out the front doors of the hospital to the Bronco.

He couldn't hold onto his curiosity any longer. "Did you happen to catch a hint of that vision that I had in there?"

Marlen opened his door and settled himself against the seat before replying. "I already told you that you had a lifetime with her. Why are you surprised?"

Paul looked at him in consternation. "You need to keep in mind that all of this is new to me. Maybe on some level I know all of this, but right here and now I'm just beginning to understand it a little."

Marlen shrugged comfortably. "It will all come back to you. In answer to your question, yes, I felt you remembering her."

"Then it was real," Paul whispered, slightly in awe of the enormity of what he was learning … or remembering.

"Everything is real somewhere," Marlen commented with a lazy drawl.

Paul looked at him quickly. "I could think of a whole lot of questions about that comment but I'm too tired right now. Just tell me where we're going and how to get there fast. I need some sleep."

"We need to head on back to Hwy. 260. Head north. When you pass through a place called Christopher Creek, wake me up."

A minute later he was asleep and snoring softly, leaving Paul to the miscellaneous meandering of his own thoughts.

CHAPTER THREE

PAUL WAS BEING IMMERSED in a world that he didn't understand. And yet he felt as if he were coming home to himself. It felt good. He couldn't wait until the next chapter unfolded. He drove through the dark night, tired but eager to see what would happen next.

Shortly after waking Marlen in the small town of Christopher Creek, they turned off the highway onto a bone-jarring road full of ruts and potholes. Soon they were headed up the side of a mountain on an even rougher road. It was almost dawn when they pulled into a tree-lined meadow. Not far away a campfire leapt in concert with the slight breeze. A lone figure, bundled into a brightly-colored serape, rested with his back against a fallen log and his feet stretched toward the fire's warmth. He didn't turn at the sound of the Bronco. Paul felt a chill run through him. It felt to him like the man was there only in body and that his spirit had departed.

Steadying himself, he killed the engine and stepped from the car. The air fell instantly silent. Not even the hoot of a night owl interrupted the vastness of the lingering night. He thought for a moment about unloading the supplies but instead decided that he needed sleep. With unspoken agreement, Marlen looked at him and nodded. Both men grabbed sleeping bags from the back of the Bronco, found a tree to curl up against, and in minutes they were asleep. Weariness won out over manners. Neither of them acknowledged the lone figure at the fire.

The dream was dark, making Paul's surroundings almost indistinguishable to him. It became clear that he was in a hallway. To the right and left of him were walls of cubicles, each the size of a coffin.

In several of the cubicles were dim lights. Beneath the lights lay figures as still as death. His stomach twisted in anxiety as he wondered if they were actually dead. Instantly he heard a voice behind him. He turned to see a small figure dressed in an aura of violet. She was five feet tall with alabaster skin pulled tightly against her bones. Her head was bald and angular. Her large, almond-shaped eyes gave back his own reflection, as if they were mirrors. She answered his questions by placing thoughts into his mind. It seemed as natural as breathing.

"These are transmutation chambers. The people within them are currently visiting other universes in spirit form. The function of their bodies will return when their spirit returns from its journey."

"Why?" was Paul's simple question.

"A physical body is merely a vehicle that is used to obtain physical results in physical worlds. An incarnation on a physical plane is nothing more than the spirit expressing itself physically. There would be no reason for eliminating these bodies during the spirit journey, only to re-manifest them upon the return of the spirit. And so they are held suspended until the return."

"I suppose that makes sense," Paul commented, turning again to look at the motionless figures. "How does one go about deciding to leave the body and take a spirit journey? What is the purpose of the journey?"

"It depends upon the personal need of each spirit and the personal desire to serve the Plan. If, let us say, a soul is manifesting in a universe and a situation in a parallel existence needed assistance and that soul is capable of assisting, one might leave the body behind in order to help." The being stretched out a paper-thin, almost-effervescent hand and laid it gently on Paul's arm. "Your mind will accept more knowledge and memory as you stretch it by allowing all possibilities. A closed mind is actually a wasted tool. Your capabilities are far greater than you now realize. As you travel through the next several years, you will come to understand yourself and your truth to a much greater degree."

As if the dream were merely an exercise of his spirit, a method of bringing him closer to his personal truth, Paul embraced the words that she offered him as a gift. An unexpected thought leapt into his mind. She answered before he could voice it.

"Yes. It could be possible for you to maintain a body elsewhere. As a matter of fact, you are doing that exact thing at this moment. This," she waved a fragile hand at him, "is your spirit. Your body is on Earth, in that sleeping bag." She turned him gently. He was looking at Earth from a vantage point that seemed to be a million miles away. His vision focused and he could somehow see his sleeping form, lying on the ground in Arizona, curled against the chill of the morning. A thread-thin silver cord shivered with life, connecting his spirit with his body.

Though it appeared that he was dreaming, Paul could feel himself react to what he was seeing. A shiver ran through his spirit as if the breath of God had embraced it. He looked away from the thin being, his soul suddenly filled with a longing that was so great that he knew it included only himself and his Creator. Steadying himself, he turned and noticed what appeared to be a huge aquarium recessed into the wall opposite the cubicles. The liquid inside glistened as if snakes of silver were etching their way through it.

As he formed a question about it, the end of the dark hallway appeared to move, opening as if it were a doorway. A small figure appeared, dressed in shadows. It was only about three feet tall. It moved toward Paul, gliding on silent, motionless feet. As it passed him, Paul could feel a brush of energy as if, for only a second, he and the figure had touched. He was astonished to feel an almost desperate sense of loss as the being moved out of sight.

He turned to follow, but with his first step the hallway became a staircase. It was spiraling, twisting, floating, through a humming mist. His arms helplessly reached as he tried to hold onto the dream. The hum of the mist grew louder until it seemed to be a deliberate torture. He watched himself grab a piece of the mist. He tore at it frantically, willing it to hold him tight enough to bring him back to its reality.

He opened his eyes slowly and shook his head in frustration as the noon sun tapped on him in an effort to wake him. He lifted his arms over his eyes, shading them. He realized that any attempt to return to sleep would be futile. Running his hands through his disheveled hair, he sat up. The sleeping bag bunched at his waist. The slight chill in the air nipped at his neck. He was looking at a small meadow surrounded by a thick forest of tall pines.

Glancing toward the campfire, he saw that the figure of the man who had been there when they'd pulled in was still there. Marlen had joined him. Kicking the sleeping bag away from his legs, Paul stood, drew on his jacket, slid his feet into his new hiking boots, and walked off in search of a place to relieve himself. A few minutes later he was accepting a cup of coffee from Marlen's outstretched hand and being introduced to the man at the fire.

The old man's face was etched and ribboned by time. His cheekbones flared out from his face, making his small, black eyes seem sunken. His lips, as thin as fingernails, were pressed around the stem of a stubby pipe. He was dressed in threadbare jeans, dusty old boots, and a red, plaid, flannel shirt that had cuffs as ragged as a desert horizon.

"This is Grandfather," Marlen said, introducing the old man.

The old man nodded and took his gaze away from Paul. The mountain air was chill and silent. Paul struggled to think of something to say but, coming up with nothing, remained in the silence that no one seemed eager to fill. He sank down and leaned his back against a rugged log, balancing his coffee on one knee.

It was Grandfather who finally broke the silence. "You got good timing," he said. His voice was low and as gravely as an old, unplowed field.

Uncertain what he meant, Paul simply nodded and waited for further explanation. There was none. The only sound was Grandfather's dry lips sucking on the unlit pipe.

After a minute Grandfather's thin, age-weakened hand gestured at the tall pines that surrounded the meadow. "While we are waiting, you should take the time to notice where you are. This Earth has much beauty to offer."

Paul agreed. The forest was thick and lush green. The small meadow was dotted here and there with patches of yellow wild flowers. Beyond them was a small range of mountains, marching across the horizon in ragged formation. It was a sight he would never have expected to see in what he had thought was a state filled with only desert landscapes.

"Let's throw together something to eat," Marlen suggested suddenly.

The words caused Paul to realize that he was hungry. "An excellent idea," he agreed, jumping to his feet.

Together they rustled through the supplies, coming up with eggs, canned ham, canned potatoes, and a large jar of salsa. When all of the work was done, they sank back against the logs and enjoyed one of the most delicious meals Paul had ever known.

At the end of the meal a shrill and haunting cry split through the day. For a strange, metaphysical moment it seemed as if it had come from a place beyond Earth, through a split in reality. The day stood still. Reality seemed to hold its breath and wait. In the small piece of the sky that loomed over the meadow, Paul looked up to see a small, dark form. It stopped, hovered, and then dived, disappearing from sight. It was his first sight of a great eagle.

The rest of the day passed lazily as he adjusted to the altitude, explored his surroundings, bathed in a nearby creek, and attempted not to eavesdrop on Marlen and Grandfather as they sat by the fire and talked in low tones. The air held a sense of unnamed anticipation. Paul suspected that, when they were ready, the two men were going to tell him what his journey was all about and what he might expect in the days to follow. He sensed that his entire life was about to change dramatically.

That evening the sun was slow to disappear, the shadows clinging to the light as if reluctant to let it go. After preparing a feast of fried potatoes mixed with corn, wild onions, slivers of canned beef, and dollops of salsa, Paul leaned back against his log, stretched his feet toward the fire, and heaved a sigh filled with peace, enjoyment, and a tinge of curiosity.

Grandfather peered at him quizzically. "You are more patient than most men I have met," he grumbled amiably.

Paul brushed his strong hand through his hair and smiled. "That is not to say that I'm not ready to hear what you obviously have to say to me. Actually, I would really like to know. I've traveled quite a ways to get here. It might be nice to know why."

Not answering directly, Grandfather began to speak. "You may not remember this, but I think it is time to remind you. All people were first created as souls. These souls are great and powerful. But these souls begin to explore existence by taking small parts of themselves, in forms that we call spirit, out to all realms and dimensions throughout existence. These spirits, as you may recall, often take on physical forms." He grinned around the stem of his ever-present pipe. "We call these forms 'bodies'. They have their ups and downs," he added, chuckling. To Paul he sounded like a lonely old horse that had just come upon a new companion.

"Anyway," the old man continued, "the point of this is that we often forget that we are souls, powerful and wise. We lose sight of the truth and settle for what we can see and hear. We learn to identify with the smaller parts of ourselves and forget the bigger parts. We make the small parts real and get to believing that anything beyond that is pure fiction and fantasy. Now, my son, it is time to remember. To call your soul to you."

Paul started to speak but silenced himself when the old man took a deep breath and continued. A small fire stood in his eyes. It seemed to Paul that his eyes were speaking of battles won and lost, both with worlds and with souls. "Do not let the world tell you what your thoughts should be or how your life can best serve you. When we do this, we lose our soul. We give our power away. It runs like the wind back to a place where it can be free.

"It was meant that the soul lead the body and the mind toward all new possibilities. The soul knows all worlds. It is not limited by this experience. It is the way of man that says that the world must consist of only what he can see and understand and label. It is a crime. A crime against all of creation." The old man sucked fiercely on his pipe, his hollow cheeks becoming more hollow with the effort.

Paul was gripped with an intensity that he had never experienced before. He found himself leaning toward the old man, as if with a closer proximity he might draw the old man's wisdom into himself. "How do I call my soul to me?" he asked tensely.

"We have prepared what you will need to begin the process."

Grandfather glanced at Marlen without speaking. Marlen immediately rose and began to stir the fire, adding logs until the flames were reaching for the sky as if they wished to dance with the stars. For the first time, Paul noticed a thick mug of unknown origin perched near the edge of the fire.

As the moon took command of the sky, Grandfather offered Paul the brew that had been steeping near the low fire for most of the afternoon. Feeling slightly apprehensive, Paul took a small sip. It tasted musty, like old grass and herbs that Paul couldn't identify. The liquid rushed to his stomach and rolled around. Feeling woozy, he scooted off of his perch on the log and leaned back against it. He wanted to hold onto the Earth for balance but there was nothing to hold onto. Instead he simply placed his palms flat against the ground beneath him and hung on with his imagination.

The sky seemed to be moving toward him. The moon appeared to want to hear his thoughts as it drifted down from the sky to peer at him closely. Seconds later he realized that it was the other way around. His spirit was swimming through the sky, embracing the night air, kissing the stars. He felt the desire to look back and saw that his body was lying on the ground, the fire smoldering nearby. Grandfather and Marlen were resting peacefully as if they were unaware of his presence between them.

But now the sky seemed to change. It was becoming a face. Or was he going beyond the sky, beyond the atmosphere, beyond the Universe? His spirit-chest began to expand with light and love, reaching toward the possibility of someone, something, beyond what and whom he had ever known. Am I approaching God? he wondered. He felt the presence of something passionately caring. It seemed to hover over the Earth, as if attempting to shelter it. It seemed to Paul that the very air he breathed was the air that this presence had breathed out of its own lungs in order to fill Paul's lungs with life. He sucked the almost-liquid air into his chest, feeling it moving through his veins, making him new.

As each breath pulsed through him, it seemed to bring new life. It erased every moment that had gone before. He breathed in the atmosphere of Earth, sensing that he was being healed with each breath he took. Soon all thoughts began to recede. The world became a dark and spiraling funnel, a force that was drawing him toward a pinpoint of light. He felt his spirit reach for it, as if he innately knew that this was the source of Life, that he had been living in a dream. He balanced on the edge between light and dark. With his spirit-feet he could feel the cutting edge that divided reality from illusion. He felt his toes curl along the edge, as if they were talons.

The light had no source. It came from everywhere. It pervaded everything in existence, making it impossible to know whether there was anything else in existence other than light. Paul tried to pierce it, to see within in or beyond it, to identify its source. Something inside of him cried out with passion and longing. He heard himself saying … it has been a long journey and I now seek my home. Show me the source of home. Show me the truth.

His words seemed to usher in an invisible pulse. Like standing in the center of a heart, it beat and pulsed around him, absorbing him. His world began to throb. He was helpless to resist. In seconds he became the pulse and it was then that he knew that he was in union with the Creator of All That Is. Indeed, he had never been separate. Only the illusion of separation had stood between him and the union he had been seeking.

And now he became a mass of atoms, unformed, new, and seeking shape and substance. The pulse was his center. It seemed to him that if not for the pulse, he would cease to exist to himself, as if he was the pulse, the heart of all that is. He began to feel his world shifting. A vision of a flat line appeared beneath him. It extended, spanning through existence from beginning to end. He lived above the line, but should he choose, he could live inside the line. Inside the line was where he could be physical and where he could live a linear existence. And there were other lines as well. Stretching across time, intersecting with each other, meeting and sharing lifetimes.

At his request, the souls that lived within the lines nearest his came into his vision. He recognized each soul. His parents, his brother, Marlen, Grandfather ... all purposeful and determined, knowing their missions without doubt. Without any effort at all he came to understand the purpose of each within his own life. Why they had spent time together, what they had learned, what they had not.

This is a grid! he suddenly realized. From somewhere beyond himself he heard the words 'grid of existence.' As if he had somehow fallen into the very source of existence itself, he felt a rush of exhilaration dash around him.

As a thought occurred, it manifested. Through time and space he sped, helpless to stop his race toward knowledge. The grid was now nothing more than a magnetized impulse, pulling him toward a realization that he needed. Home! he whispered to himself with elation.

The land beneath him sparkled with life. There were two suns, both of them shades of violet and soft blue. Like sequined earth, specks of something that looked like polished silver winked at him from the ground. He allowed himself to drift to the surface until he felt solidity beneath his feet. Fascinated, he walked slowly, examining each thing that he saw.

On his left was a thin, liquid silver stream. Beyond were cave-like entrances into low, purple hills. Somehow he knew that people resided inside and that they were wise indeed.

There was a crystalline structure on his right. Even to his

untrained eyes it appeared to be arranged in a geometric pattern. He walked on, anticipation building in his chest. He tried to swallow but found that he could not. He wondered if, on Earth, his body might be dying.

Distant, elusive memory drew him off his path. Before him lay a small meadow, dotted with colors that he had never seen on Earth. Reverence for the place was causing his heart to swell. Beyond the meadow he saw a place that he knew was his home. It stood glistening in the low, embracing light. It was four-sided, pyramid-shaped, and appeared to be made of crystal; the purest, finest crystal that one could imagine. The apex came to a point so sharp that it looked as if it could pierce the atmosphere and allow other worlds to seep through.

He started toward it but was drawn by a movement to his right. Turning, he saw four robed figures with hoods drawn over their faces and sandals on their feet. Paul's memory flashed through time and instantly recognized one of the men as a dear and trusted friend named Solomon. He walked toward the group, as if drawn by a magnet. Stopping near them, his hand reached and felt the smooth hemp draped across Solomon's arm. The man turned and Paul was impaled by the sapphire-blue stare of a man he had known for centuries.

"We are glad that you chose to have this experience," Solomon said, placing his words into Paul's spirit in a manner that sent warmth to his heart. "We will now be able to help you overcome the belief in the boundaries that have been imposed upon you by this life-experience. You are about to begin your mission on Earth. The more you allow yourself to recall your limitless existence, the more you will be able to serve in other dimensions as well. We would love to see you live beyond earthly limitations."

As if by magic, the scene began to change. Paul now stood in the center of a rounded theater, surrounded by the four men. A gigantic screen ranged around him, standing almost twenty feet in height. It seemed that he was surrounded by the Universe. The screen came alive, giving him the vision of night sky, stars, planets, and galaxies sparkling around him. A tiny spacecraft careened across the screen, seemingly out of control.

Paul watched in horror as Earth's gravity pulled the small craft closer to its atmosphere. It was almost as if he could feel the efforts of those inside, struggling to right whatever was wrong.

A soft voice insinuated itself into his thoughts. "Not long ago the gravitational device was lost on this craft. All efforts to stop it have failed. It is being pulled to Earth. Aboard the craft are some that you know. It was not your original mission to be there to assist them but on a soul-level you have volunteered to be at the site of the landing. You would have it no other way."

The voice continued. "The time of impact is soon. The place will be Aztec Peak, which is near where your physical body now rests. The military forces of Earth are aware of the craft and its approach. It's being tracked. They have calculated where it will land. They will get there not too long after the impact. Their timing will be close enough to be a threat to the rescue mission."

A light began to pluck at Paul's eyelids. It felt as if someone had poured hot gravel into his eyes. He rolled away from the light, felt solid earth beneath his body, and realized that, without wanting to, he had returned to his body and was now rolling in the dirt, hot, dusty, and thirsty ... and annoyed. With a trembling hand he touched his forehead. It was hot. He grimaced at the foul taste in his mouth. He felt a cool hand touch his arm. He opened his eyes to see Marlen offering him a cup of water. Struggling to an upright position, he wrapped a trembling hand around the cup and drained it.

He looked around uneasily. Everything looked the same. But he knew that it wasn't. Life continued in the way that it always had, but he was different. He would never be the same.

After relating his experience to Marlen and Grandfather, Paul let the silence of the night envelope him. All three men fell silent as they allowed the vastness of reality to expand their thoughts and possibilities.

CHAPTER FOUR

THE NIGHT WAS DARK AND STILL. Grandfather slept, buried beneath several thin, weathered blankets. With his foot, Paul moved one of the blankets a few inches further away from the campfire, which had been reduced to a large smolder of ashes. Marlen leaned placidly against a log, surveying the star-dappled night.

"I can't believe that within a matter of hours we're going to be meeting up with folks from 'home,'" Paul commented quietly.

"We've never left 'home,' as you call it," Marlen replied, his voice sounding as if it had issued from a distant dimension and drifted down through the darkness.

"What do you mean?"

"This is only a phase of experience. Every dimension holds various experiences, like layers. Think of the dimensions as layers, like one pancake on top of another. Even though the top pancake isn't touching the bottom one, it's still part of the whole picture. They both make up the entire plate."

"So, even though we can't see the top layer, call it Heaven or whatever you want, it's still a part of our experience?"

Marlen nodded. "A tremendous amount of the problems down here are caused by people's belief that they are somehow separated from the Source; like this lifetime is a punishment, a banishment from Heaven or something."

Paul saw him turn his head this way and that, surveying the dark landscape.

Marlen continued. "Everything that exists is existing in the body of the Source. Each person, each thing, is an integral part of the whole. Where you exist within the whole, at any given time, is

31

your soul's choice, based on what you want to experience. So, you're never far from home, as you call it."

"I wonder why I chose this place and time?" Paul speculated, not expecting an answer.

Marlen shrugged his large shoulders. "It really shouldn't matter, should it? I mean, you're here. If you spend all your time wondering why you are somewhere, you never really experience where you are."

Caught off guard by the comment, Paul laughed out loud. "You're right," he added quickly. "I never really thought about it that way."

"I suspect that you've spent most of your life wishing you were somewhere else."

"How did you know?" Paul asked with a small smile at himself.

Marlen stretched his arms and locked his fingers behind his head. "A lucky guess."

Paul hesitated for a minute. Either he was extremely readable or Marlen was extremely perceptive. Either way, it was clear that he would need to evaluate his responses to life. He was amazed by how much he had learned about himself in the short time since he'd left Sacramento. In the back of his mind a vision of Stephanie haunted him. He was aware of the magnitude of the task ahead … but where did she fit in? "I wonder if I ought to go back into Payson before we get busy with this rescue," he said out loud.

"To see Stephanie?" Marlen asked with a yawn.

Paul glanced over at him quickly. He was still surprised by the fact that Marlen seemed able to read his mind. He felt the need to defend his returning thoughts about her. "Well, it can't be coincidence that I came all the way here from Sacramento, and at a particular moment in time I end up at a particular gas station in a town that I've never even heard of … and, voila! There she is."

Marlen shrugged again. "I don't believe in coincidence. However, I do believe that just because we knew someone in a different experience doesn't mean that we need to know them again in this one."

Paul's teeth chewed on his lower lip for a minute while he thought about the comment. "Maybe I was put there at that moment so that I would know she was in trouble and would help her."

Marlen's arm lifted to point out the silhouette of a silent owl as it passed by a hundred feet above them. "Maybe she chose this experience for a reason," he drawled.

"In other words, leave her alone to live her own experience?"

"Meaning … it isn't necessarily your job to rescue her." Marlen paused for a minute, choosing his words. "Stephanie would not be in this position if, on some level, she was not choosing it. She needs to learn something and this is the way she's learning it. When she understands what it is she wants to know, she will pull herself out of it … one way or the other." He lifted one finger to stop anything Paul might say and continued. "Do you honestly think that she isn't as wise as you, as strong as you, as connected to God as you? Would you rob her of that identity?"

"I don't follow you," Paul said. But even as he said it, he realized what Marlen was implying. His emotions tangled with his thoughts as he struggled with the possibility that it might be in her best interest to allow her to have her experience. Instinctively he wanted to rescue her. Intellectually he knew it might not be the wisest thing to do.

"Paul, you know who she is. You've known her throughout several other experiences. Remember those and then tell me that she's stupid or weak or whatever. Your memories will tell you the exact opposite, which should tell you that she is choosing this experience for a reason. Why would you step in and take it away from her?"

"Maybe in order to love her again," Paul said softly.

Marlen said nothing. Somewhere in the forest night the cry of a coyote cut through the darkness, reminding them that they weren't alone.

The night was quiet after that. Paul had a lot of time to think, though for the most part, he let his mind drift, relaxing into the peace of his environment. When it was time for sleep, he fell into it heavily. It seemed like only minutes before he drifted into another realm. He was standing, facing a long, oblong table. Sitting at the table were eighteen or twenty beings not from Earth. Several were short with ivory skin. Others were taller, about five feet, and had tan skin. Still others had opalescent qualities. The one that captured his attention most was pale green with a large head that was shaped something like that of a praying mantis. At the end of the table stood a humanoid-looking man, dressed in thick leather that fit him like a second skin.

"And so it is time for the Mission to enter the next phase," the humanoid was saying. "The new Earth grid is being worked on from all levels. The old is almost disassembled. The communication corridors are in place. Some of the inhabitants are already aware of them and have been seeking contact. I am extremely hopeful that all will go well with this next phase."

The luminous green alien turned to Paul with eyes that spoke to him with the intensity of thunder. "You remember how it used to be?" she asked him. "We came and went from Earth dimension freely. We were accepted. Our assistance was welcomed. Universal peace was in order." She dropped her gaze and shook her head sadly. "I was very saddened when Earth became a place of alienation. Deprived of communication with other realms, it has fallen into a state of great disrepair."

The small alien next to her placed a gentle, three-fingered hand on her pencil-thin arm. "The Mission will succeed, Thaline," he said urgently. "Most of the preparations have been completed. We are well into the next phase. By our deadline in 2006, everything will be in place. Perhaps even sooner." The alien's large, almond-shaped eyes turned to Paul. "There had to be a time when Earth was available as a place where people were left alone to make their own mistakes and to come, once again, to a time where they desire harmony with all. I hated to see the uprise against us and the fear that followed, but I also understand the process and why it had to be."

"Does this mean then," Paul asked, "that the entire human race will begin interacting with you?"

The small being glanced at Thaline and back to Paul. "That remains to be seen. We are limited to our role of offering the opportunity. The humans will continue to have free will."

Thaline interrupted. "I understand the pain of watching as things on Earth played out the way they have. I have never seen such a rapid manifestation of walls of fear and limited thinking! It makes me shiver with dread. How quickly all other dimensions and realities were blocked from view! It was astounding to watch." Her gaze once again blazed through the dream and into Paul's awareness. "We are extremely grateful to those forerunners and workers who have taken bodies on Earth in order to do the work that will re-establish connections."

A shroud of loneliness draped his heart as Paul opened his eyes to the morning. For a few minutes he had been among friends and companions, a part of a home that felt more comfortable than anything he had experienced on Earth. He understood what Marlen had said about being content with your experience … but putting it into action was ten times more difficult than simply thinking about it.

He sat up, drew his shirt on, and leaned back against the tree that sheltered his sleeping bag. The day was already warm. He had stopped looking at clocks when he left Sacramento but he wondered what time it was. By the position of the sun, he guessed that it might be around eight o'clock. Bird songs occupied the air, calling and chattering but keeping themselves hidden among the thick branches. A faint smell of strong coffee tempted him. Glancing over at the campfire, he saw that Grandfather and Marlen were in their usual places.

Turning away, he allowed the dream to replay in his mind. His years of searching and yearning made sense to him now. He was, indeed, from another dimension. Why he had come to this one was not yet clear to him. The thought of the upcoming rescue loomed over him. He scoured his face with his hands in frustration. How he was going to accomplish the rescue was a mystery. He had a sudden, unwanted vision of military troops and all manner of assault vehicles bearing down on them and small, vulnerable, alien faces looking up at him for guidance. Wanting to escape the vision and his fear, he slipped into his boots and walked into the forest. Not long after, he found a rocky ledge that looked out over a small, uninhabited valley far below.

It was there that Marlen found him an hour or so later. "How's it goin' for you?" he asked as he sat down near Paul, resting his back against a small, scruffy pine.

Paul stared in silence at the valley below before answering. "I'm worried about this rescue. I hope we can pull it off."

"You would be a fool not to worry," Marlen agreed.

Paul glanced at him. "Thanks," he said dryly.

Marlen grinned and lifted his shoulders in a shrug. "Hey. How many times in a lifetime do you find yourself pursued by a hundred guys in military fatigues?"

"Not more than once," Paul said dryly.

Their laughter rang through the air and echoed off of the mountains on the other side of the valley.

It was a short time later that Paul began to feel a faint thrum in his chest. It was as if he had two hearts and each was beating a different tune. The moment was near. He looked at Marlen, who had been silent for quite some time. Marlen looked back and nodded without speaking. Both of them sent their vision to the sky, looking for the craft that was hurtling toward them on a path of destiny.

Paul felt calm, something that he had not expected. He could feel that his recent metaphysical experiences and the knowledge that he had absorbed during the last few days had made him stronger, more confident. He needed to believe in himself in order to pull this off. He could not allow himself to exhibit a limited vision of reality or of himself. He drew in a deep breath and thought again about what he had learned about himself.

As if it were a separate entity, an energy that existed in a space alone, he felt his memory enter his body. He felt himself absorbing his personal truth as if it was a tonic. His personal power and awareness of himself as someone from a different place and time spread through his bloodstream, lighting the fires of courage as it went. To fail in this mission of rescue would be to fail far more than himself and far more than the beings aboard that craft.

As his sense of knowing propelled itself through his body, he began to feel certain that there was much more to the coming event than there appeared to be. It was possible that it was more than a rescue mission, more than a successful escape from military forces who might use his alien friends to accomplish their own goals. It was possible that what he might experience and what he might learn could alter the viewpoint of many who lived on Earth.

Still without speaking, he and Marlen stood and made their way through the forest to Grandfather's side. There the three of them waited.

The throb in Paul's chest grew more persistent as the day passed into evening. Now he sensed that he was feeling the heart of a machine. Probably it was the vibration of the incoming craft. He willed it to continue, thinking that it might be a sign that the occupants of the craft were alive and well. But what happens when it hits? he wondered.

For a minute his calm threatened to slip away. What if they are injured? How am I going to handle it? I have no medical knowledge whatsoever. Not to mention that these are friends of mine that I haven't seen in twenty-nine years. How will I handle the emotions that will undoubtedly hit me?

He shrugged heavily, as if shrugging an unwanted hand from his shoulder. With determination he forced himself back into the place where he had been minutes earlier, a place where he believed in himself. Without thinking he accepted the plate of food that Marlen set in his hand. He had not even been aware of him preparing it. He ate without notice and was not aware when Marlen silently took the plate away.

The evening shadows grew long before the mountain chill began to chip away at the day's warmth. The moon stood low on the horizon. Venus watched brightly over the night. Out of the corner

of his eye, Paul caught a movement along the black velvet back-
ground of the night. The others saw it too. With faces turned to the
sky the three men rose slowly from their seats and stood silently
watching. Their faces glowed with wonder and a sense of awe
bathed the quiet mountain top. The craft was approaching, hurtling toward them like a train without brakes. And aboard was
another world, possibly one that offered solutions, if not salvation,
for Earth's ills.

As the craft sped toward them, Paul could not stop himself
from wondering how anyone could possibly survive the impending
impact.

The natural silence of a mountain night was shattered by
sounds that were loud enough to make one think that the world was
coming apart at the seams. The sickening sound of trees toppling,
their branches cracking like gunfire. Dust and chaos blocked the
light of the moon. The craft hit. The earth shook. And then deadly
silence.

Moving quicker than minnows in a fast stream, Paul and
Marlen flew toward the sound. Paul's heart was beating so fast that
he was alarmed for himself as well as for those aboard the downed
craft. Grandfather waited behind, a shotgun across his lap and his
old black eyes piercing the night, watching for enemies.

The craft was small and milk-white, shaped like an upside-
down cereal bowl. Wedged in between misshapen tree trunks, it sat
at a ninety-degree angle. Along the bottom edge of the craft,
innocently unaware of the impact, small lights blinked repeti-
tiously. Paul didn't take the time to notice much more. His
thoughts were on the occupants.

Skidding to a halt only inches from the silent, blinking craft, he
saw no way to enter. He circled frantically, rubbing his hands over
the surface in an effort to move the walls somehow to give him
access to the interior. There were no obvious entries. Time was
passing. A sound began to intrude. The slapping sound of the rotors
on a helicopter was closing in.

Marlen heard it too. Moving as silently and swiftly as an Indian legend, he slashed at branches and limbs and hauled them quickly to the craft, tossing them on and over the craft in an effort to hide the blinking lights.

"We're only buying seconds," Paul thought frantically. Almost in a state of shock over the possibility of failure, he did the only thing that he could think of doing. He reached inside the craft with his thoughts and desperately begged someone inside to open a door.

As quickly as an unexpected flash of memory, a small aperture appeared only inches from where he stood. Heart racing, he jumped to the entryway, at the same time preparing himself for what he might see. The inside of the craft was low. There were five small beings inside. With a rush of pity, Paul threw himself on his knees beside the one nearest to the door. One paper-thin, three-fingered hand dangled over the arm of the chair. The other rested near the instrument panel. To Paul the hand resembled the dependent frailty of a baby bird that has fallen from its nest. Paul assumed that it was this hand that had been the one to open the door.

The aliens were small, with ivory skin stretched tightly over bodies that were almost as thin as the width of a nail file. Their heads were large, with noses so small they were barely noticeable. Tiny slits made up their mouths. Their eyes were deep-set and almond-shaped. They looked exactly like they had in Paul's memories and dreams.

One of the beings was staring at Paul. His ebony eyes were so deep that they might have been replicas for the depth of the ocean. Paul gave up the hand he was clutching and moved to the open-eyed alien. He touched the unmoving arm and pulled back abruptly. It was hot ... fire-hot. How much danger are they in, he wondered.

Suddenly Paul could hear thoughts insinuating themselves into his mind. "We are in danger ... but that is why you are here. These two," and the being nodded toward the two slumped figures in the far-right seats, "cannot be helped."

Paul sensed a deep sadness in the marble-like black eyes. He took a deep breath and tried not to react to the deaths, though something inside of him felt as if it would never be healed.

"We must move quickly," the thoughts continued. "We have only minutes. The forest is too thick for our pursuers to set down close but it will not take long for them to reach us. Place your hands on our heads, one at a time, and loan us your strength. That will give us the strength we need to move from here quickly."

The alien's eyes closed in exhaustion. A pang of desperation led Paul to instantly do as he had asked. Following his intuition, he laid his hands on the bald head of each alien. A deep knowing led him to envision a golden, arrow-like shaft of light coming from above and moving through him and out of his hands. He could feel his hands becoming warm. Energy shot through his mind, his arms, his hands. He could feel it move into the aliens beneath his touch. Exhilarated, he repeated the process with each of them. Soon three pairs of grave, ink-black eyes were turned on him. It was clear that they were counting on him.

He turned to Marlen, who was standing just outside the door watching. Marlen nodded, indicating that he had a plan. One by one Paul handed the feather-light aliens down to him. As he stepped from the craft he allowed himself to turn back for an instant. His sadness at leaving two of them behind nearly buckled his knees. With an effort, he turned away. He met the imploring stare of three sets of dark eyes. He could not even imagine how it must feel to have just survived a crash on a foreign land, in a foreign world.

The thunder of helicopters was beginning to surround them. Searchlights stabbed the darkness like silver needles piercing through black velvet. Paul easily lifted one alien into his arms, while Marlen lifted the other two. Without a word he headed into the deep forest, moving in the opposite direction of their camp. Paul felt the small alien that he was carrying turn and look back as they hurried away. A razor-sharp stab of mourning gripped Paul's chest.

The weak hand that clutched his neck patted him softly. They headed into the night, following Marlen's silent path.

The group moved quickly through the forest, heading downhill. The moist-earth smell insisted its way into Paul's lungs. Several times he slipped on dew-wet oak leaves and pine needles. The intense yellow stare of an owl startled him into almost dropping his burden. At every step he cursed the noise he was making.

The moon was not shedding much light on this night. With every step he was slapped by a pine branch or hit by low-hanging clusters of oak leaves. He could feel scratches and welts raising on his arms and face. With his arms he shielded the being he was carrying as best he could. He knew he was bleeding in several places. His breath was coming hard and his legs were tiring. He sensed Marlen slowing. He caught up to him and watched in bewilderment as he stopped and set the two aliens on the ground. They were surrounded by thick forest. Directly in front of them was a tall range of mountains. Why was he stopping?

Marlen reached over and began hauling large bushes out of the ground ... at least it seemed that way at first. A minute later Paul realized that he was removing camouflage from the mouth of a cave. He stepped forward quickly to help. Seconds later he heard noises coming from the other side of the entrance. A minute later he was shocked to see two, round, intense faces appear in the semidarkness. They were motioned inside urgently. Paul took the thin hands of two aliens and urged them into the cave. Behind him he heard Marlen and the other men scrambling to cover the entrance again.

Paul's eyes widened to accommodate the deeper black of the cave's interior. Peering into the gloom, he noticed a small fire burning further back. He shook his head at the sight of perhaps twenty round-faced native Americans peering at him with bright, interested stares. Looking closer, he could see brightly colored blankets caressing the cave floor and children's toys laying nearby.

One old woman was bent near the dim firelight stirring a large pot that was hung over the low flame on a solid-looking wooden rack.

None of the occupants of the cave looked shocked at the unlikely sight of the three aliens. No one spoke as Marlen led the small group past the fire and deeper into the cave. One man rose and quickly followed. He stepped past Paul and touched Marlen on the arm. With a wave he indicated that they should follow him to the right.

The cave branched off and led to a small, circular enclosure. A kerosene lamp lit the area. Several mattresses, shrouded with blankets, lay upon the floor. As if knowing what was expected of them, the aliens moved to the mattresses. With hesitant fingers they touched and explored the blankets before finally lying down. The fact that they instantly scooted next to each other, like a pile of puppies seeking warmth, was not lost on Paul. He looked up and into Marlen's eyes. They exchanged a silent moment of pity for the lost beings before they moved away several feet in order to talk about their next step.

Paul set his back against the cool wall of the cave and sank to the floor in utter exhaustion. The emotions of the last hour had drained him. He draped his tired arms over his jean-clad knees and leaned his head on his forearms for a brief minute. Marlen squatted nearby, gazing silently at the visitors. When Paul looked up, he and Marlen exchanged brief, tired smiles.

"I feel like, in a matter of minutes, I have become a different man," Marlen said softly.

"As if your universe has expanded and you have expanded with it?" Paul asked quietly.

Marlen nodded. "That and a whole lot more." He turned back to study the visitors who were still curled next to each other, each in tight, fetal position.

"I think this may take a while to get used to," Paul admitted. "I recognize them from when I was a small child. But until now I don't think I really allowed myself to believe wholeheartedly, you know?"

"I think I know what you mean," Marlen said, his eyes fixed on the visitors.

They fell silent, their eyes fastened to the wonder of the three visitors laying so near. The soft whisper of bare feet told them that, one by one, the others were coming to observe. An air of reverence filled the room.

CHAPTER FIVE

Paul heard a murmur in the room next to where he rested. He turned toward the entry and was shocked to see Grandfather walking deliberately toward him. Marlen, not surprised, stood and walked toward him, smiling.

"You still have it!" he said enthusiastically, wrapping a strong arm around Grandfather's shoulders and leading him inside.

Paul stood and stared at them, open-mouthed. "How did you get here?" he demanded.

"He teleported," Marlen told him proudly. He grinned with satisfaction, as if he had been the one to accomplish the feat.

"Teleported?" Paul asked quizzically.

Marlen explained. "Yeah. You think yourself into another place by realizing that you are made up of energy. Then you just think your energy into another place. You use your power of thought." He chuckled, obviously pleased with Grandfather's accomplishment.

Grandfather broke into a wide, toothless grin. "I did it," he said proudly. "I thought I had lost that ability many years ago. I think I surprised even myself." He leaned on Marlen's arm, still excited but obviously tired from his efforts.

His stiff, white hair fanned out over his shoulders. It moved with his head as he turned to stare speechlessly at the sleeping visitors. "I never thought I would live to see this day," he said in a soft, awestruck voice.

The room was silent for a minute as Grandfather was allowed to absorb the impact of the aliens. "They are full of grace," he murmured. As if in a hypnotic state, he moved toward them and, with effort, folded himself until he was sitting on the mattresses near them.

"What can you tell us about the soldiers?" Marlen asked.

A wrinkled smile caressed the old man's face, almost hiding his small eyes. "I imagine they wonder where I went," he chuckled. "They came to the campsite. Of course, we knew they would. I thought they were going to be aggressive but I underestimated them."

Marlen's voice was suddenly gruff with anger. "Did they hurt you?"

Grandfather waved his hand through the air, silencing the younger man. "They didn't even touch me. They were loud and demanding, telling me that I knew what they wanted and that I was hiding something from them. They threatened to take me to their base." He shrugged his thin, old shoulders. "Perhaps they would have if I hadn't disappeared."

Paul's voice was filled with surprise. "You teleported right in front of them?"

Grandfather gave a dry chuckle that ended in a cough. "I do not think they were going to leave me in order to allow me to do this privately." He gave Paul another dry laugh.

"How many were there?" Marlen asked.

"There were only seven at the campsite. But two more were there. I sensed them. They were deep and evil, determined to stop you. They, I know, are the dangerous ones. And there were helicopters all over. A few jets flew by. They must have been involved somehow. I heard a lot of jeeps and trucks too. I am guessing that there are fifty to one hundred people out there looking for you."

Paul interrupted with some more questions. "Did it look as if they had pinpointed the crash site? How did they know about the crash? They got here awfully quick. They must have been tracking it."

Marlen answered. "Sure they were tracking it. Probably from

the base down near Phoenix. It would have been visible on their screens for quite a while. With the instruments that they have nowadays, they can track a swarm of geese. It wouldn't take anything at all for them to know the approximate crash site."

Grandfather interrupted, his voice trembling slightly. His weariness was evident. "There are lights all over that forest. You would think it's daytime. I imagine that they've found the craft by now." He turned on one hip and looked at the three visitors. "Two of them did not survive?" he asked softly.

"No." It was Paul who uttered the small word in a still smaller voice. The pain that laced through the single word surprised him. Grandfather turned to look at him. He studied Paul without speaking. For a moment it felt as if someone had asked for a moment of silent prayer. One of the sleeping visitors curled himself into a tighter ball.

"It cannot be helped now," Marlen said. His words, though spoken softly, rang through the cave too loudly.

"I don't understand why it crashed," Paul said. "I would think their craft would be sophisticated enough to avoid such things."

"From what I understand," Marlen responded, "they were helping with the energy grids that surround Earth. Their gravitational device failed. If one of the other crafts had intercepted and tried to help, that crew would have been in jeopardy as well."

Paul nodded, his eyes dark with sympathy for the visitors. He could not even begin to imagine the fear that they must have lived with as their craft plunged through space toward Earth.

"We need to wake them up and get them moving again," Marlen said, interrupting Paul's thoughts. "I think this cave is hidden well enough to be almost invisible but I also think the military will stop at nothing to find these guys. If we wait too long, we won't have an escape."

"How long will it take for them to realize that the two still on board had other companions?" Paul asked logically.

"They're just going to assume that there were more," Grandfather said.

"And the work that I did to camouflage the craft ... they're going to notice that," Marlen inserted, raising his eyebrows at Paul.

"You're right," Paul muttered.

One of the visitors stirred and lifted his head to study the three men who were discussing his fate. The other two stirred as well, perhaps sensing a change in the mood of the small enclosure. Looking into their trusting eyes, Paul felt the mantle of responsibility settle on his shoulders. It was imperative to get the visitors to safety. As if on cue, the faint sound of helicopters approaching reached the interior of the cave. Marlen and Paul exchanged glances and, as if one, rose to their feet. Grandfather rose more tentatively and moved to embrace Marlen quickly.

He stopped in front of Paul and rested his still-strong hands on Paul's shoulders. "When you have time to think more clearly, you will recognize these friends of yours. I wish you all the best in helping them to safety. When you understand, the mission will become even more important to you."

Paul looked at him quizzically but didn't ask the questions that crowded into his mind. He glanced at Marlen, who nodded, and seconds later they were being guided through a passageway that led deeper into the cave. Their guide, a young Indian boy of about sixteen, had the only light. Paul, with small, trusting, alien hands tucked into his, hurried to keep up.

Through the dark tunnel they rushed. Once in a while a lone Indian appeared, startling them, holding up lanterns to light particularly difficult passages. Paul realized that this small group of cave dwellers had known, probably even before he did, about this midnight dash for freedom.

The silence was eerie. No one spoke. The only sound was the soft, hurried shuffle of various footsteps on cold stone. Eventually the tunnel narrowed and grew darker still. They were forced to slow to a walk. The ground seemed to rumble, echoing the threat of helicopters above. Paul could feel the dank walls pressing against them. He struggled to calm his ragged breathing. He heard Marlen's steps halt.

"Now what?" he whispered.

"Smell the air," Marlen instructed quietly.

Paul sniffed. "What am I smelling?" he asked.

"Fresh air. We're close."

He started walking again. Paul followed, gently herding the visitors ahead of him. A minute later he felt a change in the air temperature. Shortly after that he was climbing a rope ladder to the surface. He reached back into the cave and hoisted the three visitors, one by one, through the small exit. Marlen followed, struggling to push his large shoulders through the small outlet.

The night was overcast with only hints of moonlight teasing the edges of the cloud cover. Paul could hear the rotors of the helicopters in the distance. He had no idea how far away they were … he only wished that they were even further. They needed to find cover. Fast.

"Do you know where we are?" he asked Marlen.

"We're not far from Fort Apache Reservation. We can find shelter there for a while. Long enough to decide what to do next."

"How far is it?"

"It's still a ways from here. About a three or four hour drive."

"The Bronco is back at the camp," Paul said, trying to hide his impatience. "How the heck are we supposed to get anywhere at all?"

Marlen held up a set of car keys and swung them gently in the bleak moonlight. Paul thought they looked suspiciously like his keys.

"We're good scouts. We're prepared for everything."

A few feet away, buried beneath a makeshift canopy of limbs, sat the Bronco. Rather than waste time asking how it had gotten there, Paul picked up each visitor and helped them into the back seat. Before he turned to get into the vehicle himself, his eyes met and held the gaze of three pairs of large, dreadfully sad, alien eyes. The impact of their experience hit him squarely in the heart once again. They had traveled millions of miles, on a mission that was meant to help Earth and its people. They had lived, for who knows how long, aboard a ship that they knew was going to crash on an alien planet. They had not known if they were going to live or die. They had lost two of their companions and had not yet had time to grieve.

Now they were going to be tossed into this vehicle and bounced along miles of rough rutted road. His heart could not fathom the depth of the misery they must be experiencing.

With a small, helpless sigh, he turned away and climbed in next to Marlen, who had taken the driver's seat. There was no choice but to continue on the path that destiny had chosen for them.

Marlen turned to him. "We need to keep low until the troops get tired of looking for us."

"That could be a while!" Paul said irritably. "We can't stay hidden forever. We're going to have to come up with something better. Do you know anyone who could hide all of us?"

"We'll figure something out," Marlen assured him.

They hit a pothole the size of a small crater and bounced out of it. The Bronco's wheels grabbed for a hold on the slippery shale road while the occupants abandoned all attempts to make conversation. For the next hour Paul was kept busy trying to find secure places to hold onto while he monitored the tortured ride of the three passengers.

The danger and darkness made their escape twice as harrowing as it might have been had it been daylight. Small rockslides followed them down the slopes. Branches slapped at them as they passed by. They slipped and slid and more than once Paul feared that the Bronco would flip over and end the nightmare for all of them. About the time he was going to scream in frustration at the time that had passed and the lack of progress they seemed to be making, the path they were on started to turn into a road. The road began to flatten out into an almost presentable passageway.

Marlen turned and looked at Paul quizzically. "I don't remember this," he said quietly.

A shudder of fear and frustration passed through Paul's bones. He could feel his jaws tense and clamp over a dozen words that he had no intention of speaking. "Are you telling me that you have no idea where we are?" he asked tightly. "That's why you're driving, you know. You're supposed to know this area like the back of your hand. At least that's what you told me."

Marlen shook his head. "I can figure it out. There are only so many ins and outs to this forest. It feels like we're coming up on a main road though. When we get there, I can tell you exactly where we are. But," he jerked his chin toward the back seat, "we're also going to be on a main road. We're going to have to hide them somehow."

Paul, who had been twisted in his seat so that he could watch his charges, now looked back at them again. Three sets of innocent eyes stared back at him.

"I shoved our sleeping bags and blankets in the back," Marlen told him. "Maybe you can see if you can cover them up with those."

No sooner had he spoken than Paul heard the sound of a large semi nearby. They were coming up on a main road. Rounding a sharp curve, they stopped dead and stared at the highway in front of them.

"It looks like 260," Marlen ventured.

"How can you tell?" Paul asked. To him it looked like every other road he had seen in the last few days.

"Just trust me on this," Marlen said abruptly.

Paul could feel the edge of Marlen's temper looking for something to slice through. It had been tense for all of them. He knew that 260 was the road between Payson and Christopher Creek. Was it possible that they were right back where they had started? He wanted to ask but he also didn't want to know the answer. He followed his instincts and fell silent, busying himself by looking for the blankets Marlen had tossed in the back. Finding them, he explained the necessity to the three passengers. He knew they understood, but he also knew that they were hesitant to comply. He didn't blame them at all. But a few minutes later they were hidden beneath their makeshift hideaway. All he could see of them were several tips of small alien fingers, clutching edges of the blankets to keep them secure.

Without further discussion, Marlen made a left onto the road. Paul figured they were headed south.

"Why are we going south?" he asked hesitantly, not liking the set look of Marlen's jaw.

As Paul figured it would be, Marlen's voice was low and tense. "Because it will be a lot closer to a hiding place than where I originally wanted to go."

"What went wrong?" Paul asked tentatively.

Marlen shrugged and shook his head. "I don't know. I must have missed the road where we were supposed to turn off to the reservation. It was just too dark out there."

Paul nodded. He had no idea where they were headed but he had to trust that Marlen knew what he was doing. He wasn't so certain a short time later when horror struck his chest at the rapidly approaching sound of a screaming siren behind them.

His thoughts careened around inside his head like pinballs in a pinball machine. He knew that he was panicking but had no idea how to stop himself. He whirled around in his seat, patting the blankets wildly, assuring himself that his charges were safe. Behind him, the flashing lights of a police car could be seen, growing larger by the second as the car pulled closer to them.

Marlen swung the car to the right and bounced them onto a road that Paul hadn't noticed. They were heading into thick forest. "They aren't after us," he said, his teeth clenched around his words. He reached out as if to slug Paul on the arm. "If you panic on me, I swear I'll knock you out cold!"

Paul swung around to face forward and glared at him. "What the heck is wrong with you?" he shouted. "I am not panicked."

"Do you realize how ridiculous that statement is?" Marlen yelled back.

Paul's eyes were huge in his head as he tried to assimilate everything including the fact that Marlen was yelling at him. They were charging down another pot-holed road with hairpin turns. They were heading into deep forest. His charges, by now, were peeking out from beneath the blankets, watching them with frightened eyes. The sound of the siren and Marlen's anger was reverberating inside his head. For a minute he thought that he might have gone mad.

Marlen glanced over at him, saw the wild look in his eyes, and promptly burst out laughing. It took Paul several seconds. He realized the absurdity of the entire situation and burst into laughter that bordered on hysteria. Gasping for breath, his teeth cracking together as they hit a small rise going fifty miles an hour, he managed to calm himself enough to ask Marlen if he had any idea at all about where they were.

"Mogollon Rim," Marlen managed to say. "Plenty of places to get lost up here." He risked a glance over at Paul before dragging his eyes back to the rough road. "Don't worry. I have a plan."

"I hope it's a good one," Paul yelled over the sound of the Bronco crashing over yet another rise in the road.

The siren seemed to reach out and wrap itself around them. Paul realized that he had gone beyond fear into a world where he'd never been before. As if it had a life of its own, the siren engulfed them. He closed his eyes and listened. He realized then that he was beginning to feel something like a weightless fog surrounding their vehicle. Before he could understand what was happening, the pursuers screamed by them, dust flying. In a matter of seconds, they were surrounded by a dust cloud so thick that they couldn't breathe.

"It's a trick," he thought. As suspicious as a mosquito in the neighborhood of a lizard, he waited. He couldn't imagine why their pursuers would have passed them by. He turned slowly, looking into the back seat where he felt a prickle of humor being directed at the back of his neck.

One of the visitors was peering at him from beneath the blankets. His eyes appeared to hold a smile. Slowly he blinked.

"What did you do?" Paul asked incredulously.

As had happened before, he heard a voice inside his head. "We lifted our energetic field."

"What?" Paul asked tensely. "What does that mean? How can you do that?"

The voice in his head calmly informed him. "You know all things are made up of energy. All you need to do is alter the energetic frequency and you alter your energetic presence in space. It's a matter of how your energy merges, or doesn't merge, with the energy surrounding you."

Paul shook his head, attempting to calm his thoughts and his sudden temper. "If I had known you could do that we wouldn't be charging around like a couple of lunatics trying to hide you."

The set of eyes blinked at him again. But now they were filled with a silent appraisal of him. "Within Earth energies it is not always possible to do the things which are simple in other dimensional energies. To maintain what we just accomplished over an extended period of time would be impossible."

Paul nodded, understanding. "That makes sense." He said, taking a deep breath to calm himself.

"What's going on?" Marlen asked, sounding slightly disoriented. "What just happened?" He shook his head in an attempt to clear his confusion.

"You're not hearing them too?" Paul asked.

"What are you talking about?" He pointed through the windshield. "Those guys just went right through us." He shook his head. "Or something. I don't know what the heck just happened."

Paul explained what had just happened and why using the technique couldn't be used to get them out of the mess they were in. Neither of them had anything more to say when they heard the dull thud of helicopter rotors coming toward them through the distance.

Dawn was just taking over the night. Paul could see that they were spinning down a road that overlooked a vast canyon. He caught a glimpse of a steep, tree-crowded cliff. If they didn't slow down it was highly likely that they were going to end up at the bottom of the canyon below. He dug his fingernails into the leather of the door handle, looked over his shoulder at his charges, saw that they had once again buried themselves beneath the blankets, whether out of fear or something else, and turned his frightened eyes back to the road. Marlen handled the car expertly, spinning them around corner after corner, bend after bend.

Paul prayed as he never had before. As if in an attempt to prove to him how out of control their situation was, he heard the faint sound of another siren. It seemed to reach through the air and wrap itself around him, as if sending him a message, telling him that there was no chance of succeeding in his mission. He smiled to himself, refusing the suggestion of failure. If this invisibility thing can be done again, if only for a few minutes, we might have a chance, he decided.

"Do you know this area?" he yelled over the noise, staring at Marlen intently.

Marlen glanced at him sideways, one thick eyebrow raised. "I doubt that there's any part of Arizona that I don't know like the inside of my eyelids," he said loudly. He pointed at the road with his chin. "They call this General Crook's trail. You know, the guy who chased Apaches around the countryside for no good reason." He glanced back at the huddle of aliens. "There's a path up here that I can get us on. It's a path ... not a road. But I can get us back into the woods a little further. Then we can stop and regroup."

Several minutes later they were barreling over more potholes and ruts, leaving the sound of sirens behind. Out of necessity, Marlen had to slow to a crawl not long after. The thickness of tree branches overhead began to make them feel safer. The noise of pursuit began to weaken. About a mile away from the main road, Marlen finally slowed the Bronco to a halt. He and Paul both took deep, tension-releasing breaths. In the back seat, the visitors unwrapped themselves from the blankets and sat up tentatively.

All business, Marlen proceeded to give Paul detailed instructions. About a mile further on they would find a small lake. It should be uninhabited right now because it was the middle of the week. Not many people knew about the lake because it was so far off the beaten track. Marlen planned on leaving long enough to find out just how serious the pursuit was and how long it might last. While he was gone, he was going to try to find someone to hide them out for a while. Paul would have to make his way to the lake alone, taking the aliens with him. He would bring back some clothes that might fit the aliens and together they would attempt to make the visitors look as inconspicuous as possible for the trip to the next hiding place.

He handed Paul a compass, repeated his directions to the lake, and watched with concern as everyone began to leave the Bronco. As the last small alien climbed gingerly from the car, he placed one thin hand on Marlen's shoulder. Paul swallowed hard as the two of them exchanged a glance filled with unvoiced recognition and trust. They stepped back and solemnly watched him maneuver his way back onto the almost-nonexistent path. When the dust had settled, Paul was alone for the first time with the friends who, he was beginning to suspect, had escorted him to the planet twenty-odd years earlier.

CHAPTER SIX

It took a while to reach the small, secluded lake. By the time they reached it, the sun was shedding light on this part of the world and the air was getting inundated with its usual July warmth. The lake lay before them, pristine blue and seemingly dropped from the heavens to serve as a reflection for the hordes of tall, deep green pines that surrounded it. A short distance away was a small stand of aspens wrapped in fragile ivory and taupe parchment, waltzing in the quickening breeze. Among the pines stood an occasional oak. Small tufts of leaves, fallen from the oaks, played at the feet of the larger trees, reminding Paul of small, restless children playing at the feet of preoccupied adults.

Tall mountains towered over the small lake on the northern side. Here there was no meadow, no span of earth that might serve as a place to pitch a tent ... if he had one. He thought with longing about the supplies in the back of the Bronco. He hoped that it occurred to Marlen to fill the ice chest with ice and cold drinks.

As far as Paul could see, his group was alone. He was winded, dirty, and exhausted. The aliens, however, seemed totally unruffled by the hike. Paul glanced at them and wished he could feel as calm. Desperate for some kind of relief, he suddenly allowed himself to fall into the lake, clothes and all, surprising even himself. He came up gasping for air, not having realized that the lake was filled with snow melt-off. Shaking his head like a wet dog, he yanked his icy-wet shirt off and stumbled from the water. For several minutes he stood shivering, slapping at himself to shake the chilling droplets of water off. The visitors stood placidly watching.

Paul smiled at them sheepishly, wondered if they realized how foolish he felt, and gestured with his hand, inviting them into the lake as well. The three of them exchanged glances and looked back at him, shy and amused. One of them, after glancing at the others, approached the lake tentatively. He timidly extended his narrow foot toward the water. It was the first time Paul had noticed their feet. They were extremely narrow, flat, and toeless, somewhat resembling the working end of a garden trowel.

One of the others joined the first, crouching next to him and cautiously touching the water's edge with his fingertips. His large eyes seemed to grow larger as he watched the water dribble from his fingers. His face was a study in delight. With bright eyes he turned to look at Paul. The look was so trusting and full of love that Paul struggled to fight back a sudden, unexpected rush of emotion.

"Do you remember?" asked the third visitor, who now stood near Paul's side. His voice was light and small, sounding like a sparrow might sound ... could it speak.

"I think I am beginning to," Paul answered, not surprised by the question. He looked down and met the steady gaze of the small being. "I was thinking that I remembered you from my dreams but that isn't it, is it? You were the ones who brought me here a long time ago."

The visitor nodded. "I am Zere," he said simply. "That is Elan and Galin. We were the ones who transported you from the Esartania, which is the mothership that brought you from Questar."

The words rang through Paul's mind like solemn bells tolling a solemn event. He sat down abruptly, forgetting his chill. Another kind of chill chased through his body, bringing wave after wave of yearning. Questar! His heart filled with the name and the elusive memories. A single, involuntary tear escaped. He looked again at Zere, noting for the first time how his black eyes were encircled with an almost unnoticeable band of gray. "There is so much that I need to remember," he whispered, wishing that somehow he could make the years disappear, that the world would somehow cooperate and bring him back to the place where he yearned to be.

Zere's three-fingered hand reached out to gently touch Paul's forehead. Paul involuntarily closed his eyes. Colors of gold, white, and vivid purple swirled before his mind's eye. When he opened them again, it was to meet Zere's gaze. It was obvious to him that a bond that had been broken had now been repaired.

Zere turned his eyes from Paul's and looked toward the heavens. His eyes now held a longing that was almost impossible to fathom. Every fiber of Paul's being recognized Zere's need to return home. His own need reached out in an attempt to soothe. For an instant their hands touched with understanding. Paul blinked away his sudden tears. Both of them turned to study the sky in a vain attempt to see their origins.

After drying in the morning sun for a while, Paul led his charges to the edge of the woods, where he would be able to see a stranger approaching and would have time to hide them. Each of them rested contentedly against a tree. Paul could feel a familiar sense of family emerging, now that he had time with them alone.

"How has it been for you?" Zere asked quietly, after several minutes of companionable silence.

Paul glanced at him and allowed the lake to draw his eyes back to it. The years had been filled with so much that it seemed impossible to try to sum it up with only a few words.

"You needn't speak of it, if you wish not to," Elan inserted. "For the most part we can see your life experience. We know that you have been challenged."

"See it? How can you see it?" Paul asked.

"In your energy field," Zere explained. "Most experiences lodge in a person's energy field. And there the energy can be seen and understood." He studied Paul for a silent minute. "The human race has forgotten that these energies cause most of their illnesses and anger and such." He shook his head slightly. "Energies can be healed, but it takes time and knowledge."

"I've heard a lot of speculation about that kind of thing," Paul offered. "I think a lot of people think it's a bunch of fantasy."

"Fantasy?" Galin exclaimed. "What does this mean?"

"It means that most people think it's fake, made-up."

"That energy is fake?" Galin echoed in surprise.

Paul laughed. "I don't think they believe energy is fake, no. But I think that some believe that it doesn't impact us and can't be changed." His face saddened. "I think many believe that nothing can change anything. That all things are simply what they are and that all we can do is simply endure."

"That is the state of the human race it seems," Zere said thoughtfully.

The three visitors studied him for a silent minute. Just as he was becoming uncomfortable under their scrutiny, Elan spoke. "Perhaps it would be good for you to understand how energies and thoughts can be easily read. It might serve you well to know how in the future."

Paul was intrigued. "I'd like to understand, yes."

"Thoughts are made up of energy," Zere explained, while studying something invisible over Paul's shoulder. "Just as all things are made up of energy, so are thoughts. They can be sent, received, and monitored once you become adept at understanding energy."

"How do I go about learning more?" Paul asked.

Zere smiled comfortably, his thin lips curving into a tiny, curved line. "Observation is a wonderful place to begin. Most souls who take on physical form seem to get waylaid from their wisdom by the simple but all-consuming needs of simply maintaining their bodies and their lives. But, if one was to set aside what appears to be the 'real world,' meaning the physical, and train themselves to focus on the entirety of existence, observing energy would be a simple thing."

"How long has it been since you lived someplace like Earth?" Paul asked suspiciously. "Do you have any idea what it would take to be able to do that?"

A sound that was similar to the tinkling of a fairy's bell rang through the air. Paul realized that it was Elan's laughter. Paul turned to him, delighted. It was sheer joy to assist these three precious beings with forgetting, if only for a moment, their precarious position.

"Watch," instructed Zere, touching Paul briefly on the knee. Without explanation, he held his hand in the air. Paul watched, shocked, as the air in front of him turned violet, and then pink, and then violet once again. Soon there was a rainbow of pastel colors dancing before them. Accompanying the colors were tones, as soft and faint as the sound of a feather falling. Paul had to strain to hear them. He felt something deep in his chest respond to the spectacle in front of him, as if his heart was desiring to escape in order to play in the morning air with this energetic delight.

"This is spectacular," he breathed. "How do you do it?"

Galin held up one long finger, stopping Paul's questions. Still holding his finger in the air, he traced what appeared to be a crystalline pyramid. Light danced off of the thin threads of crystal, creating a pastel rainbow of colors. It was large, large enough to settle over and around Paul as Galin directed it with his hands. In speechless wonder, Paul sat within it and looked out, captivated by what he considered to be a miracle.

Before he could ask more questions, Galin silenced him again by placing a single finger on his knee. Paul met his eyes and was surprised by the sobering stare that he received.

"Close your eyes and listen to me," Galin instructed quietly.

Paul did as he was asked, curious now as to what was in store for him.

"Think of yourself as simply a mass of cells, cells separated by space, for that is what you truly are. Allow yourself to accept that you are an expression of your soul, having accepted this energetic body for the sole purpose of expressing your soul in physical form." Galin's voice was hypnotic. It was lowered until Paul wasn't certain if he heard it out loud or simply within his mind. "You are not this physical body. You are simply cells surrounded by space. You are an energetic mass of energy. Nothing more. You have no limitations, other than those that you have imposed upon yourself. You are unlimited in the way that your soul is unlimited.

"Your soul belongs to a world without boundaries; therefore you exist in a world without boundaries. Within your mind and body resides the thread that connects you with your soul, with your memories, with your power. Allow yourself to release your belief that you are this body. Realize instead that you are a mass of energy expressing your soul. Feel your soul within your body. Feel your cells reach out and absorb the truth of who you are."

Like a tender, gentle breeze, Paul felt something within himself begin to shift. He began to feel larger than himself, as if he were expanding. He could actually see that he was nothing more than cells separated by space, cooperatively held together by a thread of agreement. Deep within he could feel a pulse that was separate from his heartbeat ... a pulse that might possibly be that of his soul.

He became aware that he was not separate from his surroundings. With closed eyes he could see and feel the trees, the air, and the nearby lake. A moment later it seemed that he was looking back upon himself from far above. He was a small mass of energy sitting among other masses of energy, each with its own purpose and expression. His sense of unity with himself and the Universe thrilled him in a way nothing else had ever done.

With a sudden chill of excitement he realized that he was free. From his perch above Earth he blended with the sky, observing all. It was easy to accept that he had no limitations. He was hovering over Marlen as he barreled the Bronco down a rugged road that appeared to be the same one that they had traveled days earlier. He shifted his attention and hovered above men and helicopters. The fallen craft was no longer where it had been. Men swarmed over the mountainside, directed by thoughts and voices that showed red against the deep green of the trees. For a moment it seemed to him that the trees were enjoying the part they were playing in the small scenario, being bothersome as they reached out their branches to interfere.

Abruptly Paul felt himself return to the small lake and his three companions.

"You took me quite seriously when I suggested that you had no limits," Galin said with a smile.

"I can hardly believe this," Paul said, his voice low with wonder. He looked around. The crystalline threads were gone. "What just happened?" he asked.

"That was the truth of the freedom of your spirit," Zere told him.

"But how is that possible?" Paul asked, peering at him intently. "How can I be sitting here and be out there at the same time?"

"Because this body is not really you," Zere said. "Believing that you are your body is what limits you. That belief captures most humans and burdens them with problems unlike any we have seen elsewhere. You are a vast spirit within a physical body. That is the thought you must hold."

"Okay," Paul said, tossing his hands and then setting them firmly on his jean-clad knees. "I can understand that we have a spirit in our body. I've heard about that. As a matter of fact, I saw a program that said that the human body actually loses four ounces at the instant of death. I assumed that this was the spirit leaving."

His three companions nodded without offering further explanation.

"So, the spirit is what ... operating the body?"

"In a way, yes," Elan offered. He had been silent until now, but Paul could see by the expression in his eyes that this was a subject he loved to discuss.

Elan continued. "You see, everyone has a soul. That soul is capable of sending out threads of itself, so to speak. Those threads are known as spirits here on Earth. So the spirit connects itself to the body with a thread, which connects it to the soul. So you see, there is never any disconnection with the soul, which is the True Self. But without this realization and understanding, your people believe that they are separated from their Creator, their soul, their power. This is what causes the disruption and pain here on Earth."

By now Elan's eyes were shining with intensity and fire. "Can you imagine what this world would be if everyone understood their Truth?" he asked. His paper-thin body leaned toward Paul with passion. "The soul does not recognize or realize disharmony. It does not create pain, death, illness. It is not out of order with anything at all. It knows that all things are only another expression within "The Creator of All That Is," therefore all things are a part of it. And why would one wish to do harm to oneself?" His small hand tapped Paul on the knee with vigor. "Can you see the potential for this beautiful world? Can you see the possibility for change if only everyone could know the Truth?"

Indeed Paul could. His mind filled with a vision of harmony, a world where each person was in union with their soul, where power was not fought for but accepted as each person's due, to be used for the benefit of creating more possibilities and better worlds. It was clear to him, with a suddenness that caught him by surprise, that most of the problems that he had witnessed on Earth were caused by fear and pain. If people were to believe that they were not alone, not separate from God or Heaven or whatever they believed to be their Source of Truth and Goodness, they would know peace.

He shook his head with the simplicity of the answer. Stunned into silence, he sat with heavy head and wondered how the message could be given, how it could be understood.

"You could write a book," Zere suggested quietly.

Paul looked at him with interest. He wanted to think seriously about the idea, but a sudden flock of dark clouds caught and held his attention. He had heard about monsoons. It looked as if they were going to get to experience one.

Great drops of rain began to fall without warning. He and the others moved further back among the trees, seeking shelter beneath the inadequate limbs of the pines. Within minutes they were soaked to the bone. Every few minutes Paul shook his head, casting water from his limp hair. The aliens, who were bald and did not have to worry about hair, watched as water dripped off their scalps and ran down their small faces. Paul wondered if they had ever experienced rain before.

Suddenly, before Paul could react, his three companions dashed out from beneath the trees and were standing, faces raised to the storm. A look of pure delight flowed from their wide-open eyes. Their thin lips parted slightly as they allowed the rain to pour down on them.

Paul stood watching, his heart filled with wonder. They are like children, he thought. Their innocence is captivating. Here they are, millions of miles from home, and yet they are choosing to delight in the experience. They seem to be innocent of fear. They have no doubts about the outcome of this adventure, apparently. I see no evidence of it. I don't think they're pretending. The joy I see is real.

The thoughts gave him reason to wonder about life itself and the way that people interpreted it, for it was the interpretation of events, he now understood, that influenced people's lives ... not necessarily the event itself. The knowledge being given to him was that each person is connected to the soul and everything outside the soul was an illusion ... an illusion that was being created by the soul for some unnamed purpose. What if it were true that the Universe is ordered by some greater Force than he could imagine and that this Force had created souls who, in turn, created energy masses of all forms, shapes, sizes, and differences. What if all these things they created were for the specific purpose of exploring the potential for life and living? What then would be the reason for fearing what you yourself were creating? It made no sense to look at it from any other viewpoint, now that he thought about it. He had no proof that he was living an illusion. But he had no proof that he was not either. After what he had experienced, it seemed altogether possible.

His thoughts continued. If experiences are nothing more than something that we, our souls, are creating, then why would we fear that experience? If, upon death, we do nothing more than return to that soul, why would we fear death? And is not death the greatest fear on Earth? And … if all of this is true, and our souls are out there creating lifetimes, it would stand to reason that this lifetime is only about as big as a speck of sand on a beach.

The entirety of his thoughts passed through his veins like water pouring through a empty pipe. He could feel a thrill, a sense of freedom, passing through his spine. He looked at the sky and the frolicking aliens. Without hesitating, he shed his wet clothes like they were burdens on his soul, and joined them in the rain.

CHAPTER SEVEN

THAT EVENING MARLEN APPEARED among the rain-washed trees. The storm had passed, leaving only the comforting smell of damp pine. Everyone but Paul had been resting peacefully. He was hungry and thirsty; still a victim of human needs, no matter how much he tried to think of himself as cells separated by space. He leapt up when he heard the soft brush of footsteps on earth.

"Am I glad to see you!" he said quietly, not wanting to disturb the others who were resting nearby, eyes closed and bundled close together beneath a large Ponderosa pine.

"The feeling is mutual, my friend," Marlen said hoarsely. "That proved to be one heck of an ordeal."

For the first time Paul noticed his friend's disheveled hair, sweat-stained shirt, and boots that had seen a lot of mud that day. "What happened? Did they give you a hard time? Did you bring the Bronco back with you or did they confiscate it?" He hadn't heard it drive up the tiny path.

Marlen cocked his head toward the thick brush behind him. "Come on. It's here. You can help me get the supplies out of it. I'll tell you all about it after that."

The next hour was spent hauling supplies, setting up a make-shift camp, and putting together a meal. Paul broke open a can of corn, a can of potatoes, and a tin of corned beef. He tossed it all together in a large frying pan while Marlen made a fire near the lakeshore. Together they had laced rope through the grommets of a large tarp and strung it beneath the trees. After the forest floor had dried a bit, they would toss down some sleeping bags and blankets.

"So what happened?" Paul asked, after shoveling dinner on a plate for both of them. The three visitors had refused the feast, looking at it with suspicion and distaste. Now they sat nearby, watching with interest.

"You would have thought that our campsite was the head-quarters for a drug smuggling operation or something," Marlen told them. "There were guys swarming all over the place. I'm surprised they didn't have a damn tank parked there. I met up with Mike and he went up there with me. We took a bunch of fishing gear and all. Went into camp like we had just been fishing. Raised a ruckus about them tearing our camp apart. They questioned us for hours but couldn't lay anything on us. They went on and on about wanting to know who the old guy was. They were talking about Grandfather. They wanted to know what we'd done with him." He sighed with exasperation. "They didn't let up. It took everything I had not to pop those guys. They were right in my face." He grimaced with the memory, then grinned. "I think I might have convinced a couple of them that they were nuts. That they had not seen Grandfather at all but had imagined him." He laughed. "By the time we drove out of there they were scratching their heads." He frowned suddenly. "But I got pretty worried there for a while. They didn't have any intention of letting me in or out of there. I think there must have been some higher spirits watching out for us because, logically, I shouldn't even be here right now."

Paul grinned at his words "higher spirits." "Speaking of higher spirits … I had a lesson on that today. Maybe before too long I'll be able to read your mind as well as you read mine. Better watch yourself."

Marlen jabbed at his arm with a fist, missing him deliberately. "I bet my thoughts are a lot more interesting than yours," he joked.

Laughing, Paul got up to pour them both a cup of coffee. He glanced over at Zere and the others, wondering if they might like to try some. Before he could ask, Zere shook his head no.

"What do you eat and drink?" Paul asked curiously. "You haven't had anything to eat or drink since we picked you up."

"Our understanding of life forms causes us to interact with our bodies differently than the human species," Zere informed him. "We are aware of being one with all things at all times. When we need something to assist our energy form, we simply ask it to supply us. There is a constant fluctuation and exchange of energies in our lives. Even the air assists us. It contains some of the energies and vibration that we need." He lifted his small shoulders in what might have looked, to some, like a shrug, though it actually resembled the wiggling of a fish out of water. "We partake of chlorophyll at times though. Out of desire, not need."

"You mean you eat plants?" Paul asked.

"Perhaps you could say that. But chlorophyll in liquid form. Not solid."

"And that's all? That's all you eat?" Paul asked, his eyebrows raising in surprise. To him life would be extremely boring without food, especially pizza.

Galin smiled, perhaps reading Paul's thoughts. "We find other ways to entertain ourselves." His chuckle sounded like the water of a small brook dashing over stones.

They joked and exchanged stories for another hour. By that time Paul was feeling, for the first time in his life, that he had established some good friendships. It made him feel good about the path he'd chosen, about the courage he'd shown in walking into unknown territory without fear of letting go of his comfortable but unsatisfactory life.

Zere began speaking quietly about Earth and the pollution of its energy field, interrupting Paul's thoughts. "If you consider that Earth has existed for centuries and you think of all of the events that have occurred on this planet, you might be capable of perceiving the energetic pollution that exists here. Not only do you have the personal pollution of emotional distress throughout homes and work places, but you also have the energy of the ages to contend with. For centuries you have had multiple wars, deaths, disasters, and incalculable pain contributing to the disturbance of the atmosphere.

"Earth was created as a place in which souls can physically incarnate in order to better understand themselves and existence. Earth's energy form has taken on the energetic consequences of its population. It is clogged with anger, pain, tears, and bloodshed. Like a saturated sponge, it is not capable of absorbing any more."

Paul had never thought along these lines before. But it seemed logical. If everything was energy, including Earth and the events that had occurred on it, it made sense that everything would be inundated with the misery that had plagued civilization throughout its history. It occurred to him that something needed to be done but he had no idea what the solution might be. To clean it up seemed like a task too large to even consider. Any attempt to clean the atmosphere, if that was even possible, would immediately be waylaid by the daily influx of new, negative energy that manifested from people's thoughts and actions.

Upon seeing Paul's expression, Zere was quick to explain that there were many other-dimensional societies, from near and far, that were trying to assist. Many souls from other lands had volunteered to take on physical incarnations in an attempt to bring their higher vibrations to Earth, and Light and wisdom to the problems. Most were struggling to overcome the saturation by constantly bringing Light from beyond and drenching the Earth with it. Paul, after listening with a myriad of emotions, wondered out loud what part he played.

Elan looked at him calmly. "You have choices. There are many things you can offer."

"Such as?" Paul asked. He had suffered with the dilemma for years without achieving a satisfactory answer.

Zere was smiling, his face lit up with a mischievous grin that could mean anything. Curious, and unsuccessful at reading his thoughts, Paul urged him to speak up.

"I think we've mentioned it before. You could write a book."

"I wouldn't have the slightest idea where to begin."

"We have the answer," Zere told him with a mysterious chuckle.

Paul glanced at Marlen, who merely raised his eyebrows in innocence.

"Sit back against that tree," Elan instructed. "Relax."

Paul did as he was asked. The setting sun was just topping the mountains on the horizon behind the lake. For an instant the fading rays touched his eyes and then were gone.

"Now, close your eyes. Relax," Elan said in a soft, hypnotic voice. "Let yourself forget who you are and where you are. Let the world fade. Clear your mind of thoughts. Allow yourself to let go of this reality and accept how vast the Universe is. This is a mere speck in time and space, and it does not hold you captive. Realize that you are far greater than this moment and that you are allowing yourself to exist here merely by your focus. When you allow your focus to drift without the need to control this moment, your truth will come to you."

Paul relaxed with the soft, soothing tones. He felt himself letting go of concern and stress. He felt himself begin to realize that, no matter what the momentary outcome, all things would eventually be set right.

"Surround yourself in Light, Paul," Elan continued. "The energy that is your body becomes saturated with Light. Feel yourself absorb the Light and then realize that your spirit is this Light. Feel your spirit rejoice at becoming the truth of itself. Feel the Light consume all energy, healing it, bringing it into the Light."

The vision was clear. Without hesitation, Paul followed the voice. A surge of joy rushed through his veins. His heart raced to embrace the Light. For this moment he was Freedom, unburdened by Earth reality. It was then that he began to notice a different energy entering his body. Like a fine lace, weaving itself through and around his cells, he felt threads of energy moving. As it moved through him he began to realize, with wonder and awe, that he was beginning to feel different than ever before. As if by magic, the cells of his body seemed to be altering. Some changed and some simply vanished. With internal vision, he watched himself.

His eyes became large and black and almond-shaped. His body was thin and white-skinned. That skin was tight against a small form that felt nothing at all like the body that he had known for twenty-nine years. He reveled in the sensations. They felt more familiar to him than his human skin. For an instant he was back to the moment when he had been accompanied to Earth by his five companions. A thread of human emotion tugged at him, urging him to mourn for the two aliens who had been lost in the crash. A flash of understanding whirled through the moment, bringing the knowledge that they had simply left a form behind, had moved in spirit to another world. He rejoiced for them, at the same time wishing that he could join them in their permanent freedom ... which brought him back to his original question ... why was he on Earth?

As the thought formed, he became aware of energies pressing in on him from all sides. With mental eyes he scanned the energy and was surprised to find that they all had specific forms. One by one the forms became more solid in his mind. He recognized them, as they formed. Here was Solomon, a soul he had known since the beginning of time; a friend who brought him the sense and depth of God. Here was Jacob, a soul of such spiritual depth that it brought tears to Paul's eyes. And there was Lateasha, a sparkling minx of a soul, filled with magic and light and joy that had no boundaries.

There were others, all familiar, all loved. He knew that they were in spirit form to assist him with his mission. The full impact of who he was and what it was that had been asked of him filled him at once with urgency and the imperative task of coming to a point of knowing the entire truth. Here, sitting next to him, were the friends who would help him find the way.

He opened his eyes and solemnly looked at those who sat near him. Each of them wore a different expression. All were serious and hopeful.

Galin was the first to speak. "When the truth of who you are becomes the reality which you live, rather than a momentary or fleeting contemplation, you will be prepared to go forward with your mission."

Paul answered by telling them about the memory of being transported to Earth. "It was only a few days ago that the memory came back fully. I guess maybe your proximity to Earth triggered it."

"Possibly," Elan ventured. He smiled slightly. "More probable is the fact that the time for beginning your mission is near. You see, each person awakens at a different time. There would be no point in knowing the complete truth and living in frustration, if it were not time to act upon that truth. At least, that is the case at this time in Earth's history. Many will be awakening to the truth of themselves."

Galin, who appeared to be the one who felt most strongly about changing the Earth and healing it beyond its present state of disarray, spoke up. "The energies that surround this planet are toxic and are affecting the societies that are in close proximity to it." He moved his small hand in controlled frustration. "Let me explain. All energies operate within a grid, in order to keep them contained in their present form. Such is the case with Earth. A grid surrounds it and that grid has broken down. Many, many forms of life have worked together to create a new grid as the old one broke away. But the new grid has a different vibration than the old one. It is made up of higher dimensional vibrations and threads of energy. This will necessarily affect the way in which humans exist. Because the new grid has higher vibrations, humans will be more affected by societies that live beyond their field of vision. This includes easier contact with soul, other worlds, and the Creator of existence."

Paul nodded, understanding. "That makes sense to me. But the damage here is massive. Is it going to be healed? How can we accomplish that when there's more negativity being added every minute of every day?" His voice rose an octave, displaying his frustration.

Galin's thin lips lifted in a small grimace. "True. The task is monumental. That is why there are so many from so far away who are assisting. That is why there are so many people on Earth who are from such distant origins. They have come to assist during this crucial time. Thousands are working from the surface here, as well as from above."

"I had a vision," Marlen offered, "of masses of crafts, large and small, all shapes and sizes and colors, descending on Earth en masse. And there were people waving hysterically, ecstatic with joy."

Zere chuckled softly. "The vision is close to being accurate. What you saw was a future effort that will take place. And the people you were shown are those who have volunteered to come to Earth. They are uncomfortable here and struggling to live in a way that doesn't suit them. They were overwhelmed to see their friends arrive."

"Wow!" Paul exclaimed. "I've got chills all over with that one."

Marlen nodded. "Yep. Chills are the body's way of telling you that you're hearing the truth."

Elan touched Paul on the knee and smiled. Paul felt a kinship with him. It was almost like he were looking into his own eyes.

"That's really going to happen?" Paul asked, breathless with sudden anticipation. "A convoy of ships is going to appear?"

"That's the plan," Elan said softly.

Marlen spoke up. "I think I'm going to go back out tomorrow morning and call a friend of mine. They have a place outside of Payson. It's pretty isolated. Maybe we could hole up there until you get rescued." He stopped suddenly and stared at Zere. "You *are* going to be rescued, aren't you?"

For a minute Zere and the others seemed lost, as if Marlen's words had caused them to instantly leave their bodies and transport themselves home. Zere turned slowly and stared vacantly at Marlen before answering. "Yes," he said slowly. "Yes, they plan on coming for us."

"Who?" Paul asked quickly. "What can we expect?"

"The *Esartania*, the mothership, will be transporting us. But first the atmosphere and timing must be right. We have no way of knowing the exact time." He scoured Paul's face, looking for answers. "Do you think that you can help us until they arrive?"

Paul's heart lurched with the pity he felt. He knew what it was like to be far from home. "Of course," he assured him quickly. "Whatever it takes, we'll do it."

Zere nodded thoughtfully. "I'm sorry that I felt the need to ask," he said. He shook his head lightly. "Earth has an instant affect on you, doesn't it?" he asked, turning to Galin and Elan. "For centuries I lived without fear and always knew that all things were in perfect order and everything would turn out for the best. Now, I've been here only a matter of hours and I am full of fear and doubt." He shook his head again, clearly saddened by the events.

"Look," Marlen interrupted in an attempt to change the mood. "I brought back some clothes for you guys. Mike and I hustled some up while we were out. Let's put them on you and see what works and what doesn't. If we can outfit you so that you look even a little bit like kids, it will be an easier trip out of here." He glanced at the quiet night sky. "It might be quiet now, but I imagine they'll be out early and in full force tomorrow. They're not going to give up that easily."

The three visitors stood willingly and allowed the various pieces of clothing to be draped over and around them. Within fifteen minutes Paul's ribs hurt from laughing. "He looks like Barney Fife!" he cried, collapsing into more laughter at the sight of Zere.

Marlen's hunting cap, ear flaps down, perched on Zere's head. The flaps scraped his bony shoulders. Elan and Galin stood nearby, pale arms flapping, having their own peculiar fit of amusement.

Marlen grinned but looked at Paul with raised eyebrows. "I think you need some sleep," he said pointedly. "You're getting' giddy."

Paul wished he had a camera. He wanted to savor the moment forever. Somehow, if the camera could freeze the moment and the humor, he thought the world might just understand the full extent of who these visitors really were. The fear would dissipate. Companionship between the worlds would grow, and what they had to offer would be freely accepted … without fear.

"We know nothing of your entertainment processes," Galin said suddenly. "We do not clearly understand. We recognize that many people spend much time being entertained by your television and such things. But we find it possible that this is a way in which they avoid themselves."

The statement instantly sobered Paul. "You might be right," he agreed. "I never thought of it that way."

"Life here is fairly simple to understand, in some ways," Galin commented. "But there are many who are not ready or willing to understand that things could be different."

Paul thought about it for a moment. "You might be right again. But," he added, "if it's time for the Universe to change, they might not have a lot of options."

Zere smiled calmly. "There is an order to all things," he said mysteriously. "We call it Divine Order. All things unfold as they are meant to."

Elan slid into a plaid, flannel shirt that, when settled on his small shoulders, left the sleeves hanging over his hands by a good three inches. "I once intercepted a picture wire that was being beamed around Earth for your entertainment." He studied his flannel-clad arms and looked up at Marlen. "Perhaps we could make what they call 'gloves' out of these things."

The thought of Elan attempting to fit his long, three-fingered hands into red flannel gloves sent Paul into more gales of laughter. An hour later, after the camp had been set to rights, Paul's memories and occasional giggles could still be heard. It was clear that the presence of his friends from elsewhere was lifting his spirits. He was enjoying himself immensely.

CHAPTER EIGHT

THE NEXT MORNING started with the drone of helicopters overhead. His sensitivity heightened, Paul felt the determination of the searchers. It felt as if they were scraping the earth itself in an unforgiving effort to uncover him and his charges. Contrary to what was happening around him though, he felt a tranquility. The process of accepting himself as something more than a limited human had brought him to a place of serenity.

As he slipped into his boots and jacket, a sudden thought occurred to him. He turned to Marlen, who was groggily mumbling something about needing a cup of coffee.

"Something I didn't think of until now," Paul told him. "If they were still suspicious of the Bronco, or you, when they let you go, they would be looking for it now. Maybe they even followed you."

Marlen shook his head negatively. "They didn't follow. They tried," he smiled wickedly, "but they didn't succeed." He stared at Paul for a silent, sleepy second. "But you might be right about the Bronco. As a matter of fact, you probably are right, since I evaded them." He ran both hands through his long hair, tucking it behind his ears, and looked out through the trees toward the lake, thinking. "I need to get in touch with someone who might come up here and take us out. Someone with a camper or something that we can hide these guys in."

"Do you know anyone with a camper?"

"Yeah. I think the guy I was planning on calling has one. At least he used to. He might freak out about all of this though. I don't imagine that he's used to seeing little men from other planets." He grinned. "At least they're not green."

Paul chuckled and then turned serious again. "I have a cell phone in the glove box. Do you think it will work from up here?"

"Depends on its range capability." Marlen shrugged. "Let's try it."

"What are you going to say to him?" Paul asked. "You probably ought to prepare before you get him on the phone."

The slap of helicopter rotors was closer than before, making it harder to hear. The three visitors sat huddled together, staring at Paul and Marlen with eyes that were obviously trying hard to hide their fear.

Marlen jumped up. "I'll go get the phone. I'll think of something to say. But," he added, "we need help *now.*" He leaned against a tree to pull on his boots. "It's going to take him at least an hour, maybe more, to get here … if he'll come," he added.

Paul glanced at the visitors, obviously worried. "Maybe we can create some kind of shield that will make you guys invisible."

"We can create a diversion," Zere said quietly.

"What?" Paul cried. "What can you do?" He flapped his arms in exasperation. "And why are we running and hiding if you can use some kind of trick to help us out here?"

"We prefer not to cross free will," Zere said primly.

"That sounds like something you're going to need to explain to me," Paul told him firmly. He glanced at the sky. "But right now you need to do whatever you can to help us out here. Or we're all going to be in deep trouble," he added.

Zere studied him for a minute. Finally he looked at the others and nodded. The three of them closed their eyes and went into what appeared to be a trance-like state. A minute later the helicopters veered away without explanation and were gone. Silence fell over the forest like a protective blanket.

"It is only a temporary diversion," Zere said quietly. "They think that they know where we are. Once they discover that the lead is wrong, they will be back."

"Go call your friend," Paul said tensely, addressing Marlen. "I can throw together a small fire and get us some coffee. But that's about it. I think we shouldn't risk a larger fire to cook breakfast over."

Marlen nodded, agreeing. "Some coffee would be great. That will be enough for right now."

He was gone in a flash, heading toward the Bronco. The forest enveloped him, making it appear that he had never even been there. Zere, Galin, and Elan calmly rose and helped Paul gather kindling.

By the time they had the fire going, Marlen was back. "The phone worked. Bill said he'd head up here as soon as he got dressed. I'll go out to the main road with the Bronco and lead him back in here."

"Great!" Paul said. "But maybe we should just go with you. We can wait back off the road, stay hidden until he gets here."

Marlen looked at him blankly. "Why didn't I think of that?" He shook his head. "I think the stress is getting to me." He stared with concern at the three visitors. "We need to get them dressed," he said distractedly.

Paul walked over and stuck a cup of coffee in his hand. "Here. Drink this. Then let's get this stuff packed into the Bronco. Then we'll worry about dressing them."

Marlen looked up at him with a small sigh. "Sounds like a plan." He studied Paul for a minute. "Why are you so calm and I'm such a wreck? I thought it was going to be the other way around."

"I have no idea," Paul said. He shrugged slightly. "Maybe you're taking on my stress for me."

"Well, take it back," Marlen snarled good-humoredly.

Paul turned away without comment and studied the small area of serenity around them. The deep forest and its companion lake were unaffected by the drama that was playing out in its midst. It would have been a perfect place for a vacation getaway. "I imagine this place only gets about ten people a year up here." He waved a hand at the other side of the lake. "And they come in from the other side. The road over there is probably ten times better than the one we came in on."

Marlen gulped the tepid coffee and hoisted himself up. He clapped Paul on the shoulder. "If we get out of this alive, I'll bring you back up and you can fish to your heart's content." He grabbed an armful of blankets and began folding them haphazardly. "But right now we better get busy."

Together they all struggled back and forth between the campsite and the Bronco, carrying supplies. When everything was settled, they tackled the job of dressing the visitors. After a contest with arm holes and buttons and long fingers getting caught in sleeves, and bare feet that wouldn't fit into shoes and pants that were too long, they were finally dressed. He stood back and surveyed the motley crew. It was impossible not to laugh. After their paroxysm, which the visitors took good-naturedly, they were ready to take their chances with civilization.

Paul thought about their hastily approved plan as they walked to the Bronco. Their escape, in his opinion, had been ill planned and disorganized. It was against his nature to have things unfold in such precarious ways. He was a planner; meticulously planning everything in order to assure that the end result would be the one he wanted. He didn't like unpleasant surprises. He broke the silence, offering his concerns to anyone who cared to listen.

Marlen was the first to respond. "We just have to wing it and take our chances." He glanced over his shoulder at Paul, who was the last in line as they threaded their way through the trees toward the car. "I don't see why it won't work. Bill will get here. We'll hide these guys in the back. We'll get them out to the ranch. And then we'll wait for the *Esartania*. I don't see why it won't work," he repeated.

His words impacted Paul. Something inside his chest shivered in protest. Until now, it hadn't really sunk in that his three charges would be leaving. It was illogical to think that they could stay. He had no idea why he had even hoped for such a thing. Now all he wanted to do, even though it would be beyond dangerous, was to create a way for them to stay.

He blinked back sudden tears, feeling foolish. He was glad no one noticed. His thoughts went forward to the time when they would be rescued. He watched their departure in his mind. He knew without a doubt that he would want to leave with them. How would he cope after having renewed this friendship … only to lose it again?

Elan looked back at him, having heard his thoughts and despair. For a second their eyes locked.

"My life will never be the same," Paul said quietly, his voice trembling.

"And that is exactly the point," Elan said just as quietly. He reached out and gently touched Paul's hand before turning back to the narrow pathway, leaving Paul wondering exactly what he meant.

Marlen stopped the group at the Bronco and helped the visitors settle into the back seat. After another bone-jarring ride, he swung the Bronco into a shelter of trees several hundred yards off the main road. Like a mother hen, Paul herded his companions into a tight circle and hovered over them in a silly attempt to shield them from view. The forest was thick on all sides and overhead. There was little chance of them being sighted.

It was only about twenty minutes before they heard the rattle of a truck on rough ground. Marlen stepped boldly to the side of the road to see who it was, ignoring Paul's protest.

"How else are we gonna know who it is?" he grumbled, looking over his shoulder at Paul.

They were in luck. It was Bill Madison, Marlen's friend. Bill pulled off the main road and onto the small path about fifty feet before noticing Paul and the visitors. He stopped the truck and sat staring, wide-eyed, while Marlen made his way around to the driver's side. Paul could hear Marlen talking quietly, explaining. A minute later he heard a small eruption of sound from Bill.

"What? You're kidding me, right?"

Two seconds later Bill exploded out of the truck and stood staring at the sight of the three badly dressed, badly disguised aliens. "I don't believe this," he breathed softly.

Paul studied him while he studied the aliens. He was approximately five-ten, stocky and barrel-chested, with dark brown hair reluctantly giving way to threads of silver. At the moment it was uncombed and stuck up in small spikes, making him appear somehow vulnerable. Soft lines were etched around his eyes and lips. Paul guessed that he was about forty-five years of age.

Marlen came crashing around the side of the truck, catching up to Bill. "You have to take this seriously," he said firmly, grabbing Bill's arm. "They are as real as you and I. I wouldn't have called you if I didn't think I could trust you."

Bill glanced at him quickly and turned back to the sight in front of him. "You can trust me," he assured them firmly. "I just never thought I'd see the day."

Paul stepped forward, hand extended, and shook hands with Bill. "I appreciate your help. We all do." He glanced at Marlen. "I think we should get going though. We're only inviting trouble by hanging around here."

At that instant they heard once again the distant approach of helicopters. Not even two seconds passed before they heard the chatter of wheels on the main road. Paralyzed with fear, they watched in horror as two military Jeeps sped by only yards away. Apparently intent on a specific destination, none of the men in the Jeeps looked at the thick foliage on their right. If they had, the entire mission would have been over. Paul took a prayerful second to thank the Universe and everyone in it and then, without asking, threw open the rear door of the camper and started lifting his companions into the interior.

He threw himself in after them, exchanged a hard look with Marlen, and slammed the door. Seconds later he heard the engine start and they were backing up onto the main road and heading east toward the highway. He was prepared to hold on tightly but, wisely, Bill took it slow, meandering out of the forest as if there was nothing out of the ordinary going on. Paul cast his eyes heavenward with another prayer of thanks for Bill's cool head and sat back against the wall of the tiny camper to await their arrival at Bill's place.

CHAPTER NINE

Paul felt the truck slowing. He didn't want to risk looking out the tiny, curtained window. He assumed they were in Payson. The truck rolled again, making a turn to the left. He could hear traffic on both sides of the truck. He sniffed. Sure enough. They were in town. After days of eating camp food, it smelled so good he almost swooned.

Elan watched his reaction with interest. "Your senses are most interesting," he pointed out.

"How so?" Paul asked.

"At home you were only interested in that which fed your spirit and your etheric body. Here you are uncommonly absorbed in the care of your physical body."

Paul was slightly affronted. "I would imagine everyone is," he said defensively. "It's quite an undertaking to take care of a body."

"But at home you have a body also," Elan answered reasonably.

"But I imagine that it's quite different," Paul responded. "It's reasonable to assume that it has different needs."

Elan tilted his head like a small puppy listening. "Why would you assume such a thing?" he asked, seeming to be genuinely puzzled.

Paul was struck by the question. Up until this challenge, he had assumed that things were vastly different in places other than Earth. Maybe such was not the case. He thought about it for a minute. "Well," he finally said, "from what I understand, the vibrations and energies elsewhere are a lot different than Earth. If that's true, and I think it is, than the lower vibrational places of life would need much more attention."

Zere got into the conversation. "Such as plant life?" he asked, his eyes twinkling with humor. "I understand that they take an inordinate amount of time tending to themselves."

"Are you being funny or trying to make a point?" Paul asked good-naturedly.

Zere was quick to answer. "I suppose I am trying to point out that, while life on this planet is in a state of chaos and definitely needs some reorganization, it might help to change some of your priorities. Not necessarily only you, but all people." He lifted one small finger for emphasis. "If the people wish to evolve beyond some of the life circumstances that occur here on Earth, there is no other way than to cause oneself to evolve first. Then the rest of the reality would follow suit."

Paul thought about it. "You have a good point."

Zere chuckled lightly. "It may very well be my job to point out such things."

"Do you think?" Paul asked, surprised. "Is that why you're here? Is there more to this than what appears to be an accident?"

Galin spoke up. "There really is no such thing as an accident. Or a coincidence, for that matter. The Universe is ordered. One action creates a reaction. It is simple physics. If one could learn to observe the world through the eyes of the soul, one would accomplish a greater understanding and would see that the Universe is orchestrated. Whenever a person makes a choice, the Universe reorders itself in order to accommodate that choice."

The idea was astounding to Paul. He gazed at Galin open-mouthed. "How in the world can something so vast react to one single incident or choice?"

Galin lifted one small shoulder in a shrug. "It has no choice. Energy affects energy. One cannot throw a stone into a pond without causing a ripple."

The words made a clear picture in Paul's mind. When explained so simply, it made a vast amount of sense. It seemed to him that his entire being was reacting to the understanding of the Universe through this vision. It was as if things suddenly became clear. The thought was monumental. Another thought occurred to him. "This makes it perfectly obvious to me that you are not here by accident. With your, shall we say, foreign energy, you are affecting the energies on Earth. Was that the plan all along?" He looked from one to the other for the answer.

Elan nodded without speaking. Paul thought that he looked a trifle sad at the voiced thought. Galin spoke for the three of them. "There are many reasons why we are here. One of them is you. In the near future you will come to a greater understanding of the part you play in this mission."

"Mission?"

Zere looked utterly serious as he met Paul's gaze. "There will be a Peace Mission. There are many preparing at this moment. They have been preparing for many earth years. As Galin said, with all things being energy, it is impossible for events upon Earth not to affect all things. What is occurring here is impacting all things within existence. It is essential to bring Earth and its energies into proper alignment with the rest of existence."

For Paul the task seemed too large to absorb. "How on Earth are you going to accomplish that? People have been acting the way they are for centuries. You can't honestly believe that things can change just like that?" He snapped his fingers for emphasis.

"Those who do not desire change may choose another existence," Elan said quietly. He tapped Paul lightly on the knee. "This is as good a time as any to tell you the part you play. Or at least a piece of it. We need emissaries between this world and the ones beyond. You're one of them. You'll be called upon to pass messages and to begin to open the path between worlds."

Paul gaped at him. Before he could comment, they felt the truck slow, turn, and jolt onto a rough road. The air behind them turned to dust, letting Paul know that they had turned onto a dirt road. Just as he was going to risk a peek outside, he heard gravel beneath the tires. Seconds later the truck ground to a halt. He heard the cab doors open. Assuming it was safe to do so, he reached over and pushed the camper door open. The fresh air of a high-desert morning spilled in. He jumped down lightly and looked around. On his right was a low, ranch-style house. Beyond it lay a valley that was backed by a low range of squatty hills. Fences paraded here and there. He could see several horses in a nearby corral. Behind the house was a smaller building, possibly a guest-house.

"It is beautiful," Zere said from behind him.

Paul turned. Zere and the others were still in the camper, but stacked like building blocks, peering eagerly out. He laughed out loud at the sight. Marlen and Bill joined him, glanced at the visitors, and chuckled as well.

Paul turned to Bill. "Are you sure they'll be safe here?"

"I wouldn't have brought them here if I thought any differently," Bill said lightly, not taking offense. He looked toward the house. The front door was opening. "Better have them stay here while I prepare my wife," he advised. He strolled off unhurriedly.

Paul decided that he was going to like him. He admired his immediate acceptance of the alien visitors and the fact that he had not hesitated to offer his assistance. He watched as two Irish Setters and a short, slightly-built brunette came out of the house. The dogs bounded toward Bill and, after satisfying themselves that he was, indeed, the same man who had left a few hours earlier, turned to investigate the newcomers. Paul noticed that Bill gathered his wife into his arms in a way that suggested that she was his world. For a minute he felt envious and lonely.

His attention was drawn back to the dogs as they bounded toward him with small yips of excitement. He had no idea whether his charges had ever encountered dogs before, but he knew for certain that the dogs had never encountered aliens. He moved to stop their progress toward the truck, but they dodged around him and leapt joyously into the camper.

Appalled, Paul rushed to follow them, his eyes wide with horror. From inside he heard what sounded like the gasps and grunts of a struggle. He braced his arms against both sides of the door, preparing to hoist himself into the camper, but there was no room for him inside the cramped space.

The dogs were standing over the fallen aliens. He reached wildly for the wiggling, jumping red fur of a dog, prepared to haul him off of the visitors. He heard what sounded like the squeal of a small, excited child. A gasping giggle followed.

With an anxious, stress-releasing gasp, he allowed his hands to drop.

Elan's smiling face popped up out of the muddle. "Dogs!" he cried excitedly.

Paul laughed with relief and nodded. "Dogs," he agreed.

From beneath the frolicking tongue of one of the dogs, Paul heard another giggle. "They are soft!" he heard someone say.

A soft cough came from the pile. "Their skin comes off," Galin said, sticking his head up and fighting for breath. His thin lips were covered with red dog fur.

Paul couldn't help it. He burst into gales of laughter. He didn't see Bill's wife approaching him from behind. When he finally looked up, she was there, a large smile on her face and tears in her eyes as she stood looking at the visitors.

"Oh," she said softly, reverently.

She pressed her fingers to her lips in an attempt, Paul assumed, to stifle her overwhelming emotions. From the look on her face one might assume that these were her children, who had been lost for a hundred years, and had now returned home. Paul stepped back in surprise.

Bill was there to make the introductions. "Honey, this is Paul. And this is," he looked at Marlen for confirmation on the names, "Zere, Elan, and Galin." As each name was called a head popped up and nodded. "This is my wife, Brenda." He reached down and fondled the ears of one of the dogs who had jumped down and run to sit by his side. "This is Fric and Frac," he added lovingly. "I hope they didn't scare the life out of you."

Paul extended his hand to Brenda, who took it absentmindedly, her eyes still on the three aliens. When he dropped her hand she turned to him, as if she realized that she was being impolite. He was struck by the deep violet-blue of her eyes.

"I'm sorry. I didn't catch your name," she said, apologizing.

Paul told her again while looking at her soft, fair skin, the sincerity of her eyes, the exuberant curl of her shoulder-length hair. He hoped that some day soon he would be as blessed as Bill was.

"You're so lucky to have been able to spend some time with them," she breathed, turning back to the camper. Her eyes filled again with tears as she studied the occupants.

They, in turn, studied her. Suddenly Elan stretched out a paper-thin, three-fingered hand and softly touched her cheek. She gave a soft cry, as if the wing of an angel had touched her.

"Your eyes are leaking," Elan said, his voice soft and melodic.

Brenda's eyes wrinkled in delight. "Oh! I think I'm in love with you already!" She reached out her arms. Elan stepped easily into them and allowed her to lift him from the camper. Brenda turned and began to walk toward the house with him in her arms.

Paul lifted Zere and Galin down and together they followed Bill into the house.

Paul had never before been in a house that seemed to reach out to welcome him. He felt a rush of relaxation the instant he stepped inside.

The house was decorated in the Southwest style. Soft pastels and striking whites greeted his eyes. The furnishings were simple but colorful. He felt the warmth enfold him as he stepped down the single step that separated the entryway and the living room. Through a sliding glass door at the other end of the room he could see a brick-red patio and the crystal-blue of a swimming pool. Another rush of peace enveloped him.

Brenda was watching him from the large, over-stuffed couch where she sat holding Elan on her lap, as if he were her child. She looked brightly at Bill, who was advancing to sit next to her. "So ... I want to hear everything," she told him.

Paul smiled. He liked her immediately. Just in the few minutes that he'd known this couple he had a feeling that he could trust them. "Everything?" he asked teasingly.

Brenda responded with a grin.

"I'll make you a deal," he offered, running his hand over his gristly chin, which had not been shaved in a week, "I'll trade you the story for a hot bath and a shave."

Chuckling softly, Brenda set Elan on the couch, rose, and led Paul out through the sliding glass doors and into what turned out to be a guest cottage that sat on the other side of the pool.

It was almost an hour before Paul sat down to tell his story. He assumed that everyone had discussed everything already and so he started with his part in it, the dream of another world.

Zere and Galin rested on large floor pillows. Elan laid on the couch with his head cradled on Brenda's lap. Every once in a while Brenda's hand would hover over him like a hummingbird over a flower. Paul could sense that she feared waking him, but also wanted to touch him to prove to herself that he was real. Her face glowed with wonder. She interrupted Paul's story only when he mentioned that he might write a book about the experience.

"A novel?" she cried softly. "You're going to write a novel about this?" That's a pretty incredible coincidence." She glanced over at Bill, who sat on the floor with his back resting against a large, easy chair. "I'm a writer. I might be able to help you with editing and such."

Paul sat back in his chair and stared at her. The earlier comment that there was no such thing as a coincidence bounded through his mind like a rabbit through clover. A sudden clutch of joy rose in his throat. It was quite possible that, after all his years of searching, his life might change into something that he craved, rather than endured.

When he didn't comment immediately, Brenda pointed to a nearby bookshelf. "Really!" she insisted. "I really am an author. There are two of my books right there."

Paul shook his head. "No. I didn't doubt you. I was just astounded at the way things are working out."

"It's pretty amazing, isn't it?" Again her hand fluttered, resisting the urge to caress Elan's thin shoulder.

"I was thinking it was going to be a monumental task and I was wondering if I would be able to talk myself into even thinking about it, much less writing it." Paul searched her eyes for a minute. "With your help, I might be able to pull it off."

Brenda's eyes filled with sincerity. "But you must," she insisted. "I have a feeling that your story will fill a lot of people with hope."

Paul thought that it was an odd comment to make but he didn't pursue it.

Brenda looked down at Elan and then moved her gaze to Zere and Galin who, by now, were resting against each other. "I think it would be impossible for anyone to know how much this means to me," she said quietly.

She looked up at Bill, and Paul noticed that there were, once again, tears in her eyes. "I have had dreams about them all of my life. I have even dreamt about being aboard their crafts." She smiled shyly. "I had no proof that it wasn't wishful thinking. Now I know it wasn't. I was really aboard." She looked at Paul brightly, her eyes penetrating him, gauging his reaction.

Paul looked at her thoughtfully. He wondered if, indeed, she had been aboard and if, perhaps, he had seen her but not recognized her. And was it possible that he knew her, as well as Stephanie, from another lifetime. The immediate sense of closeness that he felt to her suggested that he did. "It wouldn't surprise me at all if you actually were," he said. "As I mentioned, I've had those dreams too. And now these guys are actually here. That's proof enough for me."

Brenda breathed out softly. "I think I was," she said, her voice trembling. "I have always wanted it to be true, to know that I was accepted by them." She glanced at Bill. "Bill understands how I feel. I just feel that these beings from other places are really special and that they're dedicated to making a better reality for all of us. Not all of them," she added, glancing at Bill, "but these guys for certain. I don't know. I just have a feeling that they have a mission of some kind … that they are here to help our world get out of the mess it's in." She looked at Paul and Marlen to see if they understood.

"I think you can rest assured that is exactly why they're here," Marlen said strongly.

Paul nodded in agreement.

Brenda nodded and turned to look out through the patio doors. Fric and Frac were sitting there, staring intently. "Oh, honey, I think they're hungry. I forgot to feed them this morning. They probably feel neglected."

Bill rose immediately. "Consider it done," he said. He stopped in the doorway to the kitchen and turned back. "Anyone else hungry? I can whip us up something to eat."

"Let me help," Marlen said quickly, jumping to his feet.

Paul laughed. "I think that's a good sign that he's tired of campfire food."

Marlen chuckled. "That kind of food can only keep a man satisfied for just so long."

Paul offered to help. Bill and Marlen waved him back. "Relax," Bill told him. "Too many cooks in the kitchen and all that stuff, you know." He waved a hand at Paul and disappeared through the doorway with Marlen in tow.

"Good," Brenda said, nestling into the couch a little further. "I was feeling like I was being a rotten hostess but I didn't want to disturb this little one." Her gaze went from Elan to the kitchen door. "He is really, really good to me," she said quietly. "I'm really blessed."

Elan, apparently sensing commotion around him, opened his eyes. Paul watched in amazement as those normally marble-like eyes turned to glowing embers of love at the sight of Brenda hovering over him.

The two stared at each other for long seconds before Paul dared to speak and break the silence. He felt compelled to share what he was thinking. "What's your opinion about some of the human population actually being from elsewhere? About being here on a mission?"

Brenda raised her eyes to Paul's and smiled. "I think it's true. Some of us are extraterrestrials living on Earth. We have come to help heal the Earth and are attempting to lift and heal energies and vibrations." Her eyes widened in surprise at her own words. "Where did that come from?" she asked, shaking her head. "It felt almost as if that wasn't me talking."

Paul looked at her in amazement. "You just confirmed that you think you're one of them," he told her quietly.

She lifted her chin and met his gaze directly. "I know I am," she said firmly. "When I spoke earlier of being on the craft and wondering about it, I didn't know how much you knew and how much you could accept. Suddenly I know that I can trust you." She smiled. "I don't know why. Things like that happen to me all the time. The truth is though, I've always believed that I was one of them. I've never been totally comfortable here. I've had pretty clear memories of another place and another time."

From across the room Paul noticed that her chin trembled slightly. He nodded, remembering his own experiences.

"There were many years when I wondered what was wrong with me. I couldn't seem to fit in anywhere. No matter how hard I tried I couldn't understand what I saw going on around me." She smiled ironically. "That hasn't changed, believe me. Anyway, people always thought I was different and weird. They didn't hesitate to tell me so either. Even my parents always seemed to be angry with me for not being who they wanted me to be. But I didn't know how to change." She paused and turned to look out the window, biting her lower lip. "I have healed from that as much as one can, I suppose."

"I hope you know that you're not alone with those feelings," Paul said softly. "I had a pretty similar experience. Always looking for something but not even sure of what it was I was looking for. Never fitting in. All that stuff."

Brenda turned back to him. "I know that I'm not alone. When I was old enough to head out on my own, I began to encounter others who felt the same. I met them mostly in metaphysical aisles at bookstores," she added, smiling. "How about you? Did you find people of like mind?"

Paul shook his head. "No. Not really. I've walked this alone until now. I went to bookstores and bought quite a few books about aliens but I never met anyone."

"That's where I met Bill," Brenda explained. "In a bookstore aisle. He was reading up on the subject. That's why he's taken all of this in stride. He's been reading about them and listening to me for quite a few years now."

"I heard that," Bill called from the kitchen. "Hey, honey, why don't you take everyone out by the pool? We can bring the food out there. The fresh air feels pretty good coming through this window."

"Sounds good to me," Brenda called back. "Okay with you?" she asked Paul, raising her eyebrows in question.

"Sure."

Elan moved reluctantly from Brenda's arms and jumped lightly from the couch. He stood watching Zere and Galin uncertainly.

"They're all right," Brenda said softly, touching him lightly on the shoulder.

Elan gave Paul one of his rare smiles, walked to his side, and slid his hand inside Paul's. They followed Brenda as she led the way onto the patio.

Paul sank immediately into one of the chaise lounges. Elan joined him instantly, scooting his small body onto Paul's lap and pressing against him like a sleepy child. Within minutes he was fast asleep again.

"I wonder where they go when they sleep?" Brenda speculated. "I mean, we go there. Do you suppose they come here?"

Paul struggled to stifle a laugh. "Why in the name of heaven would they want to?" he asked, grinning.

Brenda shrugged with a smile. "You never know."

"I suppose not but...."

Marlen and Bill interrupted with trays of food, which they deposited on a nearby table. Fric and Frac instantly abandoned their food dishes and came running to inquire as to how much of the meal would be theirs.

"You look like you have your hands full," Bill said to Paul as he playfully wrestled the dogs away from the table. "You want me to bring you a plate?"

"That would be nice," Paul said, surprised. He wasn't used to anyone doing anything for him. It was a welcome treat but uncomfortable at the same time. A few minutes later he had a small table perched beside him, loaded with a plate of food and a cold glass of iced tea.

CHAPTER TEN

LATER THAT AFTERNOON Bill and Brenda invited them to nap in the guesthouse. Everyone was feeling the effects of the deep excitement and the heavy possibilities. Paul led the way to the small house, opening the door for the others, inviting them into the pleasant surroundings.

The small house was decorated in much the same way as the larger one. The furnishings were simple, the colors soft pastels and white. There were two bedrooms, one bath, and a common sitting area. The couch in the sitting area opened into a bed. It would suit their needs perfectly. Paul and Marlen flipped open the bed for the three visitors who were still eager to rest. Paul assumed that they were suffering from shock, which would cause them to need lots of sleep. After making certain that they were comfortable, he and Marlen proceeded into one of the bedrooms to talk.

"We need to talk about this military thing," Marlen said the minute he closed the door behind them. "We may be putting Bill and Brenda at risk. I would like to see us move out of here pretty quickly if our friends aren't picked up tonight."

Paul felt his heart lurch in protest. "Tonight? You think it might be that soon?"

Marlen shrugged. "I don't know." He studied Paul. "I'm with you. I wish they didn't have to go. But they do. And the sooner the better as far as safety for everyone is concerned."

"There's still so much that they can tell us, teach us," Paul muttered, stepping to the window and staring out sightlessly, his hands locked behind his back.

"I agree. But it's not like we have any say about how all of this is going to end up. It will happen the way it's supposed to happen, no matter how we feel about it."

Paul turned back to him. "That's true, I'm sure. And you're right. They're not safe here. I would hate to have anything happen to them or to any of us, for that matter."

"Maybe I should call Mike and have him come get me," Marlen suggested. "He can take me back up so I can bring the Bronco back. That way we'll have it if we need to leave quickly."

"Bill would probably be glad to drive you back up," Paul told him.

"I know he would. But I don't want him to take any more chances than he already has. Mike and I know this area better than anyone, I imagine. We can get lost if we need to."

"But the military won't be looking for Bill's truck," Paul pointed out. "They might be looking for Mike's, and they most certainly are watching out for the Bronco."

"True," Marlen agreed. "Maybe I should talk to Bill about it." He turned to leave the room but turned back, his hand on the doorknob. "What?" he asked, as if Paul had spoken out loud.

"Maybe it's not something we're going to have to worry about," Paul said glumly. "Maybe they'll be picked up tonight and it will be a moot issue." His words dropped on the floor like weights and sat heavily between them, fraught with significance.

"I'll be back in a while," Marlen said after a silent minute. He turned and left the room, closing the door quietly behind him.

For several minutes Paul stood looking at the closed door. Finally he opened it, went to a small, stuffed chair in the sitting area, and sat silently, watching his three companions sleep.

That evening was one of love shared across the boundaries between worlds. The night air was mild and softly tuned to the mood of the small group. Elan sat peacefully on Brenda's lap. Zere sat between Marlen and Bill. Galin was, much to Paul's surprise, perched casually on Paul's knee. Occasionally Zere or Elan would point out a falling star, the blinking of a comet, a spark of unexplainable light.

Paul, deep in thought, was troubled but reluctant to speak about it. Galin, reading his thoughts, finally asked him what was bothering him.

"I keep hearing all of these things about abductions, mutilations, and stuff like that. I don't understand. I've known you, and others like you, for centuries it seems. I know it's not anyone from your society who's doing these things, but who is it? Maybe a better question would be, are these things really happening, or are they products of fear and imagination?"

"Let me explain if I can," Galin answered. "Just as there are many societies on Earth, there are many societies elsewhere. There are portals through time and space, which allow travel throughout existence, through dimensions and realities and such.

"Years ago a society that Earth people now refer to as 'the greys' began to use a route that was traveled centuries ago. It was closed due to a common agreement between Earth people and those who live beyond. Earth people, at that time, wanted to live alone and make their own mistakes or have their own successes. You see? Like children who don't want to be taught any more, they wanted to be free to make their choices without direction from other worlds. And so the portal was closed. But the 'greys' opened it again."

Paul interrupted. "Who exactly are these guys?"

"They look much like we do in stature. Their complexions are grey and their faces, as well as their purpose, are more sinister. They are, in some ways, more advanced than Earth people. That is why those who have been in contact with them in your government listen to what they say.

"But they have plans of their own which do not coincide with the plans of the Elders and the Overlords and the Mission."

"Plans like what?" Paul asked.

"They would like to see it become mandatory that humans interact with their species," Zere said simply, his words bringing a sense of dread to Paul's chest.

"They would like to see the human race become dependent upon them in a way that supports the belief that humans are powerless. When people believe they are powerless they look to others to lead them. The greys are hoping that they will become those leaders."

"But who are they exactly?" Brenda asked. "Where do they come from?"

Zere answered the question. "Long ago, during the time of Atlantis, when the breakdown between Earth and other worlds became quite serious, they were watching. The leaders in their world had lost control of their own people and were systematically destroying the rebels. This left them without enough people to generate and continue their species. They looked to Earth beings for procreation. They created a plan that would benefit their species.

"They looked nothing like us at the time," Zere added. "But in the midst of the chaos of Atlantis falling, they kidnapped one of our fleets. They used those aboard to reproduce our DNA, our features, and created a clone, if you will, of us. They were able to mutate to the degree that they came to look like us, except for the color of our skin and other small details, which you would have to be very perceptive to notice. We had been interacting with the human race extensively and people had come to trust us. The greys cloned us, basically, hoping to fool people into trusting them.

"In our minds they have been unsuccessful at duplicating us because their vibratory rate is so much lower than ours. Anyone who can read energies and vibrations will instantly recognize the differences. Such things as energies cannot be duplicated … only achieved."

Everyone nodded with common understanding.

Galin took up the story. "They became outlaws in this Universe. They are a scientific community. They desire to learn all that they can about other societies with the goal of cloning them as well. They learned, by kidnapping and duplicating our species, what works and what does not. They also learned more about the technique of kidnapping versus the art of persuasion. It is, they found, more beneficial to them to have many captives who do not know that they have been duped. They attempt to cause your people to believe in them by exhibiting their intelligence and technical expertise.

"They are looking for the flaws as well as the perfection in each species. Their goal is, of course, to create a superior race by borrowing from others. In addition, they study others in order to understand them. It is no secret that, when you know your enemies' weak points, your enemy becomes your victim."

Paul was compelled to glance over at Zere. His eyes had turned to blocks of ice-cold, ebony-colored marble.

"Their purpose is to control and dominate as many civilizations as they can in order to control the power and energy and potential of this Universe," Zere said quietly, his eyes fixed on Paul's.

"But what you fail to tell them," Galin said, "is that their mission will not succeed." His voice was low and controlled, as if he were an imperious being facing a threatening crowd. "The Elohim Council, who are, in cooperation with many others, overseeing the energetic progress of this Universe will see to it that they don't succeed."

Elan spoke up. "The 'greys' are one legion against a million. They cannot possibly take control. We, meaning the societies that exist in higher dimensions, are bound never to interfere with free will. However, there is a majority throughout existence who demand that things be set right. The free will of those who choose to continue with war and separation from Divine Order will be free to live as they choose in another reality. But this existence will be righted," he added steadfastly.

"Why did the 'greys' choose Earth?" Bill asked curiously.

Galin answered. "They saw a tear in the fabric of Earth … meaning the energetic grid that surrounds Earth. They saw it breaking down and thought that they might use that to their advantage. People who saw them instantly feared them. They were able to use that fear to empower themselves. Fear and doubt rob people of their personal power. Their connection to the Divine is broken."

Brenda shuddered. "I have always had a suspicion that it was something like that. Tell me this … why is it so much easier to manifest our fears than to manifest our desires. Do you know?"

"That one is easy to answer," Elan offered. "You see, the spirit wants nothing more than to manifest the power of the soul. Any unhealed areas within the emotional body or mental body will willingly show themselves as quickly as possible in order to display to the spirit that there is something in the way of its progress. And, because like attracts like, fear will attract exactly what it fears."

"That makes a lot of sense but it does not entirely explain why desires don't manifest," Brenda challenged.

"Think of it this way," Zere offered. "Imagine the soul at one end of a pillar of light. The spirit is at the other end. The goal is to return to the end of the pillar where the soul resides. Desires live and manifest within that pillar, but fears are blocks that get in the way. You have to move the fear out of the way in order to get to the desire. The fear is the tool that shows you what needs to be healed in order to reach the desire. The fear won't move until you heal it. The desire cannot be achieved until the part of yourself that denies it, namely fear or doubt, is healed."

"That makes sense!" Brenda exclaimed.

"And that is the point," Galin said, raising one finger in the air with a show of victory. "Simplify. Human beings make things much too complicated. The more you realize that what you seek is already there, the more you will become the simple, trusting, children of joy that you were meant to be."

"I like it," Paul proclaimed.

"I do too," Bill agreed, nodding.

"Okay," Brenda interrupted. "So tell me this … I feel like I have to know this, like something or someone is pressuring me to ask you this before it's too late … whatever that means. If people realize that they are in fear and they make a deliberate, concentrated effort to overcome it, will these abductions stop? Will the 'bad guys' lose? And will they leave an opening for the higher vibrational beings, guys like you," she said, laying her hand on Elan's arm, "to come in and help the human race to evolve?"

Elan smiled serenely.

Zere answered. "There are many Masters from many ancient societies who are going to intervene and assist Earth. The 'greys' have no power to stop the Mission."

Brenda sighed with relief. "I'm so happy to hear that. I was worried that there might be a war or something."

"There has been a war," Galin offered seriously. "Unbeknownst to most people on Earth, there has been a war of energies for centuries."

"And now?" Bill asked.

"And now it looks as if we are going to win," Zere said confidently. With that hope voiced, they all agreed to end the evening.

The next morning Paul awakened with a thrill of excitement. He tossed off the covers, pulled on a fresh pair of jeans, and walked barefoot to the bathroom. Finding Marlen's door closed and the small house quiet, he decided to take a shower to wash away the grogginess of the night. He had slept as if drugged, with only vague impressions and memories left of his dreams.

With a towel around his waist he tiptoed back into his bedroom so as not to wake the others. The small house was still silent. He dressed quickly and headed for the patio, anxious to breathe in the rich air of the morning to clear his head. As he stepped into the sitting room, he realized that the fold-out bed was empty. Any calm that he had was instantly shattered. He dashed outside, his heart flapping in his chest as if it were a flag caught in a windstorm. He scanned the distant horizon frantically, wondering if he had slept through the departure of his companions.

"Good morning," Brenda's soft voice called from the chaise lounge where she was calmly sunning herself. Fric and Frac slept next to her. A small table held a steaming cup of coffee.

"Good morning," Paul said. "Did you happen to see our friends this morning?" he asked, struggling to compose himself. "They aren't in bed."

"Calm down," she advised. "They're not gone. They went for a walk. They headed out toward the pasture. They can't get in any trouble out there."

Paul was not so certain. He turned to scan the pasture area. He could see nothing. He turned back to stare at her. "You just let them walk off by themselves?" he asked, puzzled.

"Why not?" She shrugged her slim shoulders and peered at him. "They'll be all right."

"But the military is still out looking for them," Paul said, trying to remain calm. "What if they fly by here and see them out there?" He waved his arm at the pasture.

Brenda looked at him as if he were a small child making up stories. "You know better than that," she chastised him gently. "They can take care of themselves."

Paul took a deep breath and turned away from her, scouring the pasture area and the distant hills.

"For someone who is an alien himself, you certainly do worry a lot," she teased.

Paul felt a slight blush dab his cheeks. "I guess you're right. I try not to, but it's a habit that dies hard, I guess. But," he added in his own defense, "you weren't up there when those guys came looking for us. They must have had a hundred guys up there." He hesitated to speak his next thought, not certain if Bill or Marlen had talked to her about it. He decided that she needed to know. "Umm, they're due to be picked up, you know. I don't know if you know that or not. They won't be staying. I have no idea when," he rushed on, afraid to look at her in case she had not known. "I thought maybe they were gone already. That's why I panicked."

"I'm sorry," Brenda said quietly. "I guess I shouldn't have teased you. I would hate to wake up and find out that I didn't have the chance to say good-bye."

"Exactly," Paul sighed. He turned to glance at her and returned to his observation of the pasture.

Behind him Brenda made a small sound. "Look. There they are now."

Paul turned to see her pointing in the opposite direction. He followed her finger and was shocked to see his three charges being followed by something large and ungainly. The thing lumbered behind them like a devoted dog.

Brenda's chair slid loudly against the red tiles as she stood up quickly. "Oh no! What in the world? I think they've taken the neighbor's cow! I think that's what's following them."

"I do believe you're right," Paul breathed in amazement. He started toward them, stepping onto the night-dew grass, which was cold under his feet.

Elan's smile was as wide as his thin lips could make it. "Look," he said eagerly. "She was lost. She was standing by herself in that field over there." He turned and looked back quickly.

Zere stepped lightly to Paul's side and touched his arm. Paul looked down at him.

"What is this thing?" Zere asked quietly, his tone as perplexed as Paul had heard it thus far.

Paul's laugh exploded like a sneeze. "That's a cow," he told them when he could catch his breath.

"And what exactly is a cow?" Zere asked. "What does it do?"

"You explain," Paul told Brenda. "I'll look and see if I can figure out where it came from. He left Brenda to explain and turned to scan the pasture, as if that might tell him where she belonged. Elan and Galin watched him with interest.

Bill showed up, his bathrobe trailing in the wet weeds of the pasture. "She belongs to the farm about a mile down the road," he said, gazing at the cow with a small smile. "Let me get dressed and I'll take her back there."

Paul could not stop another laugh. "What are you going to tell them? That some alien friends of yours led her away in order to rescue her from Earthlings?"

Bill tapped on Paul's shoulder lightly with his fist. "I think maybe I'll just let you explain it. And then I'll tell them where to find you." He turned toward the house, chuckling at his own joke.

Laughing, Paul suggested that he hold onto the cow until Bill came back.

Bill laughed abruptly. "That should be a fairly easy job," he said, looking at the cow that was placidly chewing on her cud and calmly surveying the assortment of people around her. "She doesn't look like she's going anywhere," Bill added good-humoredly.

Half an hour later the cow was returned without incident and Bill and Paul were walking back toward the house. The sun was warm. Paul was filled with a sense of contentment. "This really seems like an ideal place to live," he said.

Bill nodded in agreement. "Yep. It's pretty close to perfect. I guess a guy couldn't ask for much more." He sighed with satisfaction.

"How long have you lived here?"

"We left California the day after we got married. This was our honeymoon and we never went back. That was six years ago."

"Where in California?" Paul asked.

"Sacramento."

"No kidding!" Paul cried. He brushed his hand through his hair quickly, filled with another sense of unexplainable coincidence. "Seems like there's no end to these coincidences. That's where I'm from."

Bill looked at him quickly. "And now you're here," he said, his tone raising with speculation. "Rescuing aliens and bringing them to us. Beats all, doesn't it?"

"I guess," Paul said. "I sure can't explain it all."

They turned into the yard.

"So where do you go from here?" Bill asked.

Paul shrugged. "I guess I haven't stopped long enough to think about it."

They both stopped and looked around peacefully. The mountains were still being touched by the soft peace of morning. The distant pastures looked freshly washed and green. To Paul, the air smelled like freedom.

"You might consider staying on here for a while," Bill suggested. "You can use our guest house while you explore the area to see if you like it."

Paul nodded thoughtfully. "Thank you for the offer. It sounds like a great idea," he said, not really surprised that the suggestion rested comfortably inside him.

The thought of possibly meeting Stephanie again popped into his mind. He nodded once again. Not a bad idea at all, he thought.

CHAPTER ELEVEN

OVER BREAKFAST, with Marlen muttering occasional, soft sighs of nervousness as he continuously glanced out the window, Paul told the others about his decision to stay in Payson. Everyone was enthusiastic. Brenda offered, again, to help him with his manuscript. Zere, Elan, and Galin expressed their pleasure by chortling over the fact that now it would be easy to find him if they ever needed to be rescued again.

Even Marlen, in a distracted manner, voiced his approval, offering to take Paul on exploratory trips around the countryside.

As he was talking, Paul noticed Marlen's tense jaw and the fact that he was paying little or not attention to what he was eating. He glanced at Bill and asked the question that had been on his mind all morning. "Did you two discuss picking up the Bronco? What's the situation?" He looked across the table at his three charges and looked away quickly, not wanting to admit the depth of the argument going on within him regarding their departure.

Bill nodded. "We talked about it." He glanced at Marlen. "He's pretty worried about putting us in danger." He looked at Brenda, caught her gaze, and they exchanged a look of purity that set Paul's heart into envy at their closeness. "But Bren and I talked about it. We would rather be a part of what little time they have here than worry about us. We'd like you all to stay until the rescue."

Paul acknowledged their generosity by patting Brenda lightly on the arm.

"I suggested," Bill continued, "that instead of bothering Mike, Marlen and I drive up to get your car while you stay here and keep an eye on things here."

Paul started to protest. "I can drive up there with you."

Bill waved him off. "Marlen and I know the country better. With two vehicles, and the danger of being followed, it would be smarter if he and I went just in case we have to separate. You would have a heck of a time even finding your way in and out of the forest up there, much less find your way back here."

Paul realized the truth of what he was saying. He shrugged within himself, accepting the plan. He would have to let them take the risk, but he hated to think of how they might feel if they were to miss the departure of the visitors, should that happen while they were gone. There didn't seem to be any alternatives though.

After they had gone, Paul offered to help Brenda with the morning dishes. Elan, Zere, and Galin dangled their feet as they perched on the stools that framed the kitchen island. The sun's rays were angled in such a way that they sparkled off of the glasses that Paul placed in the top rack of the dishwasher. That moment seemed, to Paul, to be one of the most satisfying he had ever experienced. The sense of familiarity, camaraderie, and genuine acceptance lulled him into a deep sense of peace.

The spell was broken when they all heard the crunch of gravel as a car drove up the driveway. Fric and Frac, bathed in sun on the patio, merely lifted their heads, listened, and returned to sleep.

"I'm afraid that if you were counting on them to be guard dogs, you're out of luck," Paul muttered, grabbing a dish towel and drying his hands quickly. Like the slice of a blade, the sound had cut through his serenity, leaving his thoughts scrambled, his emotions raw. His heartbeat was loud in his ears. His skin was clammy. Visions of military jeeps and angry uniformed men storming into the morning flashed through his mind. His eyes darted here and there, frantically looking for solutions without finding any. He turned to stare anxiously at Zere, wondering where to hide them.

Zere merely stared back, seemingly unconcerned. For just an instant Paul wondered if possibly they wanted to be captured, if perhaps that had been their plan all along.

Brenda grabbed another dish towel and was headed toward the front door, drying her hands as she walked.

"Wait!" Paul hissed. "We need to hide them." His pulse was erratic. A wave of dizziness hit him. He wondered, for a second, if he was going to faint. "We need a plan!" he whispered, shaking his head to clear it.

Brenda turned quickly. A look of set determination had replaced her normal, soft features. When she spoke, her voice was as flat and heavy as a steel girder. "This is my home. No one enters here unless I invite them."

For a minute Paul wanted to believe that this small woman had the ability to stop an entire military battalion. Within seconds he realized that it was a foolish thought. He glanced helplessly at her steady progress toward the front door and then, in a mad rush, snatched at the thin shoulders of his charges and rushed them down the hall that he assumed led to the bedrooms at the back of the house.

Without examining the room, he pushed them through the first door he came to, followed them in, and slid the door closed except for a crack that he could listen through. He heard the front door open. He heard Brenda's voice and, following it, the voice of another woman. He couldn't hear what they were saying.

The voices went on for several minutes. He leaned forward anxiously when he heard the front door close. Barely breathing, he waited for the sound of the car starting, for Brenda to tell him the coast was clear. But neither of these things happened. Instead he heard the women's voices again. But this time they were closer. His thoughts spun in circles as he realized that Brenda had invited the woman inside.

Paul turned, wide-eyed, to his charges. His mind registered the fact that he had thrust all of them into a small bathroom. Elan and Galin were perched on the edge of the bathtub, watching him curiously. Zere stood with his back to Paul, attempting to raise himself onto the toilet in order to peer out the window. Paul realized that they were totally unconcerned with the predicament.

Frustrated beyond reason, he turned back to the door and listened again. Now he could hear the sound of weeping. What in the world is going on, he wondered? By now his curiosity was overwhelming. He heard a murmur and the carpet-soft tread of footsteps. The door pushed against him. He stepped back and stared, wild-eyed, at Brenda.

She squeezed herself in beside him and closed the door behind her. She stared at him silently, her eyes asking for forgiveness. "I'm sorry," she whispered. "This is a friend of mine. She's been hurt. She needs to talk. I couldn't send her away." Her eyes were bright with unshed tears.

"Hurt how?" Paul asked.

"Her boyfriend beat her up. She looks pretty bad." Brenda wiped her eyes with her sleeve and looked up at him. "What am I going to do now?" She waved her hand at the visitors. "I can't let her see them but you can't stay in here for an hour or however long it's going to take to calm her down."

Paul's heart stopped, as if a sledgehammer had hit him unexpectedly. "What's her name?" he asked urgently, when he could breathe again. This, he knew, could not be another coincidence.

Brenda stared at him in surprise before answering. "Stephanie," she whispered, making the single word sound like a question.

Paul closed his eyes against a sudden swarm of emotions. No such thing as coincidence, his thoughts whispered. He took a deep breath in an attempt to calm the hive of rushing thoughts that swarmed like bees on honey in his mind.

Brenda touched his arm with a warm hand. "What is it?" she asked, her voice tight with anxiety.

Paul opened his eyes and found himself pierced by her intense stare. "I know her," he said quietly.

Brenda let out a tiny breath of surprise. "How could you?" she whispered fiercely. She waved her hand in exasperation. "You don't even live here yet. You've only been here a few days. It must be a different person."

"Trust me on this. I know her. Marlen and I helped her get to the hospital the first night I was here."

Brenda's eyes widened. "The hospital?"

"She was beat up that night too. We helped her out."

Brenda shook her head and sighed through her lips. "I have no idea what's going on in this world. How these things can happen." She looked at the closed door. "I need to get back out there." She looked at the three visitors, who were watching them calmly. She turned back to Paul. "Should I tell her you're here? She knows you. Maybe you can help her?"

Paul looked at the three aliens. "Will you be all right if I go out there and see what I can do to help?"

Zere nodded immediately. His face was soft with compassion. "Go. We'll be fine."

Without hesitation, Brenda pulled the door open. Paul followed as she hurried down the hallway to where Stephanie sat twisting a tissue between her fingers and making a vain attempt to stop weeping. She looked at Paul in shock when he stepped into the room.

Half-rising, she stared at him. "What are you doing here?" she cried.

The tone of her voice could have meant almost anything. Fear. Surprise. Curiosity.

Paul stopped where he was, just inside the doorway. "Umm, Bill and Brenda are friends of mine," he explained.

Stephanie's eyes darted from Paul to Brenda and back again. Her knees buckled, whether from exhaustion or shock, Paul had no idea. She sank to the couch and sat staring toward him, her eyes wide with surprise.

Her unusual beauty struck Paul, once again. Her cheekbones were high. Her hair was not just blonde but golden, like autumn leaves that had turned gold and were now basking in the last rays of a fading sun. Her violet-blue eyes were deep-set and framed by long, golden lashes. An artist could not have done them justice.

The thing that marred this vision of beauty was the fear that screamed through her eyes, the bruises that lay black across her fair skin, and the slash of angry red that encircled her graceful neck.

Paul wanted to weep at the sight of her. His emotions tumbled around and through each other. He wanted to protect her, to gather her into his strength and take her away. On the other hand, he was driven toward the need to destroy her attacker. His emotions clashed through him like cymbals, loud and disruptive.

Now she sat before him, her eyes as wide and innocent as a lonely child's. Her agony, as if a visible aura, was evident from across the room. Paul took the necessary steps to reach the chair across from where she sat. Wrestling with his desire to reach out to her, he threaded his strong fingers and, leaning forward, rested his elbows on his knees and addressed her quietly.

"What can we do to help?" he asked.

"I didn't expect to see you here," she said, not answering his question.

Paul waved an impatient hand and re-laced his fingers. "This isn't about me. It's about you. Obviously you need help." He wanted to point out her wounds in an attempt to shock her into realizing her neglect of herself. Instead, he cleared his throat and turned his gaze to the carpet in front of his feet. He could feel Brenda easing gently into the chair next to him.

"Paul is not the kind of guy that you need to fear," Brenda said. "You can trust him."

Stephanie snorted quietly, as if the thought of trusting any man was a joke.

Brenda rose, circled the low, oval coffee table, and seated herself next to Stephanie. She too made a web of her fingers and looked at the floor, leaning forward with her elbows on her knees. "You know," she said softly, "there comes a time when friends run out of things to say. I want to be there for you. I _will_ be there for you. But this is what, the fourth time?" She waved her hands helplessly at the coffee table. "There is enough information out there, enough books and shelters and help, well, there's any number of ways to get help."

She glanced at Stephanie quickly and back down, nervous about confronting her friend. "I want to help," she repeated. "But if you keep going back you're going to keep getting hurt." She tossed her hands in frustration and locked them again. "It's as simple as that."

Stephanie's eyes turned liquid blue as they filled with tears. "I know that," she said miserably. "But then he says he's sorry and everything is okay for a while. Actually, it's great. We get along great. We laugh. We play. We go places. We have fun. I've missed being with someone since my parents died," she said, her voice trailing off like the last wisp of a small, windblown cloud.

For a self-absorbed minute Paul visualized himself with Stephanie … laughing, playing, going places. And the end result would be love … not another beating. Rage threatened to swallow him again. He forced himself to sit still, wanting only to pace the floor and pound the air and somehow convince this beautiful woman that she deserved better. But he had watched his mother suffer through the years. He knew that a woman would leave only when she has had enough.

"What is it in your past that makes you think that you deserve this?" he asked quietly, raising his eyes to meet hers.

For an instant their eyes locked in combat. It looked as if she might throw rage at him, accuse him of interfering, toss his imperfect knowledge across the room with disdain. They searched each other, speculating, deciding. For that instant Paul set aside all thoughts in a silent effort to remind her that they had once loved. He had been shown a mere glimpse of their past life together, but it had been enough. Now he willed her to remember as well.

Instead she looked away, looking but not possibly seeing the beautiful day that was unfolding outside. "I suppose that when I lost both my parents I had to have somewhere to turn, someone to care about whether I lived or died."

Brenda caught Paul's eye and explained. "Stephanie's parents died in an accident on the highway down to Phoenix. She met this guy she's with at the hospital. I guess he was an intern or something."

Stephanie shook her head. "No. He was there visiting some-one. We met in the waiting room."

For some unspoken reason, Stephanie raised her eyes to Paul's once again. The seconds ticked by like hours while she studied him.

"I want to leave," Stephanie said abruptly. "I deserve better than this. I know that. I've always known that. I was just afraid of being alone."

Brenda was quick to respond. "You're not alone. You can stay here for a while if you like."

Paul's eyes opened wide with surprise. Had she forgotten the visitors? How was Stephanie going to react to them?

But neither woman was looking at him. Stephanie was quietly thanking Brenda for the invitation. Brenda was excitedly chatter-ing about making up a bed and tidying up the spare bedroom and bathroom.

Paul simply blinked in consternation. The bathroom she was talking about was the one in which the visitors were now waiting patiently.

Well … not so patiently.

Paul stared at Stephanie as she half rose from her chair with a scream, her hand over her mouth with shock. Rising in surprise, Paul jumped to his feet as well. He followed her shock-filled eyes and discovered that his three charges had strolled quietly into the room and were calmly standing behind him, hands clasped as if they were a singing trio facing an audience, ready to take their bows.

"What the …?" Paul cried, his voice shaking with astonish-ment.

Small, alarmed cries were still fluttering from Stephanie's lips, flying into the room like frightened birds. Brenda was still sitting, staring at the visitors while a myriad of emotions rushed across her face.

Elan looked up at Paul with large, innocent eyes. "We thought you might be ready for our company," he chirped.

Paul waved his hands through the air. It looked as if he were directing traffic. "You scared the life out of her! What were you thinking?"

"No," Elan said inexplicably. He moved toward Stephanie with surprising grace and rapidity. Before Paul could blink, he was tenderly reaching out for Stephanie's hand.

As if frozen, she watched his hand approach. As Elan touched her, her knees buckled and she sank, once again, onto the couch, her mouth open like a baby bird waiting to be fed.

"You see?" Elan said proudly, turning to Paul. "She is not dead."

Paul shook his head in frustration. "You cannot simply march around like that, thinking that you're not going to scare people half to death," he told them, looking from one to the other. "You know that! What were you thinking?" He shook his head wildly. "You're going to place us all in danger if you keep doing things like that. What if the military was to drive up right now? Would you just walk out the front door to greet them?"

Brenda's soft voice interrupted his tirade. "It's done," she said calmly. "Now all that's left to do is to explain to Stephanie what's going on."

"It's all right," Stephanie said quietly, her voice trembling with another kind of emotion.

Paul and Brenda turned simultaneously to stare at her. Elan was leaning against her leg, looking up at her as if she were a long-lost friend. Stephanie had one hand resting atop his as it rested on her leg. Their silent communication hung in the air as if tangible.

Paul shook his head in resignation. As if they had been waiting for that, Zere and Galin edged forward, coming to a stop in front of him. Paul sank to the chair and, one by one, Zere and Galin lifted themselves into his lap.

CHAPTER TWELVE

STEPHANIE WAS INCAPABLE of uttering any more words.

Paul and Brenda waited for her to speak but when she did not, Brenda spoke. "Are you all right?" she asked Stephanie hesitantly.

Paul was watching Stephanie closely. Her eyes were filling with tears as she looked down at Elan. He was not certain if the source of her tears was love or fear. "Are you okay?" he asked her, repeating Brenda's question.

Stephanie looked up at him. Her eyes seemed to blaze with fever. She stared at him as if she were seeing through him. He could feel his organs shiver, as if deep within him he were responding to something unspoken.

"It should never have happened." Stephanie said. Her tone was loud and vibrant, as if she were an evangelist pounding on a pulpit with religious fervor.

Startled, Brenda jumped with nervousness.

"What should never have happened?" Paul asked, staring at Stephanie with avidity. For a fanciful moment he thought that he was sensing her soul, her power, her Divine Connection, spiraling through time and space, entering her body with the force of a new soul.

Stephanie blinked. It seemed that, for a moment, she had been lost to herself. "I deserve far better than what I've allowed myself to receive," she stated.

The timbre of her voice was different. It seemed like, in the space of a nanosecond, she had become someone else.

"That is absolutely true," Paul affirmed. "But will you remember that?" he asked hopefully. "Will you live the rest of your life believing that?"

She blinked again and surveyed him as if she were seeing him for the first time. She nodded slowly. "I believe I will," she said slowly.

Brenda looked from one to the other. The energy in the room had heightened. The air felt electric. Fric and Frac had awakened and were peering eagerly through the glass, wanting to be included.

Paul caught Elan's eye.

"Stephanie is a friend of ours," Elan explained, his words dripping with significance.

Paul raised his eyebrows in question. Elan, reading his thoughts, nodded soberly.

The static in the room suddenly amplified. The hair on Paul's arms stood up. Before anyone could comment on what was happening, the three visitors had gathered together, and were walking away from the others, heading for the patio doors.

Shocked, Paul watched them walk until the full significance of what was happening finally moved him. He leapt to his feet and in two large strides, was beside them. They glanced up at him but, clearly, their attention was elsewhere. Paul watched helplessly as, without touching it, they moved the glass door aside and stepped through the opening. Fric and Frac, possibly confused by the sudden and explosive shift in energy, backed up, their legs stiff and trembling.

Paul followed them. With his heart in his throat, he whispered, "Must it be now?" He was not aware of the tears that streamed unchecked down his cheeks.

For a minute Paul imagined that Zere's eyes grew moist. He felt the light touch of alien fingers as, one by one, each of his friends pressed his hands with good-byes.

Paul felt as if he was strangling with the pain of losing them. "How can I lose you again?" he asked, his voice trembling.

"We will be back," Galin told him quietly.

"When?" Paul asked, his heart leaping with sudden hope. "When?"

He touched his head with one finger. "Listen. You will hear us. When the mission is complete, you will see us again."

"I don't want to let you down," Paul said, filled with sudden fear that he wouldn't be capable of fulfilling his end of the bargain.

Elan shook his head gently. "We have no fear of that." He smiled at Paul tenderly and reached out once again to touch his hand.

The air began to fill with quiet, as if an unseen force was putting the world to sleep. Paul watched, tears streaming, as Zere, Elan, and Galin walked around the pool and toward the small patch of green lawn behind it. A brilliant beam of light slashed through the sky, making the sun seem dim. He blinked and they were gone. As he searched the sky frantically he saw nothing but a large, flat, oval cloud. He stared at it, willing it to reveal its secret. Instead, it simply vanished, evaporating before his eyes.

Anguish gripped him. "Please take me home," he said quietly, knowing that it was not meant to be.

He didn't stir when he felt a touch on his arm.

"They're gone," Brenda whispered.

Paul simply nodded.

He heard her gasp a little, a small cry of pain and loss. Her quiet weeping brought him out of his stupor. He put his arm around her shoulders and drew her to his side. Together they stood, silently learning how to deal with the absence.

That night there were four at the dinner table. Marlen had decided, upon finding the visitors gone, that he too would leave. Now the four who were left were still and silent, absorbing their loss, thinking their private thoughts.

For Paul, it seemed like he had found what he had been searching for all his life and had, in a split second, lost it all again. He had no way of dealing with the pain he was feeling. Confused, and somewhat frightened of what the future might hold, he merely nodded when Brenda suggested that dinner was probably over since none of them had touched their plates.

After storing the dinner in the refrigerator they all sat in silence on the patio. Paul sat next to Stephanie, his sleeve occasionally brushing her arm. Once again he wondered if perhaps she might be his future. He had a hope, a vision, of a future that might bring them both some peace and happiness. But she hadn't even given him a hint of interest.

"It doesn't seem fair that I only got to spend a minute with them before they left," Stephanie said quietly, interrupting his thoughts.

Paul didn't know which would be worse … to spend only a minute with them or to spend days with them and have to watch them leave. Either way, it was an experience none of them wanted to have again. The pain of being left behind seemed to grip them all. He wondered how many future nights he would spend staring at the sky, hoping for a glimpse of them.

"How can they have such a major impact on you so quickly?" Stephanie wondered out loud.

Brenda was the first to answer. "I think it has to do with their vibration and their intentions. I think they operate from a place of pure love. And we respond to it."

Bill touched Brenda's arm gently. "Come on. Why don't you help me clear the table?" He turned to Paul. "Why don't you and Stephanie just relax. We'll be back out in a few minutes."

Brenda rose and touched Stephanie gently but firmly on the shoulder as she started to get up. "Just relax. We'll handle it."

"Are you tired?" Paul asked Stephanie as she relaxed back into her chair with a quiet sigh.

"Bone-tired." Her voice was a soft sigh that hung in the evening air like a whispered prayer.

She rolled her head against the back of the chair, turning to look at him. Paul could feel her intensity touching him. "What did they mean when they said that I was a friend of theirs?" she asked abruptly.

Paul had been expecting the question. "How much do you know about the bigger picture of existence?" he asked, answering her question with a question. "Do you believe that there is more than this?" he asked, waving his hand to indicate the earth.

"Of course." She grinned at him. "If I didn't before today, I certainly do now. Honestly though, I've been so busy simply surviving that I haven't given all of it a lot of thought, I'm ashamed to say."

Paul was surprised. "Why would you be ashamed?"

Stephanie shrugged. "Well, obviously there is a lot more to life. It seems pretty selfish, or foolish, or whatever you want to call it, to get so bogged down in the trivia that you lose sight of the bigger picture."

"I imagine that, under your circumstances, it would be hard not to get bogged down, as you put it."

"Maybe." She lifted one shoulder in a semi-shrug, dismissing the subject. "Anyway, tell me more. Tell me what you know about all of this," she said, scanning the sky with eager eyes.

For the next hour Paul explained what he felt to be the truth of existence. He instinctively knew that truth is revealed in stages, as one can accept and assimilate it. He also suspected that, because truth is vast, only pieces of it could be glimpsed. Depending upon where one stood when looking at the truth, one portion might appear to be vastly different than another. Only by standing outside of existence could the simplicity of total understanding be reached. From the viewpoint of a human, the layers of truth were sometimes too large to comprehend.

"And so there are layers of existence, dimensions if you want to call them that," he was saying, "that have different vibrations and that is what makes them different from each other."

"Layers of existence," Stephanie said, tasting the words. "That makes sense to me."

Paul nodded in the new darkness of the night.

"And so what you're saying is that all of these vibrations exist simultaneously?" She looked up at the sky, as if hoping for a glimpse of the layer above Earth. "Right now we are sharing time and space with other civilizations, right?"

Paul nodded again, letting her absorb the impact of the truth in her own way.

"So which dimension did your friends come from?" she asked tentatively, as if afraid of stirring up the recent pain of their departure.

"I'm not sure," Paul said, surprising himself that he didn't know. "Somewhere a lot higher than third though."

"It would seem to me that it would take a lot out of you to drop into a lower dimension like they did. I'm surprised they didn't get sick or something."

"I imagine that they didn't exactly enjoy it," Paul agreed. "But maybe they weren't here long enough to be affected too badly. I'm not an authority on it, by any means."

"Well, you know more about it all than I do," she said.

"Perhaps," Paul said vaguely. "You know," he added, following his own train of thought, "I think that they might have fallen down here on purpose. Like they intended to crash."

"Why would they do that?" she asked, obviously surprised.

"Well." Paul hesitated, not wanting her to think that he was way too far out in his thinking. "My sense is that this plane, the Earth plane, is going to make a big shift. I think the shift is going to entail moving from one vibration to the next."

Stephanie lifted herself up and turned to stare at him through the dim light. "You really think that? What would that mean? That Earth would no longer be third dimensional?"

"I don't know exactly what I mean or what's going to happen. I just have a sense that something big is going on and that my friends came down here to achieve something. Maybe they planted energy or something." He shrugged slightly. "I don't know. I can't explain it."

"Where did you come up with this? Why do you think this?" By now she had leaned forward in her chair and was staring at him intently.

Paul sat up straighter, feeling uncomfortable with her intense scrutiny. "Some of the things that they said made me jump to that conclusion. They hinted that something might be going on. And," he added, "it's something I feel inside as well. I've been feeling something going on for a few years now."

"You're serious!" she cried.

"Of course I am," he said defensively.

Stephanie thrust her hand out and touched his arm, patting him with reassurance. "But that's okay," she said. "You know what this means? This means that there's hope. That someone or something greater than us is trying to make things right. I'd lost hope," she added more quietly. "There is no life if there is no hope."

She rubbed her hands together in agitation. "Correct me if I'm wrong, but the kind of things that go on down here … they don't happen up there, do they?"

Paul shook his head, caught up in her wish for a different reality. "I wouldn't think so, no."

"Is this just a pipe dream?" she asked suddenly, speaking in a hushed tone. "I have a lot of hopes and dreams and by following them I've fallen on my face a hundred times. I have no desire to go tripping down another primrose lane only to fall down again."

"To my knowledge what I've told you is true. I don't have any proof. And everything is subject to change based upon people's choices. But there are many, many souls who desire this change. I'd like to think that together we can pull this off."

Stephanie thought about his words. "I don't have access to the knowledge you've acquired, but I hope you're right about this."

"I imagine that, one way or the other, we're going to find out," Paul smiled.

She nodded in agreement. "I'll take your word for that."

"Well," Paul told her quietly, "access your own knowledge. Find out what feels right for you."

"How do I do that?" she asked.

"You get quiet. You listen to your inner knowing. Listen to your spirit instead of your head."

"You make it sound easy."

"It is easy, once you accept the truth of who you are."

Paul looked toward the dark horizon. "This visitation caused a major change in me," he told her quietly. "I know things now that I had never even thought about before. They gave me the gift of possibility. I feel things, sense things, that I never did before. They changed me in ways that I can't explain." He breathed softly for a minute. "I'll never be able to thank them. The only way that I can show my appreciation is to pass on what they gave to me."

"Why do you suppose that they had such a major impact on you? Other than the obvious, I mean."

"For one thing, they reminded me about who I really am," Paul responded. "And with that memory came a swarm of other memories and knowledge. It could be," he speculated, "that they simply gave me permission to accept and believe in the truth of who I am."

Her voice was small when she spoke. "I wish someone could do that for me."

Paul could hear the wishes in her voice. His response was something that he had been saying to himself for almost two years prior to this visitation. "I think that, ultimately, it has to be something that we do for ourselves. I think all anyone else does is offer us the support to keep on searching until we find ourselves."

Stephanie's laugh tripped into the air like a joyous butterfly. "How profound you are, Paul!" she giggled. "How profound we all are! Do you realize that we haven't exchanged one light word since we met?"

"Light?" Paul asked, caught in the surprise of her sudden mood change. Suddenly he was gripped with playfulness. "I can be light," he laughed, jumping up.

Stephanie jumped up beside him. "Let's play," she said eagerly. "Let's run in the moonlight or something."

With a hoot he grabbed for her. Seconds later they were tumbling into the pool together. As they laughed and dog-paddled to the surface, Fric and Frac barked at them excitedly. All they could do, when Bill and Brenda appeared to find out what was going on, was grin foolishly. A minute later they sheepishly accepted the proffered towels that Brenda retrieved for them.

"We could have offered you some swimsuits," Bill said, surveying them with amusement.

"That wouldn't have been spontaneous," Paul countered. He glanced at Stephanie, who was vigorously toweling her hair dry. "I think she wanted to be spontaneous."

Stephanie lowered the towel only long enough to glare at him playfully.

CHAPTER THIRTEEN

THE DREAM SEEMED TO BE nothing more than a series of flashes. Flashes of civilization. History on Earth. Cave men were looking into the sky, pointing as crafts flew high above. But the men were terrified and the crafts did not land.

And then Egyptian pyramids. A beam of light that split the sky from craft to Earth. People were stepping into it as if it were an elevator. From Earth to craft and back again. There was no fear.

Beings from other places and times instructed men in the art of sacred geometry. And so the pyramids were created.

Stonehenge. Men were again instructed by those above. The stones were set, creating a pattern of energy in union with heaven and earth. It was a portal through time and space. Paul could see that, in the future, when stars aligned with Earth and time, the portal would again open.

Atlantis. Crafts were as commonplace as stones upon the ground. There were bonds between men and aliens that no one believed could be broken. But the struggle for power proved to be stronger than brotherhood. Paul watched as irreplaceable crystals, programmed with eons of accumulated wisdom, were transported into crafts and into caverns beneath the sea as the aliens withdrew their support from the human society. Soon after, the civilization was destroyed. The sea still housed the crystals, his vision told him. A treasure of wisdom, that all of existence could profit from, now lives on the ocean floor.

A small craft with alien beings drifting silently toward Earth. Below, a small group of Mayans waited. Alien hands. Human hands. Touching in friendship. Exchanging gifts. The craft as-

124

cended, leaving behind tiles etched with mysteries of future evolution and harmony between all worlds.

He watched as cultures throughout time worshipped and praised the aliens as if they were gods. At times there were choices made that caused the aliens to withdraw in order to allow men to discover their truth and the power of their own birthright.

Now a scene flashed before him that was unlike the others. In the dream, Paul blinked in disbelief. A man sat alone atop a mountain. Around him was a halo of pale blue light. From out of the distance came the silver glint of a craft. The man simply watched and waited, as if he had known that it was coming. Paul could feel his relief at the sight of the craft. It stopped and hovered and a light reached down to Earth to bathe the solitary man. Paul watched as the man's cells separated and shifted. He was dematerializing. Slowly his form became indistinct until Paul could no longer see him. The man had been called Jesus.

Reluctant at losing sight of the man, but eager to see more, Paul turned at the flash of a light behind him. Crafts flitted through the atmosphere like butterflies. People were being lifted away. Aliens were transporting to the surface. The exchanges were joyous and momentous. Knowledge pressed upon Paul like a hundred pounds of weight. He was filled with knowing that someday, perhaps soon, it would be time for Earth to change and along with that change the people would change.

Rays of light were issued from dimensions beyond, offering light and healing to those who chose it. The people were, indeed, changing, and their vibrations were altering as they were taught by those above. With light and knowledge pouring into them, people were evolving. A new species of Man was being born. Existence waited with a quiet hush, in awe of the transformation.

Paul heard himself sigh in the dream. It was clear that the havoc Man had created had affected the dimensions that shared the same space. Like the unstoppable waves of an ocean, the waves of energy that had emanated from Earth were sweeping through existence. Perhaps it had, in some way, changed it forever. But as his thought formed, the next one followed. Soon it would be time for the dimensions beyond to turn the scene around. Soon those energies would be sent to Earth and to Man. And the impact could not be avoided. Mankind should be very grateful that there is a kind God watching, Paul thought.

Now, half-waking, he blinked at the light-filled room. He didn't remember the moon being that bright when he'd gone to bed. He blinked again. The light was too bright. He tried to orient himself, to understand what was happening. Had he slept until noon? Was this sunlight and not moonlight? But, no. Oh, my God! he thought. Is the house on fire?

He tried to leap to his feet, to scream, to warn the others. But he couldn't move. His body was still, almost as if paralyzed. His voice box wouldn't work. With wide eyes, he attempted to look around. Only the ceiling and a narrow field of vision around him were visible.

But the ceiling was no longer there. Only light was present. A light so bright that it hurt his eyes. He was unable to close them against it. The light was consuming him. Now fascinated, Paul watched as the light entered and began altering the cells of his body. Like the vision he had seen of the solitary man, he was dematerializing. Awestruck, he watched from what seemed like a distance as his body became light, and cells, and space, and was slowly, gently lifted through the ceiling that was no longer there.

"Welcome," he heard a voice say.

Paul turned to look at the small being and then at his surroundings. He seemed to be in the midst of a huge pillar of pale, blue light. A circle of silver threads wove around the exterior of the pillar, as if it were intended to somehow hold the pillar in place. Not far away stood what seemed to be an entryway. It led into the depths of what looked to be a crystal cave with a multitude of rainbow facets looking out into the heavens.

He turned back to the being. He was small in stature, perhaps four feet tall. He wore a short, white cape with a cowl that almost covered his facial features. Paul felt as if he knew him. His voice, when he spoke, trembled slightly, like the single note of a singing dove that carried with it a message. His welcome was something Paul had waited for without realizing it.

"Where am I?" he asked.

"This is the Arcturian Stargate," the being advised him. He turned to look toward the crystalline entry. "You are free to explore any dimension you choose."

Paul looked at him, puzzled. Before he could speak, he was answered.

"The Stargate is a portal of energy, held by us, the Arcturians. It is used to pass from one dimension to another. I have been advised that you are at a point in your evolvement that will allow you to experience this without undue damage to the life you presently live on Earth."

Without further explanation, the being took Paul's elbow firmly and led him into the penetrating warmth and energy of the entryway. Looking up, Paul could see that the interior of the Stargate was faceted by multitudes of crystalline faces of various shapes and sizes. Most seemed to be entryways into tunnels of light, though some seemed to lead into seemingly endless voids.

The being led him firmly toward a set of three crystalline facets. "These are the three that I have been advised to show you. You may choose one or all." He peered at Paul with interest before continuing. "The path you choose will not cause you to lose the paths that you do not choose."

For some inexplicable reason, Paul was relieved to hear him say that. With an eagerness too all-encompassing to entertain the thought of looking back, he stepped through the energetic veil directly in front of him. Instantly he was in another place and time.

Twin moons hung suspended in the rose-colored sky. The ground he stood upon was soft and spongy, almost like a liquid, partially frozen, though the entire atmosphere was warm and comforting. In the distance sat a low range of heather- and heliotrope-draped mountains. Beyond the mountains hung a single, brilliant, golden star, so close to the surface of the planet that Paul felt as if could reach out and touch it. The light in the atmosphere seemed to be that of full daylight, but Paul could see only the two moons giving off their soft light. He recognized the place as being the same one he had visited during his vision quest on the mountaintop.

"Welcome."

Paul heard the single word and turned. He saw a robed man. The robe was plain, full-length, pale tan, and tied at the waist with a thin rope. The cowl was up, obscuring the man's face. On the man's feet were simple sandals. Deep within, Paul recognized him. His heart leapt with familiarity and joy.

"Solomon?" he asked, extending his hand.

"Indeed." The single word was filled with welcome and tenderness. Solomon stepped forward and placed his hand in Paul's, wrapping his other hand around it as well.

"I recognize this place," Paul said, looking around after studying Solomon's face for a brief, loving moment.

"As well you should," Solomon responded, his deep voice ringing with humor. "This is Questar. Your home away from home."

A sudden understanding and knowing about where he was swept through Paul like a longed-for memory. "Questar," he repeated softly. The sound upon his tongue was almost reverent. "As close to home as I can get, is it not?" he asked.

"Indeed," Solomon repeated. "Come. You will want to visit the home you have here."

Paul fell into step as Solomon turned on the wide walkway. In perfect companionship, they strolled together, not needing to speak. Paul knew that this man had walked beside him through centuries, had been his friend, companion, confidante, and even savior a time or two. A sense of serenity and homecoming, so potent that it threatened to overwhelm him, swept him into its embrace.

Along the path they passed a shoulder-high range of hills where cave entrances were dotted like doorways along a shopping mall. He remembered the scene from the earlier vision that he'd had. He also knew that they were headed toward the crystal pyramid that was his home. Looking at the scene more closely, he noticed that a thin stream of liquid silver separated the caves from the pathway. Paul knew that, should you choose to enter one of the caves, which housed Masters and Overlords and those of equal wisdom, you must first walk through this stream. The liquid would penetrate your energy field and instantly purify it, causing any incompatible energy within your field to shift in order to accommodate the higher energies that comprised the residences of the Masters. He vaguely remembered a dream he had several years ago where he had done just that. He struggled, with no success, to recall the face of the Elder that he had met at that time.

On the opposite side of the pathway was a surprise of forest. Tall, white trees with branches that hung low to the ground. Low, round, vibrant burgundy trees sheltered beneath the taller ones. Bushes of various hues of violets, purples, and fuchsia huddled together, making the forest impassable.

Between the patches of forest were a wide variety of fields. Some appeared to be strewn with blooms that looked like orchids. Others were filled with tall, waving threads of forest-green grasses with thick burgundy veins. The leaves twisted around themselves at the base, as if protecting something within.

As they walked around a bend in the road a large, rectangular, crystalline building came into view. Beyond it a wide stream of liquid crystal flowed, placid and silent except for an occasional tinkle of sound. Before Paul could become captured by the unseen but clearly felt interest of the large building, he sensed something on his right. His head turned and instantly he was filled with such a depth of homecoming that his eyes filled with tears.

Before him sat his home … the crystal pyramid. Four-sided and angled in such a way that the single star in the sky seemed to embrace every facet of it, the crystal rose almost twenty feet into the air. The interior was clear and Paul could see a serene meadow on the other side. The pyramid had a perfect view of the mountains, the streams, the forest, and the meadow. Without knowing what he would do when he reached it, Paul walked toward it. As if it were reaching out to welcome him, the aura of the crystal embraced him. As he neared it, he knew that he was going to walk directly into it, though it appeared to be a solid form.

And he did just that. The cells of his spirit became liquid, as did the crystal. The two energies merged as if they were one. Paul knew that he had found his home.

He sensed that it was necessary for his energy to merge with that of his home. He wandered through the energy of the pyramid, touching, feeling, communicating. He absorbed his home and its energy as if he were a man dying of thirst and here was crystal clear water. When he felt complete, he exited and went in search of Solomon. He found him lounging near the stream.

Paul sank to the ground near his comrade. The deep heather and rich burgundy grasses welcomed him. Now that Paul was nearer to the stream, he could hear the soft liquid whisper of the stream's movement. A hundred yards or so away stood a tall, winged creature, sunning itself and cooling its long legs in the stream. On the opposite shore another low-to-the-ground creature munched on mauve-colored moss.

"It seems like a long time since I've been here," Paul sighed, forcing himself to relax and accept the moment, knowing that it would have to end.

"It has been quite a while since you've actually lived here, but not so long since you visited," Solomon told him.

Paul scanned the landscape, seeking to etch it into his memory. He had no idea how much of this experience he would retain once he returned to Earth. "I seem to recall a dream about this place," he said out loud.

Solomon nodded. "You were here not long ago."

Paul peered at him. As if sensing that Paul needed all of the memories he could gather, Solomon reached up with one hand and pulled the cowl of his robe away from his face. Paul looked into the unsheathed, startlingly blue deep of his eyes, which spoke of eons of time, volumes of suffering, and countless lifetimes.

His hair was white with threads of silver. A small, neat beard graced his small but firm chin. His face was lean, his cheeks slightly sunken. His skin was tanned and showed his wisdom with thin threads of lines crisscrossed around his eyes. The revelation of himself caused Paul to instantly love and revere him as someone who had been with him always.

"Solomon," Paul said softly, not resisting the urge to reach out and touch the older man on his weathered cheek.

"Indeed," Solomon said softly, his blue eyes twinkling with humor and understanding. He had been in Paul's position often enough. It was not so long ago that he had taken a physical form and Paul had served as his guide-in-spirit.

"You walk with me," Paul marveled. "I mean, in spirit form while I'm on Earth. I've seen you. I remember now. I know for certain that I've sensed your presence."

Solomon nodded. It brought him great joy to know that, from this point forward, Paul would easily be able to communicate with him. Most spirit guides who walked on Earth are never acknowledged. It was always a blessing to have the communication barriers erased.

"So tell me why we're here," Paul said suddenly.

Solomon studied him gravely before answering. "You have a large job to do. In order to accomplish it you need to have as much information and as many contacts as you can achieve. By that I mean contacts with those of us in other dimensions who can help you."

Paul did not speak, letting him continue.

"As you pass through the Stargate on your way back, I would like you to remember to ask the Arcturians to unlock the codes within your physical brain. This will help you achieve even more recall."

"Codes? What codes?"

"There are energetic codes in the human brain which keep you from recalling who you are and why you're on Earth. Some people are ready for those codes to be activated, unlocked, if you will.

These are the people who are ready to assist others. To help Earth move into a higher dimensional experience."

"Who placed these codes?" Paul asked curiously.

"Your soul places them before you incarnate and then, as you mature, releases the locks that surround your knowledge and memories," Solomon explained. "On Earth, which is a place comprised of limitations and rules, there are certain things which are commonly accepted so as to hold Universal chaos to a minimum." He smiled. "Chaos is easily created on so many levels on Earth that there simply must be some sort of regimen instituted, you see."

Paul nodded in understanding.

"Some of the codes are necessarily placed before your spirit enters your body, so that your physical body is in alignment with that which you have chosen to experience in your lifetime. Too much knowledge and memory can sometimes conflict with the experiences that you need to have. Other codes are temporarily in place and easily activated when the time is right."

"I can understand why you would want to enter the Earth reality knowing, or believing, certain things," Paul commented, "but why would you choose to have codes which make you forget who you really are and where you're really from?"

"It is quite simple, really. The Earth plane serves as a place of learning, a place for exploring life, soul, existence. When a person is faced with a mystery, they dig deeper, try harder, to understand and to learn. The Earth plane, because it has a dense energy, causes most people to work more diligently to understand things, which stimulates growth for all of creation."

It was as if a light bulb had gone off in Paul's mind. "I see. If you knew everything beforehand, you wouldn't be open enough to try to interpret events in a different way. You would see them one way only, from the viewpoint of your origins."

Solomon nodded, pleased. "Exactly. But ..." He held up one finger, causing Paul to become aware that he was going to make an important point. "There comes a time when one moves away from a self-absorbed life, if you will permit me to address it that way, and into a life which serves all. When the time for this comes, the layers of unreality and illusion begin to fade away. The spirit begins to unite with the soul and together they shed the layers of energetic illusion in an attempt to awaken the physical body and mind so that it can be utilized to serve humanity, rather than self."

"I have a feeling that this is going to be happening to me," Paul speculated.

"Indeed." Solomon smiled with satisfaction and pulled his cowl back over his head.

Seconds later Paul found himself spiraling down through a gentle tunnel of light toward what appeared to be a spacecraft made of crystal. Only when he got closer did he realize that he was approaching the Arcturian Stargate. A pang of regret slashed through him at the thought of re-entering the limited vision of life as seen from an Earth point of view.

I have a job to do, he reminded himself. He settled into the thought and waited the few seconds that it took for his spirit to enter the Stargate.

The same being was waiting for him. "Greetings," he said quietly. "I trust you found what you were looking for?"

"Indeed," Paul said with a smile.

CHAPTER FOURTEEN

Having secured a promise that the codes that could be unlocked would be, Paul continued his journey back to Earth. He had a job to do. He was eager to get on with it. What he still did not know was how Stephanie was going to fit into his future. After a shower and a shave, he slid the door of the guesthouse open and ventured onto the patio, anxious to find out how she was after a night of rest.

She sat on the patio, dressed in the same clothes that she had worn the day before. But Paul could see that someone, probably Brenda, had washed them for her. Fric and Frac flanked her on either side, like red-haired statues guarding something. They merely raised their heads at his approach. Uninterested, since he wasn't carrying any food, they closed their eyes and drifted back to their dog-dreams.

Stephanie greeted him softly. "Good morning."

"Morning. How did you sleep?"

"Pretty good. And you?" She lifted a slim hand to block the early morning sun from her eyes as she watched him pull a chair closer to her.

There was a small table nearby and on it rested a steaming cup of coffee. The smell drifted toward Paul, tempting him. He excused himself, headed into the kitchen to beg a cup, and found the kitchen empty. From the back of the house he could hear the shower running. He assumed Bill was preparing for work. Feeling a little guilty, Paul helped himself to a cup of coffee and meandered back outside.

"It feels like I should be getting up and going to work too," he said, negating his words by plopping down on the chair next to Stephanie.

She looked at him, genuinely shocked. "Do you live here?" she asked. "I was under the impression that you were from California."

"Well, that's true. I live in Sacramento. But I've decided to move here."

"Why?" she asked abruptly.

Paul shrugged. "Plenty of reasons, I suppose. I really like it here. It's fifty times quieter, for one thing. Has about three hundred thousand less people, I imagine. It's beautiful. Peaceful. Who could ask for more?" His eyes scanned the serenity of the horizon, as if punctuating his speech.

"Do you have work already?"

Paul glanced at her, surprised by the hint of anger that he'd detected beneath her words. "No. Not yet. I have some savings that I can live on for a while."

Stephanie reached for her cup and wrapped both hands around it, as if she needed the warmth, though the day was already warm. She peered at him intently. "But you do have to go back and get your things, right?"

Paul shrugged again, unconcerned. He had not accumulated a lot of belongings. He had always thought that it was easier that way. Now he realized that it might also have been due to the fact that he had never fully accepted Earth as his home. "I can make a quick trip back. Probably make it there and back in a few days."

Her tone had become more mild. "And where will you stay when you get back here?"

Paul gestured toward the guesthouse. "Bill and Brenda suggested that I stay here." He glanced around. "It could not have worked out better. Actually, it seems almost as if this thing was divinely orchestrated."

For a minute Stephanie's eyes clouded, as if her heart had suddenly become lost in some personal, unanswered desire. She nodded absently. Paul heard her murmur but he could not hear her words. When he asked her, she would not repeat them. She merely shook her head and turned away, gazing at the distant hills as if looking for something that she knew she would never find.

"I really hate to see you so sad," Paul said quietly.

She spun her head to look at him. "Why do you care? You don't even know me."

Rather than take offense, Paul reacted with compassion. He thought that he might understand her pain. He definitely understood that she was reacting from a lifetime full of memories that had nothing to do with him.

"I think that I might know you, even though we just met," he said gently. "And, if I really don't, I would like to."

The gentle tone in his voice caused her to pause and study him. "Why?" she asked curiously. "I am nothing to you."

"First of all, no one is 'nothing' to me," Paul informed her quietly. "Everyone who exists is important to me. That's the way it should be. We're not in this alone. We're a huge group of people having an experience together and, as such, we should care about each other."

Stephanie tilted her head, looking like a cautious bird that feels the need to study the lay of the land before feeding. "You are a very different kind of person," she informed him.

"Maybe. Maybe not. Maybe there are lots of others who think like I do and you just haven't met them yet." He smiled.

"Well, that could be true. I don't know. I just feel like you care about me without even knowing me and I don't understand that. I don't even get the impression that you want anything from me … and that's odd."

She wrinkled her small, upturned nose and peered at him intently. "I'm not certain whether you're a con man or whether you're being genuine."

"I wish you weren't so suspicious," Paul said abruptly. "It shouldn't be that difficult to believe that there are people out there who have no bad intentions, no hidden agendas."

Stephanie laughed out loud. "It sounds to me like you were raised in some isolated burg in the middle of nowhere, rather than a big, noisy city. For your age, you seem pretty naïve."

Paul was slightly offended. "I wouldn't call myself naïve."

"When it comes to this planet you are," she asserted. She pointed toward the sky. "You might have friends out there who are totally trustworthy but right now," she tapped the arm of her chair for emphasis, "you're here and this is the real world. People don't go around with their hearts on their sleeves. Someone is liable to come along and slice it off for them."

The depth of her cynicism was now obvious to him. It sorrowed him. He could see the need to be realistic and to protect yourself when it was necessary. But to live your life with the assumption that everyone would hurt you if you gave them a chance, well, that wasn't really living at all. He realized that, through Stephanie, he was learning more about himself. He didn't want to live in fear. He wanted to experience what he could without filtering life through an emotional meter first.

He glanced at her set and stubborn face and decided that it would do no good to argue with her. He wondered what he could say to help her heal her fear and bitterness. He wanted her to be free of pain. Perhaps, he thought, it's something we could learn together.

For a minute he allowed himself to fantasize about a future with her. She was in an easy chair nearby, reading contentedly. Her soft breathing kept him company. Her skin was unmarred by bruises. Her pain was forgotten. Together they had formed a union, a bond that could not be broken by time or distance. Life's concerns had fallen away once they learned how to share them with each other.

He had no idea that his vision was playing across his lips in the form of a large grin until she called his attention to it.

"Hey. What are you thinking about with that big grin?"

Caught by surprise, Paul flushed and searched for something to say. Luck was with him as Brenda, looking as fresh and eager as a morning colt, danced through the door carrying a large bowl of fruit in one hand and a platter of hot, buttered toast in the other. She looked spring-like, dressed in a soft, free-flowing white linen tunic with a vivid, leaf-green leotard beneath. She was barefoot, with her toenails polished bright red.

"Good morning, you two," she cried. "Isn't it a great day?"

Paul greeted her, though not as enthusiastically as she had.

Stephanie looked at her for a minute, eyebrows raised with suspicion. "Why are you so bright and cheery?"

"Don't be a grump," Brenda said cheerfully. She set the food down on the table and dragged a chair toward it. "Join me while the toast is hot," she invited.

Paul pulled his chair to the table and turned to help Stephanie. She had already picked up her chair and was hauling it awkwardly across the short distance. He stood, watching her, having caught her look of warning. When she was seated, he sat as well.

Brenda looked at him brightly, a clear-eyed look full of mischief and intent. "What say we get started on that book of yours today?"

Paul blinked rapidly and stared at her, caught off guard.

"What? Not eager to find out if you can do it or not?" she teased.

"Not particularly," he drawled.

Brenda peered at him intently, searching his face. "But you should already know that you can do this. There shouldn't be any doubt. They wouldn't have asked you to do it if there was any doubt about your ability."

"I'm not quite as certain of that as you are," Paul smiled. "Besides, if I'm going to move here, I'm going to have to go back and get my things, close my apartment up, and things like that."

"Are you stalling?" Brenda asked playfully.

"No," Paul claimed, setting his fists on the table and glaring at her teasingly. "I'm trying to live in a logical manner, taking care of first things first."

Brenda lifted one shoulder and chuckled. "I guess you have to do what you have to do." She smiled at him pertly. A sudden thought occurred to her. "Hey! Maybe Bill and I can drive with you. We can help you pack your stuff. It will be three times quicker. Besides, I could visit Jessica, my friend. She and I have been talking about getting together for months now."

Paul hesitated. For just an instant he'd had a vision of a woman. It had been too fleeting to capture it. Could it have been a vision of her friend? "Let's find out what Bill thinks about it," he suggested. He helped himself to another piece of toast and thoughtfully watched the two women talk about their plans for the day.

When the two of them left the house some time later, Paul understood that it was for the purpose of getting some of Stephanie's clothes and belongings and bringing them out here. She was going to stay in the guestroom for a while. Just long enough to decide what she wanted to do next. She had made it clear that she had no intention of returning to her boyfriend. He hoped she would have the strength to do as she planned. If she returned to her boyfriend, Paul wouldn't understand at all. He felt too weary to even think of the possibility.

But he also knew that things are not always as simple from the inside as they are when you're standing outside. He watched them drive away in Brenda's bright yellow convertible, their hair dancing happily in the breeze, and prayed that everything would work out the way they had so glibly planned. A feeling of foreboding came over him, and he wondered if he should have gone with them. Shaking his head, trying to push away the uneasy feeling, he headed for the guesthouse.

Once inside he found a CD player and a small stack of CDs. He put one on that looked interesting and settled back to relax and wait for their return.

The music soothed him to a point where he felt an almost-hypnotic peace wash over him. He set down the book he was scanning and closed his eyes in relaxation. He was not surprised to find his spirit drifting, to see himself spiraling away from his body without concern.

Again he was aboard a craft. But this time it was different. The control room was large and oval. A huge screen hovered over the control panel. Gigantic windows framed it and gave him a vision of the galaxy beyond. He recognized it instantly. He had seen it quite often in dreams. But this time there was a figure in the stately chairs that fronted the control panel. Whoever it was felt familiar to him. He stepped up behind the figure and waited for him to realize that he was there.

The being stood as soon as he realized that Paul was behind him. The face that turned to look at Paul was familiar. Triangular in shape, his head was bald, the nose almost non-existent, the mouth too small to notice. What caught and held Paul's attention were the almond-shaped eyes. The gaze struck him with power and significance. The uniform he wore was tight fitting over a thin, bone-angled frame. Without understanding why, Paul instantly recognized the authority behind the eyes. In his mind Paul referred to him as "Commander."

"Paul," the being said abruptly, speaking only with his thoughts.

"Commander," Paul acknowledged, bending his head slightly, and allowing his hand to be taken.

The Commander's hand wrapped around Paul's and the fingers of his free hand wrapped around Paul's forearm. The greeting felt familiar.

"The name is Korton, in case you've forgotten."

The name rang through Paul's spine as if it were an attempt to jar his memory loose. Within seconds it was successful. With Korton's hand still locked with his, Paul's mind reconstructed scene after scene from the past.

This was the craft that he had been on before he had been placed on Earth. This was the home of Zere, Elan, and Galin. And there were others. Many others. A petite face with vividly clear eyes drifted just out of his reach. The name "Zo" darted into his thoughts. His lips curled with delight.

As if his name had been called, Zo entered the room and glided quickly to Paul's side. He was just barely three feet tall, had a bald, triangular-shaped head, and wore nothing over his ivory skin. His torso area looked awkward in comparison to his long, pencil-thin arms and short, thin legs. His features were insignificant except for his eyes. They were deep black, almond-shaped, and distinct only because of the humor and compassion that poured through them. Paul knew him instantly.

Pleased to see each other, they stepped into an awkward embrace. Zo stepped back, laughing, the sound clinking around the large room like the sound of a small, metal wind chime. Korton stood back watching the exchange with a serious expression on his face. Paul could not read the look.

"I have heard that you were almost prepared to return," Zo cried out loud. His voice was small and harmonic, like a melody heard from another room on a clear and quiet summer's day.

Paul smiled gently. "I wish it were true," he said. "As it is, I'm only visiting."

Zo stretched his tiny lips into a grimace that was meant to be a smile and reached up to touch Paul's arm. "Do not be concerned. Now that you have remembered, you will visit often, I'm sure."

Paul glanced quickly at Korton, taking note of his lack of expression. "I pray that's true," he told his small friend, turning back to him. He glanced back at Korton who, by now, was dividing his time between watching the huge screen and the exchange between Paul and Zo. "I assume, sir, that I have been drawn here for some other reason than to simply visit?" he asked.

Korton nodded abruptly. Without speaking he turned back to the control panel and touched a small button. Paul heard nothing, but seconds later he felt a presence behind him. If he would have been clothed in skin instead of spirit, his skin would have crawled with recognition. He turned and looked into the eyes of a woman that he had loved for centuries.

"Eia," he whispered, dropping his eyes in an attempt to conceal the impact that she'd had on him.

She smiled gently. In her realm all things were known. He could not hide from her. There was no reason to hide. In her life there was no judgment. Besides, she loved him as well … but she called the experience by another name.

Though she was only five feet tall, she carried herself with an attitude of authority and grace. Her thin neck was slender and elegant, supporting her large head in the center, rather than along the back, as it was with humans. Her skin was alabaster and luminescent, emanating with a light that came from deep within. Her eyes, though large and almond-shaped like the others, were different in that they were lined with grey. It was obvious that she was proficient in projecting her thoughts through her eyes. They spoke with more understanding than Paul felt he could comprehend or handle. She was reducing him to tears without having spoken a single word.

"Paul," she said quietly. "It's wonderful to see you again."

He had been touched by the melodic tones of Zo's voice. But Eia's voice penetrated his heart. He knew that the tones that emanated from her had the ability to heal him and to make him forget.

"I am pleased that the time has finally come for us to remember each other," she told him. "There is much to do. Come with us," she added, turning to Zo with a businesslike air. "We have a gift for you."

He followed them into a hallway that extended away from the large control room. She stopped at the first doorway on her right and gestured with her hand. The door slid open soundlessly. Paul could only stand and gape at the magnificence of the interior of the room.

On every surface, crystalline shapes shimmered and beamed, casting rainbow-like shadows across the room. There were crystals of every size, shape, and color. Set on pedestals and laid in pillow-like cradles, they radiated an energy unlike anything Paul had ever experienced. Along the wall to his right were instruments that he could not comprehend. His eyes returned to the crystals in an attempt to remember each and every one of them.

Eia turned to him and touched him gently on the arm. She smiled when he turned to meet her eyes. "Follow me," she instructed softly.

She led him through several aisles that were abundant with crystals. She was leading him to the far recesses of the room, toward the right side. Paul guessed that it would be the surface that was directly against the exterior wall of the gigantic mothership. When she stopped, it was to stand in front of what seemed to be a throne made of crystal. Pure and clear as untouched water, it stood almost six feet tall. The interior of it was smooth and curved. He stared at it, speechless.

"If you like," Eia invited, gesturing at the chair with an elegant sweep of her hand.

Surprised, Paul realized that she was inviting him to sit. He had no idea what to expect. Since his knowledge of energies had been awakened, he assumed that he was in for quite a ride.

After hesitating only a minute, he did as she requested. He nestled against the cool of the crystal and waited.

CHAPTER FIFTEEN

Paul spiraled back through time, back to the day when he had agreed to an incarnation on Earth. The place was Questar, except that this time the colors were more vibrant, the air more glorious, the moment more poignant and fraught with significance. The tall, translucent green woman that he had seen briefly in his previous visions was beside him. She appeared as she had then, her form resembling that of a praying mantis. He knew her as Thaline ... and the bond that they shared was far, far deeper than he had understood earlier.

Once again he was at the thin, silvery creek. His heart reached out for it with yearning, seeking a way to hold him there for eternity. Thaline stood beside him, her large eyes filled with a compassion that he had, before now, not realized was possible.

Her thoughts were gently, almost tenderly, placed into his mind. "When the Council meets again, I will inform them of your decision."

Paul nodded, as he had done when the actual event had occurred thirty years earlier. He turned to watch a burgundy-winged bird dart across the shade-dappled stream. "I worry about the outcome of this mission," he thought solemnly, gently placing the energy of his thoughts into her mind.

"I know that you do. But keep in mind that the Earth will ascend to a higher vibration one way or the other, whether you are there or not, or whether you accomplish all that you have chosen to attempt. It is destiny. It is time."

She studied him, her eyes full of love. "And also remember all that you have learned throughout the centuries. Don't allow the pain of your experience to blind you to the truth of who you are."

Paul glanced at her swiftly, wondering if he was misreading the thoughts she was projecting to him. He had never known her to use words such as these, emotions such as these. Her serene face didn't allow him to read beyond her words.

"But our participation will ... or could..." he changed his thought abruptly, "make an enormous difference in how the Earth people experience the shift."

Thaline nodded gravely. "Indeed." And now she shook her head negatively. "But the chance that there will be enough people who will understand why we are intervening is questionable. The amount of work to be done is phenomenal. The amount of people who can overcome the challenges and energies that saturate the Earth is small in comparison to those who will seek to keep things status quo." She shook her graceful head once again. "It will happen either way. I pray that they understand enough about energies to accept that. Even though end results are inevitable, the way in which that result comes to pass is optional."

Paul noticed a movement behind her. Solomon, his hands tucked into the sleeves of his robe, as was his habit, walked into his vision. He stopped beside Thaline and looked down at her peacefully.

"Are you prepared, my Solomon?" she asked lovingly, looking up at him with eyes of tenderness.

Solomon smiled at Paul before replying, his eyes filled with a wry humor. "Indeed. In fact, I believe that I am more prepared to depart than our friend here."

"May 6, 2006," Paul muttered. "I will be, what, in my thirties?" His eyes searched Thaline's, already hoping for a reprieve from the decision that he'd made. "I will do all I can until then. But I will, most certainly, be thrilled to see you again ... and relieved."

He reached for her hand impulsively. She laid her delicate fingers in his grasp willingly. Her touch calmed him immediately.

"You will tell Ashalana good-bye for me?" he asked, still searching her eyes ... for what he no longer knew.

Thaline nodded without speaking.

"She will be here when you return," Solomon said quietly.

Paul glanced at him solemnly. "I understand that. But I wonder ... will I be the same? Will I change with this experience?"

Solomon smiled and shook his head slightly. "Of course you will change," he assured Paul. "You will be far wiser."

"I pray that I have no regrets when this is over. I remember clearly the last time I attempted an incarnation on Earth. I became so entangled in the energy and emotion and the belief system that I lost my original intent, my purpose for going there in the first place."

Solomon studied him without speaking for a brief moment. "You have grown quite a bit since that time. It was long ago. And your mission is quite different. This time you are returning for the good of humanity. Last time you were there in order to learn more about yourself and to serve out some karmic relationships. The two are quite different."

Paul laid his hand on Solomon's arm urgently. "I have no words to thank you enough for accompanying me. I feel certain that, with you sharing your energy with me from the spiritual dimension, I will be able to hold the faith this time."

Solomon's eyes twinkled with humor. "You have been through enough experiences for me to rest assured that you will, as you say, keep the faith. But I have a feeling that, when your physical mind recalls the date of your reunion, you will repeat the date so often that I will get tired of hearing it." He chuckled lightly.

"That doesn't speak well for the time that I'm going to be down there," Paul said quickly, immediately understanding the words and the implication. It would not be an easy lifetime. "If returning becomes my sole focus I imagine that there will not be much joy for me on this journey."

"Your joy lies in knowing who you are and what you have to offer to Earth, to those who will listen," Thaline told him quietly. She touched his chest briefly. The touch felt like a brand of love that would never be erased. "If you reach only a few, you will have done well," she assured him.

When Paul looked at Solomon, his eyes were blazing with passion. "Think of it," Solomon said, now using his voice, so enthusiastic were his thoughts. "When the vibrations of Earth are heightened, there will be communion once again. The Earth will be a place of peace, rather than a place of karma. No longer will the beauty be sacrificed, the possibilities be ignored, the truth be shadowed! It will, indeed, be glorious."

He took Paul's arm and shook it gently. "I know that you harbor a touch of regret about your decision to return, and that you fear that the sacrifice will be too great and you might fail. But think! You will be participating in an event that has never occurred before in this area of existence! A great and glorious opportunity, my friend."

Paul grinned at him. "I have a splendid idea. We can share the glory together. Instead of you going with me in spirit, why don't you join me and take on a physical body? Or … you can be physical and I'll be in spirit. That way you get to share more of the experience."

Solomon pretended to look appalled. He shivered his thin frame as if in repulsion. "I think not," he responded. "It was my turn last time we teamed up. I will hold the faith in the higher dimension and let you work on the lower." He smiled mischievously. "It is only right that we share equally."

Paul grinned at his friend. They had been together for thousands of years. They would be together thousands more. But when they met again, both in the same vibration, it would be for a different reason. In the meantime, there was a job to do.

"May 6th?" Paul whispered, his eyes turning back to Thaline.

She nodded soberly and reached out with pencil-thin arms to embrace him.

They all felt the vibration at the same time. Their eyes turned to the sky. Above them they watched the approach of the lightship that would transport Paul. As he traveled, his soul and spirit vibrations would be altered, the codes overlaid. In two weeks time he would be prepared to enter the physical body that awaited him on Earth.

He took a deep breath and, after another small, steadying embrace with Thaline, he and Solomon walked the short distance to the place where they would be lifted aboard.

The small lightship that was transporting them entered the huge portal of the mothership, the *Esartania*. Stationed in the fifth dimensional energy above Earth, it housed over one hundred thousand beings. It hovered, unbeknownst to those below, with the sole purpose of assisting Earth and its inhabitants. For over a century it had held steady, its crew patiently interacting with Earth beings during their dreamstates and meditations.

Passing from Earth to the craft and back again, various people used their dreamtime to weave threads of energy from the fifth dimension to the third, all in preparation for the changes that were coming to Earth.

Still feeling as if he was seated in the crystal throne inside the crystal room, Paul knew that, in this vision, he was inside the *Esartania*. He knew that, if he explored, he would find living quarters down the hall outside and to his right. He knew also that he would find medical rooms that were available for the healing of the energies of those working on the third dimension. He recalled that he had, at some time, made use of those medical services during what he had thought, at the time, was dream state. Now he realized that he had astral-traveled and that his spirit had actually been aboard for healing purposes.

He also knew that he would discover the darkened hallway and the glass-enclosed cubicles where bodies laid in wait for the return of their spiritual energy. He could find, across those cubicles, the huge container of liquid that he had envisioned not long ago.

In the crystal room where he now sat were crystals with so much knowledge stored within them that it went beyond the imagination. Some of them were from Atlantis. Some from civilizations beyond Earth. Some had been brought from other realities, which had since perished. All of them contained energy that, when released, had the capability of healing or teaching or otherwise benefiting those who accessed them. Some of them, he knew, were replicas of those on Earth. When they were activated, it would stimulate the replicas on Earth, and the energies of all would combine and saturate the environment around them.

He also knew that, in the lower part of this huge craft was a huge transport bay where he had been delivered by the smaller lightship that had brought him from Questar.

Without warning his spirit and awareness were dropped into his body like a stone that had been dropped from the top of the Eiffel Tower. His heart thundered in his chest. His throat ached. His insides quivered like a frightened child.

What had happened that had dropped him from the fifth dimension into the third like a rock?

Outside, Fric and Frac were barking wildly. Using furniture as a support, Paul lifted himself and shakily walked to the sitting room window. Outside was a small parade of cars. Authority and anger bristled from them like cold blasts of snow through an open door.

The first car pulled to a stop only yards away from the Bronco, which was parked beneath a small elm tree. Both doors popped open. From the passenger's side emerged a tall, portly man dressed in a uniform that was laden with various stripes and badges. From the driver's side another man stepped, not so steeped in honors and authority … possibly only the officer's chauffeur.

One by one, as the cars pulled to a halt, doors popped open and soldiers slid out of them like bread from a toaster.

Fric and Frac stood back, barking wildly, but apparently intimidated enough by the numbers to not approach. Paul grimaced, tugged on his shirt, stuffing it into his waistband, and stepped out to confront them without a plan.

"May I help you?" he asked mildly, facing the first officer across the top of his car. His voice, he hoped, held no sign of his inner quaking.

"Is that yours?" the man barked, pointing at the Bronco.

Paul turned deliberately to stare at the car. He turned back slowly. The officer was taller than he'd first thought. His heavy jowls shook with unvoiced anger. His closely shaved chin was set so tightly that Paul figured that it wouldn't budge even if he hit it with a two-by-four. He ignored the dogs completely, as if they didn't exist and weren't making an appalling amount of noise.

Paul nodded ... calmly he hoped. "Yes. It's mine. Is there a problem?"

"You bet there's a problem," the officer snapped. He flicked his eyes across the top of the car toward his chauffeur.

The glance was as sharp as a knife. Paul wondered how the man managed to survive it.

His eyes snapped back to Paul. Paul could feel the weight of them even though there was a distance of about thirty feet between them. "You trespassed on military property. You stole government property. Now get your butt back in that house, get your shoes on, you're coming with us. Sergeant, accompany that man inside," he snapped.

"No way!" Paul cried. Even though fear raced through his insides like a panicked racehorse, he had no intention of going quietly. "You can't just waltz in here and order me around!"

Would they, could they, simply pick him up and cart him off? No one would know where he'd gone. They could lose him in a prison for the rest of his life and no one would ever know. A movement, a sense of danger, pulled his attention to the last car in the line-up. The door opened. A tall, thin man exited. Dark glasses hid his eyes. A dark hat hid his hair. And a dark trench coat hid the rest of him. Paul felt a chill of dread and fear crawl over his skin.

"I suggest you follow orders, boy." The officer's voice dripped with ice and authority.

Paul turned back to the commander, dragging his attention away from the other man. Was this, he wondered, the man of darkness that Grandfather had mentioned? He suddenly sensed, more than heard, something that would hopefully postpone his doom. He looked toward the road and saw a dust cloud trailing behind Brenda's convertible as it sped toward them.

The car had barely stopped before she was out of it and stomping toward the first car in the line. She stopped only yards away from it and set her hands firmly on her hips. "What the heck is going on here?" she snapped.

"I'm fairly certain that this man is a felon," the officer snarled, glaring down at her. "If you own this property and you're harboring him, that makes you a felon as well. I suggest that, if you don't want to get arrested along with him, you go inside that house and stay there. My men will be in to ask you some questions when I'm done out here."

"They will not!" Brenda blazed. "This is private property. Do you have a warrant?" She stomped her foot in fury. "You still haven't told me what this is about."

"I'll explain this only once," the man said calmly, with steel lacing his voice. "This man trespassed on military land. He has stolen government property. We are taking him with us. And if you want to go with him, keep talking."

"What military land?" Brenda asked quickly. "There's no military land around here."

"There is nothing that says I have to explain this to you," he told her with an exaggerated show of patience.

"The only place that I've been," Paul interrupted, looking at Brenda, "is here, other than the dinner that I had in Flagstaff." He raised his eyebrows, trying to pass her a silent message. He turned to the man. "However, I loaned the Bronco to some friends of mine, who took it camping up near Young. Is that the land you're referring to?"

"There's no military land up there," Brenda claimed loudly. "If that's what you're saying, you're dead wrong."

"There is now," the man said savagely. "I'm not going to stand here and argue with you." He turned back to Paul. "Get your shoes. You're coming with us."

Faster than a sprint-runner, Brenda was in her car and back out, holding a cell phone. "I can have the authorities here in a heartbeat," she stated calmly, brandishing the phone like a weapon. "If you have proof, or a warrant, or anything at all that supports your claim, you better show it to me now. Otherwise, get off my property."

"You are hindering a government investigation," the officer said stoutly, piercing her with a glare that would have felled a lesser woman.

"As a citizen of the United States, I have rights," Brenda snapped. "And that means that you have to have just cause. And I believe, gentlemen, that is the one thing you don't have."

The officer turned back to Paul. "You can come with us quietly or we can have the locals haul you in. Which is it going to be?"

Paul shrugged as casually as he could manage, trying to appear as unflappable as Brenda. "I know for a fact that I haven't done anything wrong," he stated flatly. "Therefore, I think you need to come up with some proof before I go anywhere at all with anyone."

The officer changed tactics abruptly. "What are the names of the men who borrowed your truck?" he snapped.

His minion reached into his breast pocket and drew out a pen and a small notebook, flipping it open with a snap.

Paul flinched inwardly. There was no way that he was going to send them in Marlen's direction. "They are friends of some friends. I only know their first names."

Scorn dripped from the officer's words. "You gave your vehicle to some men that you don't know so that they could take a jaunt in the woods for an entire weekend. Is that what you're telling me?"

Paul lifted his shoulders in a what-can-you-do kind of shrug. "My friend told me that they were okay guys." He flipped a hand at the Bronco which, since the entire adventure had begun, looked much the worse for wear. "You can see that it can't get hurt much worse than it already has," he pointed out. "I wasn't too worried."

The officer's eyes slitted as he looked the Bronco over. He knew that he had to concede that point. "Look," he said, changing his tactics once again, attempting to be the good guy now. "There's no reason why I have to cause you any grief. Just tell me the names of these guys and I'll go hang this on them. Sounds like you weren't even there so why should you take the heat."

Paul began to relax, realizing that they weren't going to haul him in. "I can give you their first names. That's all I have. Sorry."

"What did these guys take?" Brenda asked suddenly. "You said they stole government property."

The officer, for the first time, looked slightly flustered. "I'm not at liberty to say."

"Why?" Brenda asked. "If there is something being stored out there that's going to put us in danger, I want to know about it. Are there secret silos of radioactive material out there or what?"

The officer shook his head. "There's nothing that should concern you." He cast a glance at his chauffeur, who looked back at him blandly.

"But I *am* concerned," Brenda insisted. "I had no idea there was even a military base out there, much less that you're storing something dangerous."

The man rolled his eyes in exasperation. "There's no dangerous stuff out there, lady."

"Well, I don't know that for sure, now do I? I'm going to have to go out there and see for myself. I know you guys keep all kinds of secrets." She looked over at Paul. "You and Bill and I can go there this weekend and check this out." She looked back at the officer. "Exactly where is this base?"

He blew out a sigh. "There's no base, lady." He waved his hands as if trying to wave her away. "Forget it." He turned back to Paul. "Just give the sergeant the names of the guys who borrowed your truck and we'll get out of your hair." He quickly ducked back into the car before Brenda could question him any more.

Paul made up two names, which the sergeant wrote down. It was clear that he didn't believe a word of what Paul was saying.

"Give him a card and tell him to call us," the officer growled from inside the car.

The sergeant pulled a card from his pocket and handed it to Paul. "Call us if you think of anything that might help."

Paul took the card and stuffed it into the pocket of his jeans. He turned toward the man in black. For an instant, they were locked in silent combat. Even as the man turned away to get back into the car, Paul knew that they weren't done with him. It was a temporary respite from the danger that, he felt certain, was going to haunt him for quite a while. He and Brenda stood together, watching the small parade as it pulled out of the driveway. They only turned away when the dust cloud had settled.

"How the heck did they find us?" Brenda asked shakily, her eyes snapping with a myriad of emotions, including fear.

"I haven't the faintest idea," Paul answered, filled with his own fear. His entire body was shaking uncontrollably. He drew a trembling hand through his hair and blew out a huge sigh of relief. "I need to do something to calm down. I'm shaking like a leaf. I think I'll go take a hot shower." He attempted to stop his hands from shaking. "I was meditating when they pulled up. Dropped back into my body like a stone, which didn't help the situation at all."

Brenda touched his arm quickly. "I've had that happen. I hate it. If you want, you can come in and I'll fix us some iced tea."

Paul shook his head. "Thanks but I think I'll take a quick shower, wash off some of the sweat," Paul said. "They really had me going."

"Okay. I'll go in and call Bill and let him know what happened. And then go back and pick up Stephanie. She's putting some things together and she wanted a little time to herself before she came out. You want to drive back into town with me to get her?"

Paul looked at her anxiously. "You think she'll be all right by herself? He won't come back there, will he?"

Brenda shook her head. "I doubt it. Anyway, this is the way she wanted it. She insisted. She doesn't think he'll hurt her again. She said he was just upset about losing his job. He took it out on her."

"Well, he'll be out of a job today just like he was yesterday. What makes her think that today will be different than yesterday?"

Brenda nodded in agreement. "I know," she said with a sigh. "But she needs to do what she needs to do. This is her lesson, not yours or mine. She told me she could handle it and then pushed me out the door. She wanted to be alone."

"Okay. Guess there's nothing we can do about it." Paul glanced tiredly across the horizon. "Sure. Let me know when you plan on leaving and I'll go with you."

"I'll honk the horn. It will be about an hour."

"Okay." He headed for the shower while she went in to call her husband and let him know about the visit and the threats.

CHAPTER SIXTEEN

DURING PAUL'S SHOWER a cloud of desolation fell over him like a blanket. He attempted to shake it, thinking of the good times he'd experienced during the last week. His thoughts returned, again and again, to Stephanie. He hoped that she would choose to let down her walls and let him in. He knew it was too soon, but it didn't stop him from hoping. He wanted a friendship with her and hoped that it would grow into something more.

In essence he had no family. There had been no communication since the last time they had gathered, nearly two years earlier, beneath the façade of Christmas. The false cheer. The words unspoken. The recriminations not so carefully veiled. The lack of understanding carefully camouflaged beneath innocuous words about the weather. He had come to the conclusion that it was in everyone's best interest for him to go his separate way. It served no purpose to be false to oneself or others, in his opinion.

At one point he had looked at his mother, wondered about her silent suffering, and had been unable to shape the words that he would have liked to say to her. Later, as he helped her in the kitchen, he had tried to share his feelings with her, his concerns for her. She had shut him up with an abrupt demand that he mind his own business. Since that time, he had.

After that, he had gone through a brief, frenetic search for a lady who would share his life completely. Looking for love. Looking for solace. Looking for a new family.

Before he could stop himself he was weeping under a weight of absolute grief, with no understanding of what was happening. He decided that, perhaps on a sub-conscious level, he was telling himself that she wanted nothing to do with him, and his tears were telling him that there was no hope.

He managed to contain his tears, toweled himself dry, and walked slowly into his bedroom. Without thinking he pulled on fresh jeans and a T-shirt. Padding barefoot into the living room, he stood looking wearily out the window. Fric and Frac were sleeping peacefully in the shade of the patio, their feet twitching occasionally with a dog-dream.

The sun pounded on the exposed pastures and the low hill beyond. It looked hot and miserable. When the phone rang and it was Brenda, asking him if he wanted to drive into town with her, he politely declined. He watched her drive off with a wave. He smiled to himself, feeling good about his new-found friendships. But he wanted to re-think his decision to move to Payson. Should he return to Sacramento? Should he give up his job there, as he had planned to? It might be far safer to think of this past week as nothing more than a break in his routine, a temporary diversion. He found himself releasing a long, weary sigh.

Walking back to the patio, he sank into a chaise lounge, intending to mull over the decision of whether to stay or go. Within seconds he had sunk into a dreamless sleep. The sound of tires on gravel woke him up. Turning, he saw Brenda's convertible pulling up near the front door. He rose and walked toward her, puzzled when he saw that she was alone. He grew even more puzzled when she didn't exit the car but instead merely sat there, her forehead resting on the steering wheel. His heart filled with dread and he ran the last few steps to the car.

"What is it?" he asked her, his voice shrill.

She glanced at him quickly, her face unreadable. But there was no way to avoid telling him what she had to say. "I went to Bill's office to talk to him before I picked up Stephanie," she began. "When I left there, an ambulance blew by me, heading toward Stephanie's house." She looked up at him apologetically. "It's a small town," she explained feebly. "You can pretty much guess what's going on." She sighed heavily. "Anyway, I had a bad feeling. I followed it."

She touched his hand, which rested on the door beside her. He shivered, knowing what she was going to tell him.

"They had to take her to the hospital again," she said softly.

A soft moan escaped him. He caught her eye and silently begged her to tell him that it wasn't true. She pushed the car door open and gently put her arms around him like a mother comforting a child.

"You only left her for an hour," Paul said softly. "An hour. How could anything happen in an hour?"

Brenda lifted her shoulders with a small helpless motion. "I'm sorry," she said quietly. "I wish I didn't have to tell you this. I wish it didn't happen."

"How bad is it this time?" Paul asked.

She stepped away from him, wrapped her arms across her chest, and stared out at the distant hills. "Pretty bad," she said reluctantly.

Paul locked her gaze with his. "Tell me," he ordered. "I'm going to find out eventually."

Brenda's eyes shifted away from his, causing his heart to lurch. She hadn't told him everything yet, he knew.

"I came back to get you. I think you need to go to the hospital with me. She asked for you."

The ground beneath him dropped away, he felt himself spinning. He forced himself to take a deep breath and gain control over his emotions. "Let me get my shoes. I'll be right back."

There was no conversation as they raced back to town. The sun and wind were relentless. By the time Brenda parked the car in the hospital parking lot, Paul was drenched with sweat. Running through the double doors, he searched unsuccessfully for a familiar face, hoping to see Marci, the nurse that he had met earlier.

"Can I help you?" a nurse's aide asked, seeing Paul search the lobby with wild eyes.

"Stephanie Alder," Brenda said quickly, having come in behind Paul. "She was just brought in."

The aide led them to the waiting room, informing them that

she would send someone out to talk to them. Paul paced until a nurse showed up. He and Brenda faced her urgently.

"You know that she's been here twice in the last few days?" the nurse asked, searching their faces.

Both Brenda and Paul nodded.

"And ..." Paul prompted impatiently.

The nurse glanced at him and clasped her hands in front of her, eyes downcast. "She has a lot more damage this time."

Paul closed his eyes briefly, attempting to shut out the information and the pain. He started to turn away, instinctively wanting to escape. He stopped himself, turning instead to confront the nurse. "You might as well tell us everything," he told her.

"Are you family?"

"That doesn't matter," Paul informed her angrily. "That's only a word." He waved his hands in frustration. "We're the only family she has. We're her friends."

The nurse stared at him silently for a minute. "She sustained a lot of injuries," she finally said. She turned toward the door. "I'm going to send Dr. Cameron in to talk to you."

As if summoned, the doctor appeared in the doorway. He raised his eyebrows questioningly at the nurse. "Is this Stephanie's family?" he asked.

The nurse glanced at Paul and Brenda. "These are her friends. Apparently she has no family."

Dr. Cameron's eyes shifted away for a minute as he absorbed the information. When he looked back at them, Paul knew what he was going to say.

"I'm sorry. We did all we could but it wasn't enough. She sustained internal injuries and her brain was swollen from the trauma. We took her to the operating room but we were unable to save her. I'm very sorry."

Without speaking, Brenda turned toward Paul, walked into his arms, and rested her head wearily against his chest.

Over her head, Paul stared at the doctor, who met his gaze before turning away in sorrow. Paul blinked, watching his departure. Surely he had more to say, he thought. Without a doubt he was going to turn around and tell them it had all been a mistake. Another doctor was going to appear in the hallway and tell them that, by some miracle, Stephanie had opened her eyes and talked. Certainly there would be a miracle….

Paul looked down at Brenda's head against his chest, felt her shaking, heard her sobs. He shook his head in confusion. This wasn't real. He was still asleep on the patio and he was dreaming.

For minutes he stood, stunned, with his arms around Brenda. The two of them were alone now. He forced himself to accept the departure of the nurse and the doctor. That was the first step he needed to take, he reasoned. His thoughts were cautious, treading around the truth with soft sighs of denial. He allowed himself to accept that Brenda was weeping. When he felt her tears soak through his shirt and stain his chest, he finally knew, without doubt, that hope was gone.

Reeling on his feet, like a boxer who had been hit too many times, he swayed, holding on to Brenda for support. As her sobs lessened, she realized his pain, and gently led him to the nearby chairs. Following the urging of her hands, he allowed himself to be pressured into sitting. Once in the chair, he dropped his head into his hands. There he sat, absorbing the loss until Brenda finally pulled him into a standing position. He allowed her to lead him to the car. Without thought he handed her the keys and allowed himself to be driven back to the home that wasn't really his, where Stephanie no longer would bring with her the breath of possibility and love.

Dinner that night went mostly uneaten. They had all pretended but now they had set their forks aside.

"I guess there's nothing anyone can say at a time like this," Bill said quietly. He set his elbows on the table and tented his fingers.

"I had decided to try to gain her trust, to try to build a friendship," Paul said, his voice barely above a whisper.

Brenda nodded without speaking and reached for her napkin to wipe at her tears. "It was already obvious to me that you were going to try," she said quietly.

Paul looked at her, surprised. "I didn't know you were aware of that."

Brenda's smile was sad. "I'm aware of a lot of things," she said bleakly.

Bill nodded. "Indeed she is," he assured Paul. "Unfortunately," he added quietly, "just because you find someone it doesn't always mean that it's going to work out this time around."

"Obviously," Paul agreed sadly. He looked from one to the other. "How do you live with not knowing? I mean, how would you bear it if you lost each other?"

Bill and Brenda exchanged a look of love so deep that Paul drew back without thinking, concerned about interfering.

Brenda answered his question softly, her eyes not leaving Bill's. "You thank God for what you have and you don't allow yourself to worry about tomorrow. You cherish. You love. You give all that you have without hesitation. And you pray that, when things get rough, you don't forget why you fell in love in the first place."

She smiled at Bill and reached out a hand. He took it, curling his own over it like a protection. Paul was torn between envy of what they had and fear of finding it for himself and losing it.

As if reading his thoughts, Bill spoke up. "You can look at it this way, Paul. Reality is actually an illusion that we're all creating. Call it out-picturing, if you will. Your soul exists in another place. And it sends its spirit into space in an effort to learn, or maybe only to entertain itself. We don't know." He shrugged lightly. "Maybe all of this is nothing more than a dream. We have no way of knowing. But your soul is at peace. Your truth remains what it is no matter what you experience. It's only within this dream or illusion that the pain is real. Your soul doesn't feel it. It acknowledges the experience but not the pain. Maybe if we could learn to live the truth of our souls, we could stop the pain."

"I never thought of it that way," Paul said thoughtfully.

Bill shrugged again. "Well, when you dream, you generally aren't able to control the dream. And how much does your dream affect your life after you wake up? Not much, I imagine. And so, if we are a dream within a dream, the exterior part of us is not affected by this dream. Does that makes sense?"

"It makes a lot of sense," Paul agreed. "I'll have to give that some more thought."

The words, the thoughts, might have been only mere ramblings as Bill sought to distract Paul from his pain. Perhaps they were true. Perhaps they were not. But they deserved more thought. If he found them to be even partially true, he might discover that there was another way to live his life. He wanted to change his life, himself. Maybe this was the doorway through which he could walk to find the answers.

His reality had taken a dramatic turn since leaving Sacramento. He wondered where it would all lead. It seemed obvious to him that the world, with or without his agreement, was leading him into another reality, another experience. But if it was true that each person created his or her own reality according to a soul need, it was also true that, on some level, he was creating this experience, this sudden dash from a fairly normal life to the path he'd been on recently. What was it, he wondered, that had caused him to suddenly awaken to all of the possibilities that were now being introduced to him?

It only took a second for him to realize that the turning point had been the dream, the memory, of having come from elsewhere. He was from another place and time. Now it was only a matter of learning what to do with the knowledge.

CHAPTER SEVENTEEN

STEPHANIE WAITED FOR HIM on the other side of time. The night was dark and as deep as a bottomless cave. Paul stood facing her. Her hair flowed with the breath of the unseen moon, stirring his yearning. The chocolate-brown, effervescent gown that she wore swirled around her like a distant memory.

Paul merely stood in his dream and watched her, waiting for her to speak or dance or disappear.

She moved toward him and stood, smiling as tenderly as if he were a newborn. Finally she lifted a hand and, with a touch as light as a passing feather, brushed his cheek. "Hello," she whispered. "I just wanted to say hello."

"Why," he asked, knowing that she would understand the question "… why did you leave?"

"What you wanted and what could have been would not have been the same. My soul has a path to follow."

"Why?" he asked again.

"We choose to live and we choose to die," she said simply.

Which was no answer at all.

He merely watched her. She was the teacher, he the student.

"I needed to be who I was," she explained. "I needed to follow who my soul needed me to be, not who you needed me to be."

"I hated the place you were in," he said, surprising himself.

She nodded. Now her hair was the only moonlight. It breathed as if it were alive. "To die by the hand of another is to learn that we die by our hand alone."

He felt himself question her.

"Until we understand that we are all one, and that we are forever, we teach ourselves that we do not truly know who and what we are. Perhaps more importantly, we learn that only we create our experiences. When I lost my parents, I lost my will to live. I needed to join them." She smiled. "And I have." She waved a vague, beautiful hand. "But now I understand that we were never parted, even when it seemed that we were. I learned many things. This is only one."

"I am compelled to understand this theory ... that we create our own reality," Paul said. "I don't completely understand."

Her voice was like the whisper and promise of spring. "It is fairly simple. In the depths of our being, often in places that we never think to look, are hidden things that we think or believe. They keep us from absolute Truth, the knowledge of who and what we are. These things come from far and near, but always it is something within us that draws them to us.

"We allow ourselves to believe in the illusion because we know that it will teach us something. We can learn by allowing ourselves to live the truth of our power. You see," like the brush of an angel's wing, her hand touched his cheek, "all things serve to challenge us, to make us strong, to complete us in a way that, when we are complete with our exploration, we will never be swayed from the Truth again. Then," and here she smiled with a touch of grace, "we are strong enough to become Creators. We will have passed beyond the need to be co-creators."

"Then it's true that we are merely here practicing to become more like our Creator?"

She smiled again. "We always are and always have been as one with our Creator. Like children, we are learning to become adults."

She nodded, a wise and endless soul. "We are free to choose who and what we wish to be. We are Light alone. We are shape-shifters. We become what we choose to become in an effort to discover the Truth of who we are. We grow into our Truth. We grow into our soul."

"I would have chosen to be with you," Paul told her quietly.

"I am only one. There will be another."

With that a progression of visions glided him through lifetimes. There was Eia, Sandi, Brenda, Stephanie … and the nameless woman of his dreams.

He felt a thrill of hope that the woman of his future might be the woman of his dreams.

With that thought the dream was ended, as abruptly as if he had been thrown against a wall. He sat up groggily, wrapped his arms around his knees, and stared into the dim light of four a.m.

Her memory lingered, like the scent of a perfume after the woman is gone.

"What are your plans?" Bill asked later as they sat on the patio eating breakfast.

Paul pondered the question before answering. As each day passed, he was more determined to live a life that his soul needed him to live. How he would go about that, he wasn't quite certain. But he was going to try.

"I talked to Jessica last night," Brenda said, interrupting his thoughts. "She said that if you came back and then drove here again, she'd drive back with you for a visit. If that would be all right with you, that is." She glanced at Bill. "That would be better than us going there, I think. Bill's going to be loaded with work for the next two weeks. And I wouldn't want to go without him. I'm pretty certain that you don't want to wait two weeks, do you?"

Paul shook his head. "No. If I'm going to make the move, I'd rather do it and get it over with. Get established here."

He patted Fric's head absently, staring unseeingly into the distance. Turning back, he spoke abruptly. "That's it. I'm going to do it. I have a book to write. I'm going to go get everything sorted out there and then get back here and get to work on the book. You can call your friend and tell her I'll be happy to give her a ride back, if she wants."

Brenda's smile was large. "Yes!" she cried, raising her fist in victory. "I was hoping you'd say that!"

Paul pushed his chair back from the table, picked up and began to stack dishes, and headed for the kitchen with them. "I'm going to throw a bag in the Bronco and head out then. I imagine I'll only be gone a week or so." He paused in the doorway. "You going to call your friend and let her know I'm coming?"

Brenda pushed back her chair, stood, dropped a kiss on Bill's forehead, and said, "I'm doing that right now. She'll be thrilled. So am I. I haven't seen her in a coon's age." She paused and looked at Paul seriously. "By the way, she's a professional psychic. I hope you can handle that."

Surprised, Paul thought about what she'd said. "Why wouldn't I be able to handle that?" he asked after a minute.

"Well, she reads minds," Brenda said hesitantly.

"Who around here doesn't?" Paul asked with a short laugh. "Seems like damn near everyone I've met in the last week reads minds." He shrugged lazily. "So I guess you're telling me to keep my thoughts clean?" he asked, smiling to show that he was joking.

Brenda nodded with a smile. "Well, at least try," she joshed. She turned away. "Anyway, I thought I'd better at least warn you." Laughing, she entered the house to make her phone call.

An hour later Paul was on the road again, alone but happy. He had a plan, a purpose. It was going to be exciting to see how it all turned out. He fleetingly thought of Marlen as he passed through Flagstaff. He decided that he'd go up for a visit when he got back from Sacramento. He also decided that he'd stop at the same restaurant on his way back through Flagstaff, just to see if Marlen might be there once again, waiting, possibly ready to guide him on another mission.

The trip seemed endless. The dreary, repetitive landscape left him plenty of time with his thoughts. But they were random thoughts, darting and dashing away from memories and longings. Driving into Sacramento, he had to shake his head several times as the familiar sights forced him to realize the changes within himself.

It seemed like, the last time he had seen this town, he had been another person … in another lifetime. He sat for a minute, staring up at the blank windows of his apartment. Random thoughts about where his life would lead him made him hesitate to return to the past. Stephanie's face lingered in his mind's eyes.

Shaking himself out of his lethargy, he grabbed his duffel bag, climbed the stairs to his apartment, and shoved the door open. The stale air inside rushed out, thankful for the escape. Dropping the bag on the floor, he walked to the refrigerator, pulled the door open, and scowled at its contents. It was bare except for a half-empty carton of orange juice, a half-cube of butter, and a disgustingly stale, cellophane-wrapped sandwich that had several bites out of it.

Shutting the door, he picked up the phone to call Sandi. The conversation was brief but not unpleasant. Just as he'd predicted, she'd met someone else. She was ecstatic and he was pleased for her.

A small thrill of freedom raced through his chest as he dropped his apartment key into the landlord's hand and his letter of resignation into the mailbox two days later. The Bronco held the boxes of things he hadn't thrown away. The rest of his belongings had gone to a charity shop. His last stop before leaving Sacramento was Jessica's duplex.

He pulled up in front of the building, noted the small, neat, tree-shaded yard, and walked up to the door with a happy whistle. Nothing but the unknowable future stood in front of him.

When Jessica opened the door to his knock, he was silent with recognition. He studied her, trying to remember where he'd seen her before. Her honey-blond hair was pulled back in a single braid, wisps of it escaping and dancing gently with the slight breeze that was attempting to sneak through the open door. She wore jeans, sneakers, and a white T-shirt with a huge yellow happy face splashed across the front. Her attitude was complacent and self-assured. She greeted him casually, waving a slender arm to invite him in.

"Obviously you're Paul," she said, sticking out her hand for a brief handshake. Her voice was low and throaty, sexy. "I'm almost ready. Let me toss my toothbrush into my bag and I'll be right back."

As she walked from the small, sun-lit room into a dark hallway that obviously led to the rest of the house, Paul didn't stop himself from watching her leave. It was happening again … she looked familiar. The thought of having known her before, the recent, unbearable pain of loving and losing so recently, all of these things caused him to want to bolt back out the door. It wasn't too late. He could drive away and no one would be terribly hurt by it. Especially him.

"Where'd you go to school?" he called down the hallway. He hoped, with all his heart, that they had gone to school together. Maybe that was why she looked familiar.

"Lincoln." She called back. "Bren told me you grew up here too. Where'd you go?"

"McClatchy." So it wasn't at school that they'd met. He hesitated. Turned partially toward the door, he looked at it longingly.

She walked back into the room where he waited, a large, black duffel bag hooked over her shoulder. She wasn't a standard beauty. Instead she had a classic, underlying attractiveness, subtle and camouflaged by her casual treatment of herself. She wore no make-up. Her jeans were faded. She had changed into a full, white blouse that billowed around her lean form as if she were wearing a trimmed-down parachute. Her cheekbones were high, her lips full, and her eyes deep-set and several shades of green.

She stood for a second, studying him silently, and then gave herself a nod that could have meant anything. "I think we'll do all right," she said enigmatically.

Paul tilted his head, studying her in return. "What does that mean?"

She lifted one thin, elegant shoulder in a shrug. "I think we'll get along all right. It's a long drive," she added.

Paul nodded in agreement. "That it is! I just drove it and it's a bear." He looked around quickly. "You ready?"

She followed his glance, taking one last look before leaving. "Let me check lights and locks and I'll be right with you."

A minute later they were in the Bronco and heading toward I-5.

"This is no coincidence, you know," Jessica told him as they moved out of the city traffic and onto the four-lane.

Paul glanced at her sideways, suddenly pleased to be sitting beside her. She was pleasant to look at, though he wished that she would smile or otherwise indicate that she accepted him. "What's no coincidence?"

"That you were the one to pick me up and that we're driving all this way together … perfect strangers almost."

Paul smiled mischievously. "I doubt that we're perfect strangers."

"What do you mean?"

"You're involved in metaphysics. Brenda told me you were a professional psychic. And so you must know about past lifetimes. And you probably already suspect that we've met before. I know that I do. Suspect, that is."

"Is that right?" she asked, turning slightly on her hip to face him. "What makes you think so?"

Paul shrugged and smiled at her lopsidedly. "Just a hunch. You look very familiar to me."

She gave him a laugh and then a smile, which instantly made her seem more likable.

"Is that a line you give every woman you meet?"

Offended, he glared at her. "No."

"Sorry," she said, holding up a defensive hand. "It may not be a line you use, but that's a question I ask. Seems most guys see me differently than I see myself. And I guess I've gotten defensive."

"I guess I can understand that," Paul said, feeling better after the explanation.

"Anyway, how'd you meet Brenda and Bill? I understand you're staying in the guesthouse? Brenda said you had quite a story to tell, but she didn't elaborate."

Paul chuckled. "I guess you could say that I have a story, yeah."

"You want to tell me?"

He looked at her sideways. "How much do you believe in extraterrestrials?"

She gasped, her eyes widened. "Oh, my god! You had an encounter, didn't you?" She faced him squarely, her face eager. "Tell me!" she demanded.

He told her the story. They had hours on the road. The story was fairly thorough.

She read the emotion behind the story. "I'm so sorry," she said softly.

As they talked quietly into the night, switching places so that she could drive while he rested, Paul came to understand that she had placed a veneer around herself. He was pleased, even gratified, that, as time passed, she slowly let her shields down so that he could see the truth of who she was.

At two in the morning, they pulled into a rest stop, took advantage of the facilities, and leaned against the car, munching some snacks and looking at the starlit night.

"Wouldn't it be something if they were to show up right now?" Jessica said quietly, her voice mirroring the velvet silence of the air around them.

Paul stared at her, caught up in the romance of the evening. "Right now I'd probably have trouble deciding if I wanted to stay here or go, if they invited me."

She turned her eyes from the sky to his and studied him peacefully. "I wouldn't. I know that somewhere out there is my home, but I also know that I have work to do before I can leave."

"What kind of work?" Paul asked instantly, his senses suddenly alert.

"One thing I know is that we have a mission together. I would venture to guess that we're going to be sharing the same road for a while."

"What's the mission?"

"To bring awareness to people and to help re-establish trust between worlds," she said, her tone simple and clear.

Paul smiled. "That's asking a lot."

"There's a lot of others who crave it," she countered. She continued, her words drifting softly into the vastness of the night air, as if the Universe was listening and absorbing them. "Earth has been going downhill for quite a while. The energies of everyone and everything have muddied it up so bad that even Masters who have come to help are having trouble remembering who they are. The option that the Council has come up with is to create a replica, based upon the foundation of this world, and those who choose to can re-establish themselves there. It will appear to be like Earth, but it will a replica and it will have a higher vibration and intention."

Paul stared at her. "Do you think that's what's going on?" he asked in a hushed tone. "I've been trying to figure out how they were going to manage cleaning up the energy around Earth. I mean, even while they're working, at cleaning it, tons more of emotional energy is being dumped." He stared at her. "So you think they're creating another world?"

Jessica smiled gently at him. "Not them. Us. All of us combined. Those of us who desire to live a reality of our own making. We don't have to be victims here. And that's what you and I can help people understand."

"You're not kidding, are you? Just how are we going to accomplish that?"

"You're going to write a book," she said lightly. "And we're going to be given a huge volume of new information to share with people. I don't know yet how it's coming, but it's coming. Then we're going on a lecture tour. And after that, I'm not sure." She stared up at the sky once again. "Maybe the *Esartania* will beam us up," she said wistfully.

A chill ran through Paul that seemed to have originated from the depths of his soul. If he had any doubt about her authenticity, it was gone now. The name of the mothership could not have been pulled out of thin air. She knew. "Have you and I met on the ship?" he asked quietly.

Jessica nodded. "Yes. I remember you from there."

"So that's where I recognize you from?"

She turned to him. For an instant Paul felt as if she had reached out and enveloped him, but he realized that it was her energy, her heart. "From there, but also from another place and time," she told him softly. "If you're supposed to remember, you will."

"Let's go," she said gently, touching his arm lightly. "Who's driving?"

"I will." He walked around the car, slid into the driver's seat and within minutes he was alone as she fell lightly into sleep.

When they drove into Flagstaff hours later, Paul suggested that they stop at the restaurant where he'd met Marlen. He went in, half-hoping that he'd meet him again. But the restaurant was almost empty. The few customers who were there didn't even look up as they slid into a booth. After ordering, Jessica excused herself and headed to the restroom with her duffel bag. When she came back, her face was pink with scrubbing and she had changed into a fiendishly bright yellow pullover sweater. Paul blinked every time he looked at her. She didn't seem to notice.

An hour and a half later they were pulling into Bill and Brenda's driveway. They had stopped in Payson to phone and alert them. Brenda was waiting in the driveway, Fric and Frac sitting by her side like sentinels.

The two women exchanged hugs and excited greetings. Paul exchanged hugs with Brenda. As all of them moved into the house, Paul excused himself, telling them he needed a hot shower. He crossed the patio and stepped into the guesthouse. He realized that he had grown accustomed to it. It felt almost like coming home.

He glanced around, dropping his bag on the floor inside the door. Wait a minute, he thought. He blinked. There, tucked into the corner, was a corner desk unit, an office chair, and a computer set-up. A pole lamp lit the area softly. He couldn't believe his eyes. He shook his head, unable to believe that anyone would go to this much trouble to help him. Involuntary tears of gratitude slid down his cheeks. He bent his head in gratitude, briefly breathing in the sense of love that permeated the gift.

I hope I can prove worthy of this, he thought, allowing the enormity of the task in front of him to weigh him down momentarily. With a rueful smile, he picked up the phone and punched the intercom for the main house.

CHAPTER EIGHTEEN

"I HAVE A SCHEDULE that I stick to when I'm writing," Brenda was telling them.

A platter of various types of doughnuts had been waiting when he'd joined them after his shower. He had groaned at the sight but had picked up a lemon-filled one that was slathered with chocolate icing.

Now he dabbed at his sticky lips with a napkin and nodded. "It's going to take enormous discipline, I imagine."

"It does," Brenda assured him. "And it will be more so for you, I imagine. This is a new area to you. You're going to want to explore, go places, do things. I've been here quite a while and so it's easy for me to settle down and make myself work. I write best during the early hours. Then I exercise and shower. And then Bill and I take a walk when he gets home." She rubbed Frac's ears lovingly. "We take the dogs, of course." She shook her head at Fric, who was begging for a bite of doughnut.

"I'm worried about what I'm going to say," Paul admitted.

Jessica snickered. "You're going to be so full of information we won't be able to shut you up."

"How so?" Paul asked.

"You're going to be an open channel. They'll be passing information through you like a funnel." She grinned at him and brushed at her sugar-coated lips.

"You make it sound easy," Paul said.

"It will be easy. They'll do all the work. All you'll have to do is listen."

"What will they be saying?" Brenda asked curiously.

"They'll be giving him info about their worlds, Earth's evolution, energy grid systems and how to work with them. All kinds of things," Jessica finished pertly. "Things I don't even know." She laughed gaily to show that she was joking.

Brenda smiled at her affectionately. "Hey, why don't we go get a river-fix?" She clapped her hands on her thighs, realized that she'd gotten powdered sugar on her pants, and brushed at it feebly.

"A river-fix?" Paul asked.

"Yeah. There's a wonderful place on the other side of town. The Verde River runs through there. There's a small area where you can sit on the boulders and just be quiet for a while. It's beautiful."

Everyone agreed. With the top of the convertible down and the day slowly heating up, they made it to their destination an hour later. Paul stepped out of the car and looked at his surroundings.

There were rolling hills, a meadow with a few cows serenely mowing the grass with their teeth. A small mountain shaded the area. Down a gently sloping hill, the river wound its way across the Earth's surface. Trees and bushes that he couldn't name lined the shore.

Avoiding the cow patties, they walked until they reached a grassy area where an old oak twisted across the horizon, having chosen to grow sideways rather than upright. Brenda sat down next to the river, suddenly silent and seemingly withdrawn. Following suit, Jessica found herself a solitary spot nearby. Paul sank down next to a tree and rested his back against it. He found himself relaxing. He felt the years of tension slowly draining out of him, unwinding the tension within as if it were a tightly woven ball of yarn. He closed his eyes until he heard a quiet gasp of astonishment come from Brenda.

Snapping his eyes open, he found that the sky was darkened by something vast overhead. It was huge, greyish, and circular and it hovered directly above them. Completely encircling it was a wide, pronounced rainbow. The object took up almost one-fourth of the sky. The rainbow was linked to another circle of light. This one was hyacinth blue. Linked with it, in the northwest part of the sky, was another circular rainbow. It wasn't possible. But it was.

He blinked. His eyes were open. He wasn't dreaming. He tried to speak, to call to Brenda and Jessica. But his voice was frozen. It seemed that the world had gone silent … including him.

He stared at the object, open-mouthed, shivering with amazement.

Scanning the sky, looking for more, he watched as streaks of rainbows danced here and there. Each ended in an upturned wisp, as if an angel's wing had brushed through it like wet paint. The rainbows waltzed, floating through the sky as if they had taken possession, if only for a minute, of Earth's reality.

The greyish shape continued to hover. Motionless. Soundless. Paul understood that it, or the beings aboard it, were watching. He had not seen the craft that had taken the three visitors. Could this be it? Were they returning to offer him his freedom? With a knowing as deep as Truth, he knew that he was hovering on the edge of another reality. He was prepared to stay or to go. In truth, he wanted to leave. He wanted to return to Questar. The book that he was planning to write fell into a pocket of insignificance as he thought about the enormity of existence and how small an impact he could make in such a vast arena.

Closing his eyes, he murmured a brief prayer, asking to be lifted away from Earth, returned to his origins. All of his past yearning surged into his heart, leaving him breathless. What could he do to convince them to take him home? He could think of nothing that he could say or do that would persuade them one way or the other. The large ship simply sat above, silent and impenetrable.

Paul's thoughts began to race. It was as if his spirit was viewing the ship from the inside and tossing the vision into his mind. He saw the intensity of the crew, felt the depth of their concern for the human race. His heart burst open and he was filled with the enormity of their compassion. As if he were absorbing history, he felt himself draw the full measure of their caring into himself. For a minute he imagined that he could see history through their eyes.

With a thrilling, frightening internal vision he watched the history of Earth unfold. He felt and understood the impact that the events of the world had upon the worlds around it. He knew, with an almost fatalistic certainty, that the time for change was rapidly approaching. Intervention would be essential. Earth could not heal itself. There would be help from beyond. People would not remain in ignorance much longer.

He saw the skies fall open, revealing thousands of crafts from other worlds. They moved slowly toward Earth, bringing with them awareness.

A movement in the tree-embraced meadow on the other side of the river caught his attention. A robed Master stood calmly watching him. Blinking, Paul shook his head. The man had not moved when he brought his eyes back to the spot.

The robe was hemp-colored and had wide sleeves, beneath which the Master hid his hands and forearms. His feet were sandaled. He gazed steadily at Paul, as if willing him to hear across the distance. Not knowing what else to do, Paul cleared his thoughts and attempted to receive the energy of the man's mental voice.

"Walk across the water and join me," the man urged.

Paul looked at the tumbling water as it leapt and cascaded over the moss-covered boulders. He felt himself resist. There was no way that he could accomplish that. Things like that only happened in the Bible.

"It will be easy," the man assured him.

Paul didn't agree. He reached what he thought might be an acceptable compromise. He closed his eyes and willed his spirit to join the man. Instantly he was beside him. As if he were physically there, he felt the man's hand take his own. They turned and moved into the meadow. There a circle of Masters waited. The man who held Paul's hand moved to the circle, joined his free hand with that of another Master, and nodded to Paul to take the hand of the Master on his left. Before Paul's eyes dropped closed and he joined in the prayers of those around him, he met and held the gaze of the man directly across from him. He then saw the nail wounds in the man's hands. He recognized him.

What was said or done was beyond Paul's memory when he suddenly found himself back beneath the tree where his body was leaning. He opened his eyes and looked up. The craft still hovered silently. He had no idea how much time had passed. Wispy, angel-winged clouds drifted across the bottom of the craft, as if they too were hoping that the doors would open and heaven would descend.

And then it seemed that the craft was lifting, pulling away. Paul watched with numbed disbelief as it, still rainbow-enwrapped, grew more distant. Then, as quick as the blink of an eye, the sky was what it had been ... sapphire-blue, calm, dotted here and there with an innocent puff of cloud. Mouth hanging open, Paul stared. And then with a suddenness that shocked him, he was enraged. Tears sprang to his eyes and poured down his cheeks like rain.

How could you do this? he wept, shocking himself with the depth of his emotions. How could you leave? How can you do this to me? How can you leave me yet again?

Shocked to the core by his reaction, his rage, the depth of his pain and sense of betrayal, Paul bent his head to his knees and wept inconsolably. The fact that he was sobbing like an abandoned child dismayed him as much as the words that were flying through his mind.

It took several minutes for him to gain control again. Wiping his tears with his shirtsleeve, he forced himself to his feet, using the tree for balance. He felt weak, exhausted, ancient beyond words. He turned toward Brenda but she wasn't there. He opened his mouth to scream. Had they taken her and left him? The scream died on his lips as he caught a movement and spotted her bright red blouse moving a hundred yards upstream. She was wading out of the water, her eyes on him. She waved excitedly.

"Did you see that?" she cried. "Were you watching?" She threw her hand up and leaned back to look at the sky. "Did you see?" she cried again, stumbling in her excitement.

He caught her arm as she tripped. Her face was blush-pink, her eyes sparkling with excitement. She hopped nervously from one foot to the other, staring at him anxiously. "I wanted to yell at you but when I tried to talk, nothing came out." She shook his arm. "Did you see it? I wasn't imagining it?"

Paul studied her soberly. "I saw it. It was definitely a craft."

"And the rainbows?" she cried excitedly. "You saw them too? Rainbows don't do that! They don't go in circles and dance all over the sky like that." She shook his arm again, like a puppy shaking a toy.

"I know," Paul said wearily, setting his hand over hers as it tugged on his sleeve. "I saw it all. You're not crazy. It was real."

"Did you think they were going to land? Did you think they were going to take us? I thought so. I really thought so." Her words bounced like tumbleweed in a windstorm. "I'm surprised we're still standing here. I thought they were going to take us."

"I did too." Paul's words were heavy. It seemed like an effort for his skin to be draped over his bones. He shook his shoulders and looked wearily at the sky. It remained the same. There was no craft in sight.

"Are you all right?" Brenda asked suddenly. "You don't seem very excited."

For a minute Paul stared at her intensely, searching her eyes, willing her to understand him. "I'm all right," he assured her. "I'm just really, really angry."

"Angry?" she asked, her voice rising in surprise.

"They left us here," he said bitterly. "I don't understand how they could to that."

Brenda studied him quietly. "You're really upset, aren't you?"

"Don't you feel betrayed?" Paul asked her seriously. He took her arm and shook it slightly, emphasizing his next words. "You came here to help. You took a body and you've been helping where you can." He peered at her intently. "Don't you see? You sacrificed your home and your family to come here. You've been here a long time and, if you're anything like me, you want to go home. You want to know peace again. You want to walk on your own land, eat your own foods, hold your own family ... know your own truth again." He stared at her sadly. "Aren't you angry that they didn't take us home?" he asked quietly.

Brenda looked at him thoughtfully, allowing her own thoughts to catch up to his. She shrugged lightly. "I can understand why you're angry. I want to go home too. But right now I just feel joy. They were so close that you could almost reach out and touch them." Her eyes filled with tears that she didn't shed. "They showed us that they're here, that they're supporting us, that we're not alone." She tilted her head at him, willing him to hear her words. "They couldn't take us home and so they brought a little bit of home to us. Do you see?"

Paul nodded thoughtfully. "I should be grateful, not angry," he said, chastising himself.

"You can't help your emotions. Don't beat yourself up about them," Brenda said softly. "That's not being fair to yourself."

"Do you think that, if they could, they would have taken us?" Paul asked quietly, searching her eyes with his heart.

Brenda nodded with a small, tender smile. "I think that, if they could, they would love to offer us a ride home."

Paul turned his face to the sky again, not realizing that more tears were running down his cheeks unchecked. He didn't notice when Brenda slipped her hand into his and stood next to him, smiling and crying up at the sky. A few minutes later, Jessica joined them. The three of them stood silently together, watching the sky, hoping for a return.

Finally, by common, unspoken agreement, they turned toward the car. The trip back to the ranch was silent, each of them consumed by their own thoughts. It seemed there was nothing to say. The power and magnificence of what they'd seen had dulled their senses.

Paul knew that he had been changed yet again. In what way, he couldn't yet say. All that he had experienced, through his years and his searching, seemed to have evaporated into nothing more than a dreary, fragmented nightmare. All of the reasons that he had imagined for his life on Earth seemed to have been invalidated by the enormity of the events of the last few weeks. When life on Earth was set next to the vastness of existence, it looked less significant than one second of an entire lifetime. He knew that there was nothing, and no one who could explain why his heart was so heavy. He wondered how long it would be before he returned to some semblance of himself.

Two days later he was still wondering. Two days after that he was still lost to himself. He wandered the sun-drenched roads of the small valley aimlessly, not noticing his surroundings. He drove the Bronco to the hills and mountains surrounding Payson and he wandered there as well. The beauty went unnoticed. His search was internal. Finally he stopped driving and walking and merely sat in the guesthouse in front of the blank computer, or sat and stared into the depths of the pool.

It was there that Jessica found him at four a.m. one starlit, moonless night. "How are you?" she asked, her voice a bodiless whisper in the darkness.

He heard her sit down in a nearby chair. "I'm all right," he said, peering into the darkness. "How are you?"

"I'm all right too." She sighed quietly. "I feel changed though."

Paul nodded, understanding. "Exactly. I think we're in the process of trying to find ourselves again."

"That's a good way to put it."

She hesitated. Paul could almost hear her deciding if she should say what she was thinking.

"I want to tell you, Paul, that you look different since that visitation. It changed you in some way. I mean," she added, "some physical way."

"Different how?" Paul asked.

"I guess I would have to say you look more like an ET than you did before. Something around your eyes, I guess."

Paul gave her a small smile, though she couldn't see it in the darkness. "I didn't know that I resembled one before, and now you're telling me that I look even more like one." He chuckled lightly.

Her voice was serious. "Oh, sure you did before. You could see it clearly in your eyes. But now it's even more evident. It's almost as if you lost part of yourself, but replaced it with more of yourself, if that makes any sense at all."

Paul nodded to himself. It made sense. A piece of him tugged at his heart, seeking freedom. But it stood to reason that if he was in this place and time it was for a purpose. The opportunity to leave had been there several times and he was still here. The simple fact was that he was making an unconscious choice to stay. The simplicity of the awareness caused him to smile at himself.

Obviously he was not alone. Not far away slept Brenda, another who was from other worlds. And possibly Jessica as well. Why were they here? How was it possible for the Universe to orchestrate their meeting, all of them coming together over the miles? He turned to Jessica, acutely aware of the sense that there were other energies reading his thoughts. "Do you wonder why we're all here, why all of these things have been happening?"

He could feel her nod in the darkness. "How could I help but wonder?" she asked quietly. "I've always noticed patterns in my life. Now it seems that the events are taking us somewhere. I don't see where yet ... but I have a feeling that we're going to find out fairly soon." She paused. "I consider all of this to be a validation," she added.

"A validation of what?"

"That our mission is about to begin. I think we've just been coasting toward this minute. Marking time. Waiting."

"And what do you think that mission is?" he asked, almost fearing the answer.

"I think we're here to help tie up the loose ends of one piece of the Plan and help start to build the next piece," she told him, adding more mystery to his already muddled thoughts.

Unaware that she had confused him, she continued. "I've been shown the energetic grids that surround Earth. I've watched the old ones get dismantled and the new one replace the old. I've watched portals be put in place. Energetic gateways, I guess you could call them. I think this world is about to collide with another one. A higher reality that can't help but affect this one."

She turned to him. Dawn was stretching itself over the horizon and he could see her eyes, wise beyond her years, holding secrets not yet revealed. "Higher dimensional realities are going to merge with this one. It will be confusing for a while as people try to understand where they are and what's happening. It will be push and pull of emotions and beliefs and everything else. I think the end result will be two realities coming out of this one. Those that can handle the new one will adopt it. Those that can't will stay in the old one."

Paul stared at her, assimilating her words. "You mean, you think that the reality that has made up Earth for thousands of years is going to separate and become two different realities? Two different worlds?"

"Something like that," she said softly. "I don't quite get the whole picture yet but that's what it feels like. I was pretty brash and certain when we first met and talked about this." She smiled wryly at herself. "Now I have to admit that I may not know everything."

Paul chuckled. But her explanation rang through his body like a huge church bell as he allowed himself to think about it. Every cell of his body reached out to embrace the possibility that she was right.

Reading his willingness to entertain the possibility she'd mentioned, Jessica continued. "As far as I understand, existence is in layers, like pancakes sitting in a stack. These layers, I call them dimensions, all have a different vibration. I call this their 'rate of existence.' Well, the unhealed parts have a lower vibration because they're not filled with light and love. The higher dimensions are living in the same space but they vibrate at a higher frequency and therefore we can't see them."

Paul nodded. Her words made the picture even clearer for him, confirming what he had been thinking since discussing the bigger picture of existence with the alien visitors.

"I believe that Earth's vibrations are going to heal. At least some of them. When they heal to a point of separating from the unhealed parts, two realities will exist. Does that make sense?"

Paul nodded without speaking.

She chewed on her lower lip, thinking. "I don't quite understand it all. I just know that something is going on and that a whole lot of people are going to be really surprised."

Paul couldn't stop the smile that leapt to his face. He chuckled. "Yeah. I think I agree with you on that."

Like ice melting on a summer day, the possibilities melted into Paul's brain. He realized that their conversation might be interpreted as way beyond far-fetched. But he also realized that he, given his knowledge, could not afford to bend his beliefs in order to fit what was commonly accepted on Earth. To do so would only be enabling the old ways to continue, causing the healing to remain only a wish rather than a reality. As unhappy as he had been on Earth, he wanted to allow each and every opportunity for change.

Along those lines, he glanced at Jessica, wondering once again, if she would allow herself to open the door of possibility between them. He still had no recall of the life they'd spent together, the one that she'd hinted about.

As if she read his thoughts, she turned to him with an enigmatic smile. "I hear Brenda in the kitchen. I think I'll go visit with her and help with breakfast."

"Why don't I make breakfast for everyone?" Paul suggested. "You two can visit while I cook."

Jessica shook her head lightly. "No. Let us do it. Why don't you think about how you're going to start your book." She stood up, brushed at her hot-pink sweatshirt, and walked toward the house. Stopping, she glanced back over her shoulder. "You're going to have to bite the bullet some day soon, you know," she said, grinning to show that she didn't want him to take offense. "I don't mean to push you, but I really want to read your version of the story."

Leaving Paul wondering what she meant, she turned and sauntered through the door. Fric and Frac, abandoning his company for the possibility of food, laid down near the doorway, noses pressed to the screen door.

CHAPTER NINETEEN

AT BREAKFAST the four of them talked about a trip up the mountain to visit Marlen. Jessica thought she might head back to Sacramento in a few days. Paul, not wanting to look at that possibility, had brought up the idea of the journey up to the campsite.

"Why not?" he asked cheerfully. "We could all use a break." He looked across the table at Bill. "Especially you. You've been working while the rest of us just kind of hang out."

Bill lifted his shoulders in mock defeat. "If you all insist, I guess I can talk myself into a day off."

"We'll get everything together today, while you're at work, and we'll leave when you get home, if you can leave a little early," Brenda suggested happily. "That will give us three days up there."

Everyone agreed. The next afternoon the Bronco was loaded and waiting when Bill pulled into the driveway. After he took a quick shower and changed clothes, the four of them piled into the crowded Bronco. Fric and Frac perched precariously on top of the supplies, woofing quietly every once in a while, vocalizing their excitement.

Grandfather sat calmly puffing on his pipe as the Bronco rumbled to a halt near the small clearing where Paul had first been introduced to him. Marlen was nowhere in sight.

Hopping from the Bronco, Paul walked quickly to the old man's side and squatted down beside him. "It's good to see you, Grandfather," he said, touching the old man's shoulder awkwardly.

Grandfather's eyes were piercing, though tired, as he studied Paul intently. "You have continued the journey of discovering yourself," he said stoutly. "It is good to see you also, my friend," he added, nodding his head in apparent satisfaction at Paul's appearance. He turned slightly, glancing back at the vehicle. "You have your new friends with you?"

"Yes." Paul waved at the Bronco, inviting the others to join him. "Where's Marlen?" he asked, glancing around.

"Marlen went to Flagstaff. He should return soon though."

While Fric and Frac busily explored the area with tails held high, looking like fuzzy red periscopes scouting out the scene, Paul introduced everyone. Grandfather waved at the nearby logs as an invitation to sit. When everyone was settled, he turned his gaze back to Paul. "So how are things in Elsewhere?" he asked, chuckling at his own humor. The chuckle turned to a cough, causing Paul to study him with concern.

When the cough stopped, Paul answered. "I'd say things are pretty good. The Universe is meandering along like it always has. I've been thinking about the book I'm going to write. Planning it out in my head."

"No one else can read it if you leave it in your head," Grandfather said dryly.

Jessica gave a quick snort of laughter.

Paul glared at her and turned back to Grandfather. "I'll write it. I just have to plan it out first."

Grandfather nodded without comment, surveying Paul with his piercingly intuitive eyes. "I don't doubt that you will, my boy."

Paul leaned forward, a serious expression on his face. "How have you been, Grandfather? I've been worried about you."

Grandfather waved his pipe through the air negligently. "Do not waste your concerns on an old man. You are young. You have many years and many missions to accomplish. Mine are almost done. It is simple."

Paul shook his head. "It's not simple. If you're not well, I want to help you. You look tired."

Grandfather grinned around the pipe stem of his ever-present pipe. "I am old. I am allowed to be tired."

Paul sighed in exasperation. "You know what I mean," he insisted.

"When it comes time for me to go home, I will rejoice," the old man said. "I want you to do the same." His old eyes turned toward the sky. "It will be good to return home."

Paul glanced with concern at the others, who were listening carefully. "Is there anything we can do for you?" It was clear that his concern was valid. The old man was preparing for his death.

At Paul's thought of death, Grandfather turned his head abruptly, his face fierce. For the first time Paul caught a glimpse of a man who had been a warrior. Startled, and a little bit afraid, he waited for the reprimand that he knew was coming.

"I can still read your thoughts, my friend, and I do not accept them," Grandfather growled, his voice filled with pride and arrogance. "I am not preparing for my death. I am preparing for my return home. I have served long and well. It is my right to return to my home with joy, not sorrow and weeping." He waved his pipe at the landscape. "It has been a struggle here. I have learned much. I hope I have taught more. But now I look at freedom and it looks wonderful." He scowled at Paul. "Don't use your standard of death to entrap me."

Paul stumbled an apology.

Grandfather softened his words. "When you change your thoughts, you change your reality," he advised them. "To the degree that this world will allow, at least. With thoughts that limit me to death instead of re-birth, you send me to that place. I do not want your energy thoughts, if you choose to think of death that way."

Paul blinked. He had never fully absorbed the impact that thoughts could have. Now he saw clearly what the old man was trying to show him. He vowed to watch himself more closely in the future. "I apologize, Grandfather," he said sincerely. "I was not thinking correctly."

The old man eased up even more, stuck his pipe back in his mouth, and puffed with apparent unconcern, the matter already forgotten. "That, my friend, is exactly the problem," he said with a small grin.

With that, Bill could not restrain a burst of laughter. Jessica joined in, her eyes twinkling with amusement. Paul allowed himself a chuckle at his own expense but made a silent commitment to monitor himself more closely in the future.

The grumble of an engine interrupted the moment. An old battered Jeep thundered into the parking area and braked to a halt.

"Hey!" Marlen called, jumping from the Jeep with a grin. "Good to see you!" He thumped Paul on the shoulder enthusiastically, pumped Bill's hand, and gave Brenda a quick, awkward hug. He turned to Jessica, waiting for an introduction. When Paul had introduced them, Marlen turned to Paul with eyebrows raised in question.

Paul shook his head quickly, negatively, putting a stop to Marlen's speculation.

"Did you come up for the weekend?" Marlen asked, glancing at the Bronco filled with camping supplies.

"We did," Paul assured him. "Speaking of which, we have an ice chest with some cold drinks and another filled with food. Help me unload them, why don't you?"

The two walked away from the others.

"So what's new?" Marlen asked quietly. "I can tell that something's going on."

Paul sighed deeply. "I have some bad news for you. Stephanie didn't make it. She was hurt again. There was nothing anyone could do to help."

Marlen looked at him in shock and leaned a stiff arm against the Bronco, bracing himself. "You're kidding," he said softly. He lowered his head sadly. "I'm sorry, man. I know that you were hoping."

"Yeah," Paul said slowly. "But it wasn't meant to be, I guess."

Marlen shook his head. "I had a feeling that it wasn't going to be, but I didn't want to tell you."

Paul shrugged lightly. "I think I knew it myself but didn't want to admit it."

Marlen jerked his chin toward the others, who had settled

themselves around the campfire once again. "So what's with Jessica? Is this another possibility?"

"I'd like to think so," Paul told him. "She's not even entertaining the possibility, I don't think … but I am. She's pretty terrific."

Marlen nodded in agreement. "I can see that. I can see a connection between the two of you." He paused for a second, thinking. "But I can't track the future on this one. Seems like the lines of energy are shielded from view." He stared at Paul thoughtfully. "That's pretty uncommon. I wonder why."

Paul lifted his shoulders in a shrug again. "I haven't got a clue. I can't read it, or her, at all."

Marlen grinned. "Since when is that new?" he teased.

A small gust of laughter escaped Paul's lips. "True," he crowed. "So true."

Marlen quickly sobered. "They took the hovercraft and the ones who didn't survive. I haven't heard anything about it on the radio or through the grapevine. They did a great cover-up."

Paul nodded solemnly. "I didn't hear anything either. They came out to the house and harassed us a bit, but Brenda scared them off."

Marlen grinned. "Sounds like her. She can be a brave little thing."

Paul smiled. "Made me look bad," he said agreeably. "She went at them like a little mad hen while I stood there and wondered what the heck to do."

Marlen laughed out loud. "Come on, buddy," he said, clapping Paul on the shoulder. "Let's get this stuff unloaded."

At the sound of grocery bags, Fric and Frac popped instantly into view, tails high and wagging eagerly. As Bill stirred the fire to build it up, Paul and Marlen slathered barbecue sauce on chicken pieces and wrapped potatoes in foil, stuffing them into the hot ashes to bake. The aromas filled the small meadow, bringing a sense of complacency to everyone.

When night fell, it fell hard, obscuring the sky before anyone realized it. Thick clouds blocked out the stars and the moon's light as well. By the light of a lantern and a few flashlights, they managed to erect the tents. After everyone was settled, Paul found that he couldn't sleep. He pushed the tent flap aside and wandered toward the warmth of the fire. Grandfather was there, as usual, his pipe hanging loosely from his fingers as he dozed. Paul wasn't surprised when Marlen slipped silently onto the log next to him.

They sat in companionable silence for several minutes before Paul spoke. He told his friend about the craft that had hovered over the river that day and how he had felt since then. He tried to explain, as best he could, how he wanted his life to change and what direction he wanted to take. In the dark he could sense Marlen nodding his head as he listened. He added that, on occasion, he was able to see and hear those who lived in spirit, especially Solomon.

"It's a great thing, isn't it?" Marlen asked quietly. "To know that you're not alone."

"I wish it could be a constant thing," Paul said.

"It would call for keeping your energy at a constant frequency that is compatible with theirs," Marlen told him. "That's not easy to do. Our energy gets caught up in emotions and thoughts and business. We get side-tracked."

"As a society, we've got a long way to go, I think," Paul murmured, his eyes closed in relaxation.

"Yep," Marlen agreed sleepily.

A light from somewhere began to urge Paul's eyes open. Startled, he sat up and looked around. "Marlen?" he said urgently.

"What?" Marlen grumbled. He was leaning back against a log, almost asleep.

Paul reached out a fist and slugged him lightly on the leg. Opening his eyes, Marlen sat bolt upright.

"My Lord!" he whispered hoarsely.

"Again," Paul said reverently. His eyes misted over as he stared at the bottom of the hovering craft that sat directly above them.

Soft lights blinked rhythmically around the circumference of the craft. The clouds had turned to softly lit strips of rainbows, lighting the dark sky. An unearthly silence settled upon the Earth.

Somewhere in Paul's mind he registered the sight of Grandfather, sitting on his log, calmly setting his pipe aside as he gazed upward.

The night registered no sound at all as the bottom of the craft slid open, revealing a pale, golden light within. A small figure stepped into the doorway and stood, a dark silhouette against the pale light. A ray of light emerged and began to slide through the night toward the surface of Earth.

Paul stood, his breath rushing in a way that suggested he had run forty miles in ten minutes. The hair on his arms stood upright. He lost all sense of time and place as he moved, almost hypnotically, toward the ray of light. Just outside the small circle of light, which had fallen only steps away from Grandfather, Paul was stopped, as if an invisible hand were pressed against his chest.

He struggled with the invisible force, attempting to move away from its influence. He knew that, if he could manage it, when he stepped into the light he would be lifted into the craft. He wanted it with all of his heart. In that moment, he released all of his need to make a life for himself on Earth. He felt his spirit reaching for the craft. He felt his spirit weeping at the pressure against his chest. A memory, as if it had a life of its own, struggled to remind him of his purpose and the need for his story to be told. Reason argued with desire as he tried to move beyond the invisible barrier.

An instant later the small figure that had stood in the doorway of the craft was standing before them. Paul recognized him as Zere. Paul, Marlen, and Grandfather stared at him, waiting.

Zere caught and held Paul's eyes with a penetrating stare that took his breath away. He seemed to have grown in stature, matured in authority. He was, to Paul's senses, no longer someone that he could laugh and joke with but rather someone who stood with authority and presence. Paul waited, his heart frozen with anticipation, for what Zere had to say. But Zere stood silent as if waiting for something.

Paul felt the air beside him stir. Jessica slipped her hand into his. He felt her trembling with emotion. "I bring you the next direction for your mission," Zere told them. "In the days of long ago, our society brought to Earth some tiles. Encoded upon those tiles were mysteries from our world to yours. We gave to the people the secrets that we have learned, and we hoped that our worlds would unite. These tiles were given to a small renegade group of Mayan people. Before the tiles could be revealed, the people were killed by others. In Belize, where once the Mayan lived, the tiles wait. They are ancient. When the codes are broken, this world will have knowledge that it may use to open the gates between worlds. Treat the tiles with reverence and care. They will lead the people to the next step in their evolution. The tiles are not what they appear. The secrets are hidden within. Read beyond the symbols.

"You will be pursued. You will be misunderstood. You will be challenged. But you will not be alone. We will be with you.

"It will not be easy, but then," his lips curled slightly in a small smile, "there is not much worthwhile in this reality that *is* easy." He became solemn again. "But this too will change. We gave these secrets long ago, but they were lost. Let them not be lost again," he said softly, piercing Paul with his words and the depth of his intensity.

Paul felt the mantle of responsibility fall onto his shoulders as if it were physical.

As suddenly as he had appeared, Zere was gone. Paul had lost the urge to follow. He waited for the light to fade, the door to close. But it didn't. He glanced quickly at Jessica and back to the open door. What was happening?

As he watched, wide-eyed and mournful, Grandfather shrugged away the thin blanket that draped over his shoulders and, with a joy unlike anything Paul had ever witnessed, walked into the circle of light.

As he stood in the doorway of the craft, he turned briefly and stared into Paul's eyes. "Soon," he said. "You will follow soon."

Paul heard the promise whispered from the realm above as the great craft closed its doors and silently moved into the world beyond. With a muffled sob of emotion, Jessica turned to him. Without thought he wrapped his arms around her to comfort her. But over her head, his eyes remained on the now-empty sky.

Zere's words told him all he needed to know. The mission had begun.

UNIVERSAL PRINCIPLES

EXISTENCE/EXPERIENCES

AUTHOR'S NOTE

ONE OF MY GOALS is to share with others my vast array of paranormal experiences. This goal "came into being" as I accepted an increasingly larger picture of existence, following my life-after-death episode. It's my sense that, as we open our minds to the greatness of existence and the other worlds that exist beyond our current vision, we will become a much wiser and more compassionate society. The "Other Worlds" series is one of the ways I've chosen to share what I've seen and heard. Perhaps saying that I "chose" this is not the correct way to put it. Actually, this series of books was placed into my energy field, the first one while I was in dreamstate, and the others while I was meditating. They were placed, of course, by other-dimensional beings who desire to communicate with those in this dimension. It is my understanding that they would like to create an energy of peace that will flow through the energy field of our planet. In *Called* you read about Paul, Brenda, and Jessica having an encounter while at the Verde River in Arizona. This amazing incident was an actual event that occurred in 1997. The area where it happened had quite a few trees and, in making the artistic attempt to display the vastness of the craft, I took the liberty of creating a "deserty" atmosphere so that I would have more sky, rather than a canopy of trees. Below the artwork are two paragraphs from Julie and Lynne, the two women who experienced the encounter with me. It was my thought that you'd enjoy hearing from them as well. I'm looking forward to sharing the "Other Worlds" series with you. For me, being able to verbalize and share the abundant gifts of knowledge and possibilities that I've had shown to me is fulfilling my life-long dream and desire. The Universe we live in is vast and wonderful and each of you is and always has been a vital part of it. It is my hope that by reading the messages in this series you will be open to experiencing even more of it and perhaps even begin to have the joy of your own "other-worldly" experiences.

"They [aliens] were always real to me. But this experience, seeing that fantastic craft and all of those rainbows—things that aren't possible—it did something to my inner being. It was life-changing for me. The effect of it will last forever. It was beautiful, magnificent. I was torn. Part of me wanted to leave with them but then the other part was worried about how my husband would get along without me. I wanted to go but then there was a part of me that was afraid to go, afraid of the unknown. I honestly didn't know if we were going to be taken or not because they were so close. I was just awe-struck. The artist in me was trying to take in all of the visions at one time and I was pretty overwhelmed by it all. I felt really, really bad for Lauren when they left though. She was just devastated at their leaving. Heartbroken, I would have to say. I remember everything as clear as if it happened yesterday and, quite honestly, I wish we could have the experience again. As hard as it was for all of us to deal with our individual emotions, I think we'd all relish the chance to have them that close again."

—Julie Williams, Contactee and Witness

"The plan wasn't to go down to the river and wait for a craft to appear, that's for certain. The three of us had simply decided that spending some time at the river together would be a great idea. We hadn't been there very long before, almost as one unit, we all turned and looked up. It was almost like we had been silently called. This massive, massive craft was directly overhead. It hadn't made a sound. There was no hint that it was coming. It simply appeared and took over the sky above us. Never in my life did I imagine I'd see anything like this. It was surrounded by circular rainbows, which is impossible, but that was the way it was. And the rest of the sky had rainbows scattered around like clouds. It was the most awesome, incredible thing I've ever seen. And this craft was huge. It was so close it felt like we could reach out and touch it. I certainly wanted to. It was compelling, life-altering. I had always had a trace of doubt about aliens, whether they existed or not. This experience left me without a shred of doubt, without a shadow of doubt. It was one of the most total heart experiences I've ever had. It changed me profoundly. I wish everyone could experience what we did that day. There's no fear in me now. There's no doubt. If they were here to harm us, they were close enough to do it that day—and they didn't. I could feel the impact of their thoughts and feelings for us. The day changed me. There's just no doubt about it. We were sitting on the bank of the river and then suddenly there it was. We couldn't have moved even if we'd wanted to. The incredible impact that it had on us almost paralyzed us. We were frozen to the spot, captivated by the energy of the thing and the beings who were inside. This visitation, that's how I think of it, changed all three of us. It will impact every day of my future. I believe that each of us was affected differently. Perhaps it was meant to be that way. Maybe the beings on the craft meant to touch the secret parts of each of us, hoping to impact each of us in the greatest way possible. They succeeded. My life will never be the same."

—Lynne Shelton, Contactee and Witness

WHAT READERS ARE SAYING

"I loved this book. It filled me with hope and smiles. I am *so* ready for the next one! (and the next and the one after that….)

—Kris Bilyeu, Portland, Oregon

"One of the best books I have ever read. Once I started it, I couldn't put it down. *Called* has changed my life dramatically and inspired me to find my 'spiritual path.' The story that I read never really leaves my thoughts daily. I think it will always be with me and this is an added plus. This is the first book that seemed to jump out and answer my questions before I finished thinking them. I was impressed and amazed."

—Vickie Connell, Blaine, MN

"An exciting and insightful book that helped me to open to greater understanding of why I am here. This book (*Called*) helped me to realize what I have been feeling about outer dimensions to be true."

—Anna, Newport, Oregon

"I loved learning that what I always felt is true was written in this book as to be true!"

—Sharon, Hawaii

"I had just finished a documented book about alien visitations and the military's perpetual cover-ups when Lauren Zimmerman's book (*Called*) was sent by a friend. Coincidence? I think not! I loved reading her 'novel,' and I suspect it will resonate with so many of us around the world who feel that the 'shift is coming.' I simply cannot wait for the next in the series! I feel such hope and excitement!"

—Nancy Leonard, Waldport, Oregon

"Serious but entertaining … this book looks to be a future classic."

—Bob Brennan, Waldport, Oregon

"I found *Called* to be thought-provoking, very well written, and suspenseful and most of all … very validating."

—Elaine Correia, Waldport, Oregon

"We need to hear what this book has to say NOW!"

—Anja, Waldport, Oregon

"*Called* helps human beings become open to endless possibilities for themselves and the Planet Earth."

—Ruth, Waldport, Oregon

"As I read *Called* (Chapter 18) I was surrounded by a brilliant rainbow. It provided me with the comfort I was seeking and I was overcome with joy and emotion."

—An anonymous reader via e-mail

"*Called* will keep you in suspense, take you on a fantastic adventure, touch your emotions deeply, and offer new information as teachings with sincerity and gentle humor. If you enjoyed *ET*, you'll love *Called*. It grabs your attention and curiosity on page one and doesn't let go until you've finished the book!"

—Nancy Brennan, Waldport, Oregon

"This book represents one person's experience and journey toward spiritual enlightenment, during a time of great change in

Man's development. The author has taken a topic of consider-
able controversy (i.e. 'are we alone and have we been visited')
and woven an intriguing story of awakening, awareness, and
hope for the future. Set in a time of one man's questioning his
purpose and search for answers, the author crafts an enjoyable
story that can be read as fantasy or fact-based. I found myself
reading and re-reading each page as I searched for the deeper
meanings hidden in the development of this story. It is a timeless
and never-ending story that will make for a good read for adoles-
cents and adults alike."

—Jimmy Brown, Tigard, Oregon

"*Called* was a fun and entertaining book to read. It brings
forth an important and timely underlying message for us all to
remember."

—Gary Burda, D.C., Newport, Oregon

INCREDIBLE "COINCIDENCES" SURROUNDING *CALLED*

Three readers have reported being shown the cover art of
Called prior to seeing the actual book. One reader from Canada
reported being shown the cover five years earlier, during a dream in
which ETs presented the cover to her, bringing it out of the craft
and hanging it in the air above her.

Another reader reports being told by an unseen being that she
was to drive to Yachats, Oregon (from Lake Oswego, OR). She was
asked to go directly to a bookstore and ask for a person named
"Lauren." She did as she was requested ... ending up at the exact
store where Lauren, the author of *Called,* had appeared a week
earlier.

ABOUT THE AUTHOR

LAUREN ZIMMERMAN is the author of the fiction series entitled *OTHER WORLDS: The Series. Called* is the first of the series and will be followed by *The Mayanite Tiles, Peace Mission,* and *Choosing Universes.* In addition, she has authored and illustrated two children's books as well as several fiction and non-fiction manuscripts. She also hopes to create *OTHER WORLDS: The Children's Series* as her personal contribution to the next generation in order to assist them in remembering their spirit.

Lauren has been a mystic and spiritual counselor since a life-after-death experience in 1974. This experience captured the attention of radio listeners nationwide after her interview with Art Bell on the Art Bell radio program in 1998. She has taught and counseled in California, Arizona, and Oregon.

She weaves the experience of 1974 with her daily experiences and gives readers a unique vision and possibility of the world we live in. She plans to release a book about her other-world experiences sometime in the near future. You can visit her web site at ... www.oneworldhealing.com.

OTHER WORLDS: THE SERIES

presents

CALLED

I awakened to the truth … I am from elsewhere.
Upon waking I was called to rescue a fallen craft.
Some of my brothers lived. Some did not.
The opportunity to leave with them
slipped through my fingers like rain.
I remained to tell my story … and the story of what is to come.

THE MAYANITE TILES

The tiles are found, a gift to earth from another world.
Long buried and fragile, they are brought to the surface of earth
and to the surface of our minds.
They speak of possibilities. They speak of hope.
They challenge us to believe.
They tell of others who offer hope, who teach,
who bring the truth.
Humankind will rise to greet them.

PEACE MISSION

From every corner of reality they come … peaceseekers.
Their destination is earth.
They bring wisdom. They bring hope.
They bring the opportunity for each person to live their truth.

CHOOSING UNIVERSES

When all was said and done and I was finally freed
from a reality that could not fit my soul,
I made my passage into truth.
Of this I speak.
I will tell you of my journey that you may follow …
if you choose.

THE MAYANITE TILES

Volume Two of
"OTHER WORLDS: The Series"
by Lauren Zimmerman

PAUL'S HANDS TREMBLE as Jessica hands him the ancient tiles. The cave is dank and reeks of bats and tainted water. But he no longer cares. He holds the mystery of worlds beyond Earth ... mysteries that could change the entire human species.

But he and Jessica are not the only ones who know of the tiles. The others who know don't want them revealed. The taste of fear boils in Paul's mouth as he turns and confronts the man who has slid silently into the cave. As he stares at the gun in the man's hands he accepts that there seems to be no escape from certain death.

But those who brought the tiles to Earth so long ago have no intention of losing them again. Paul stares at the holograms of the alien beings who have materialized in front of him. If they can do this, he thinks, imagine what they can do to help this world.

With danger from seen and unseen beings, Paul and Jessica race across the border into the United States. Safety is no more certain there than it was in Belize. With their minds and hearts set on the successful exposure of the secrets, they work together to overcome and understand the forces that are working against them.

All the while, the secrets of the ancient, alien tiles are slowly unraveled. One circumstance after another reveals the mysteries of worlds beyond Earth and the societies that are waiting to reunite with Humankind. Each day brings new revelations and under-standings and together they plan the future for themselves, using the wisdom from the tiles to form a new understanding of existence.

But the future never comes to pass. Paul paces, stunned into silence, as he deals with the fact that nothing he believed about his future is Truth. Dealing with loss and confusion, he gathers his strength in an attempt to create another life for himself.

On Silver Wings

A Mystic Tale from Celtic Lore
Elfie Leddy
ISBN: 1-57733-080-3, 520 pp., paperback, $21.95

Little does Tannis MacCrae, a famous sculptor living in Canada, suspect that an earlier incarnation of herself has set into motion events that will challenge her beliefs about reality. Her first inkling is the disturbing dreams that bring into her orderly, reclusive life a man like no other, inflaming long denied desires. As past and present begin to interweave, Tannis discovers Taenacea's mystic Celtic heritage and the age-old relationships which surround them both, offering the chance for healing or further pain. On Irish soil, the story comes full circle. Tannis must utilize the lessons of the past to create a future once hoped for in the mists of Celtic lore.

From Another Side of Time

Britina Bovet
ISBN: 1-57733-088-9, 184 pp., paperback, $14.95

Many of Earth's people have already been evacuated, but to save those who remain another world is desperately needed. Earth's laws require that the local ruling system approve the evacuation. But on Enseha the Hierarchy has been illegally instituted by Earth people, and patriarchal laws still prevail among the natives . . . well, most of them. Duncan MacEnzie has trained his daughter, Belinda, as a warrior and raised her to rule. No one expects the Hierarchy to sanction the union between Belinda and Stuart, son of Enseha's most powerful lord, but when it is approved, Stuart must obey his father's orders and reluctantly weds Belinda. Stuart gradually becomes aware of a scheme beyond his wildest imagination—that is, if nothing goes wrong . . .

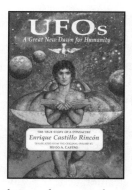

UFOs

A Great New Dawn for Humanity:
The True Story of a Contactee
Enrique Castillo Rincón
ISBN: 1-57733-000-5, 272 pp., 42 illus., $19.95

In the early 1970s, the author met a man at a movie theater in Caracas, Venezuela, and began a friendship lasting four months. Three years later, this same "man" greeted him as he was taken on board the Pleiadean ship for the first time. Enrique was later to board space ships four more times over two years. A highly respected engineer, known for his genuine credulity, he dramatically changed his life to research these amazing encounters.

Beyond Death

Confronting the Ultimate Mystery
Christopher Scott
ISBN: 1-57733-077-3, 244 pp., paper, $16.95

Beyond Death is a dizzying, mind-boggling odyssey into previously uncharted territory in the dimension of the Spirit. From scientific, mathematical, and spiritual points of view, this books provides support for the continuance of life beyond death and for the Divine Mind that designed the delicate balance of transcendent elements from which all life is formed. Additionally, Christopher Scott takes the reader to a "spiritual magnet" known as the Winchester Mystery House in San Jose, California. He provides cogent evidence that the House is actually a repository of universal secrets and esoteric knowledge. The author further solves the mystery of Sarah Winchester's hidden numerology and Hyperdimensional Spirituality incorporated in the amazing anomalies prominently displayed throughout the House.

Summer with the Leprechauns
A *True Story*
Tanis Helliwell
ISBN: 1-57733-001-3, 208 pp., 12 photos, $13.00

At first you won't believe it . . .
then you will!

During a summer spent in Ireland, Tanis Helliwell was befriended by a Leprechaun. His urgent message for humanity: "Humans are harming our own environment and theirs." With charming style and humor, Ms. Helliwell recounts the instructions from the Leprechaun on how humans can interact with elemental beings, as well as revealing the fascinating relationship she developed with this delightful fellow.

". . . *an Irish jewel, far more than a simple 'fairy tale' . . .* "

"*Tanis is a spiritual evocateur and deep seer who opens us up to other voices . . . other realms. . . .*"

—Jean Houston, author, *Search for the Beloved* and *A Mythic Life*

Through the Eyes of Spirit
Jenny Crawford
ISBN: 0-931892-32-5, 128 pages, $11.00

Seeing *Through the Eyes of Spirit,* Jenny Crawford shares her unique perspective as a medium, explaining how spirits communicate through her and why these moments are so precious. She gives examples of the help, as well as the resolution of deep sadness, that communication with loved ones in spirit provides for many people. Jenny says, "To me, the true work of a medium is to link these people with their loved ones in the spirit world, to provide them with peace of mind, hope, and encouragement to continue with their lives on the earth plane, knowing that their loved ones in the spirit world have gone on and are safe, well, and happy."

One hundred and two oracular readings
inspired by the Dolphins

A Guide to
the Dolphin Divination Cards
A guide for the use and personal interpretation
of the Dolphin Divination Cards
Nancy Clemens
ISBN: 1-57733-017-X, 384 pp., paper, $18.00

Each reading is designed with a short preface for quick, easy reference, followed by a longer teaching and explanation. Woven through the readings are friendly counsel, a universal spiritual understanding, and an environmental message.

Dolphin Divination Cards
Nancy Clemens
ISBN: 0-931892-79-1, 108 circular cards, $11.00, boxed
Words of counsel and affirmation on round
cards that fit comfortably in your hand

Draw a Dolphin card whenever you feel the need for inspiration. Let synchronicity and your own inner guidance collaborate with these *Divination Cards* inspired by the joy, love, and liberation of our Dolphin brothers and sisters. They can be used as a focus of meditation or as an affirmation. *The Dolphin Divination Cards* reveal the archetypes underlying our everyday lives. *The Dolphin Cards* are a good "ice-breaker" at your next get-together.

Hawaiian Aumakua Cards
M. Lucy Wade Stern
ISBN: 0-931892-39-2, 36 illustrated cards,
144-page hardcover book, $19.95

A beautifully colored deck of 36 cards and an illustrated book of guidelines. When all 36 cards are laid out in a "reading," they reveal personal patterns in present events.

Your Mind Knows More Than You Do
The Subconscious Secrets of Success
Sidney Friedman
ISBN: 1-57733-052-8, 184 pp., hardcover, $22.00

You will learn to tap into the subconscious, making its vast knowledge more readily available. More important, you will learn to feed it your wishes so it can help make them come to fruition. You will learn *The Subconscious Secrets of Success*. Concise, quick, yet packed with information, *Your Mind Know More Than You Do* is about:

- how to make your wishes come true
- how to predict and shape the future
- how to heighten your creativity
- how to attain contentment

Miracles Through Pranic Healing
Master Choa Kok Sui
ISBN: 1-57733-091-9, 434 pp., hardcover, $25.00

Miracles Through Pranic Healing—all you need is a willingness to help yourself or your loved ones and to follow the step-by step instructions. The results will follow. Within a week or two simple ailments can be healed . . . difficult ailments may take longer. This is the basic text used in Pranic Healing courses all over the U.S. While many Americans only work with seven basic chakras, in this process Master Choa also uses the minor chakras in the hands, feet, fingers, throat and neck. His methods for activating healing energy enable you to work with other people without the energy drain that many untrained intuitive healers experience. This is a useful introductory text, containing basic instructions, for any naturally sensitive person who has an interest in this form of healing.

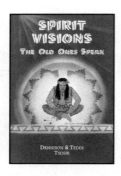

Spirit Visions
The Old Ones Speak
Dennison & Teddi Tsosie
ISBN: 0-57733-002-1, 384 pages, paper, 6x9, $19.95

This book will change your way of looking at the universe, forever.

Dennison Tsosie did not think he would be a Healer or Shaman—yet that is where his life path has led him. The information in *Spirit Visions* reads like an Indiana Jones adventure, giving new twists to the legends of the lost Ark and the Holy Grail. His predictions of natural disasters and political upheavals are balanced by visions of new discoveries to help heal our planet and ourselves.

"Spirit Visions has allowed me to pull together in a cohesive manner all of the other works of prophecy that I had already read. He is giving these teachings not to frighten us, but to let us understand love and how to survive in the times ahead." —C.L., Benton, KY

Now Is the Hour
Native American Prophecies and Guidance for Earth Changes
Elisabeth Dietz & Shirley Jonas
108 pages, 1-57733-029-3, $10.00

Counting on his fingers, a Hopi elder stood and spoke, "You have been telling the people that this is the eleventh hour. Now, go and tell them: THIS IS THE HOUR!

There are ten things to consider—Where are you living?
What are you doing? What are your relationships?
Are you in the right relationships? Where is your water?
Know your garden. It is time to speak your truth.
Create your community. Be good to each other.
Do not look outside yourself for the leader.
Then he brought his hands together in a clasp and said,
"This could be a Good Time."